A Rebellion
In
Canile

By
D.A.Episcopo

A Rebellion in Canile
Copyright: David A. Episcopo
Published: 23rd May 2014
ISBN: 978-1-4951-1483-0
Publisher: David A. Episcopo
The right of David A. Episcopo to be identified as author of this
Work has been asserted by him in accordance with sections 77 and
78 of the Copyright, Designs and Patents Act 1988.

Table of Contents

Foreword:

Complacency; often a more dangerous enemy than any other, this was the enemy that left the Lykos of Canile open to manipulation. Neil Canaan, an outspoken member of the Lykos parliament, had finally succeeded in gaining the vote to send more troops to the southern border that divided Canile from Katzen, the nearest continent to the south. Katzen is inhabited by scattered tribes of giants, these 'Kats' towered at least a foot or two taller than even the largest Lykos breed. Though primitive, the Kats were master stone-masons and craftsmen and due to their many tribes and limited land, Canaan feared they would soon try to expand their territory into Canile, and he was right. Four months after bolstering their southern borders a patrol brought in what was left of a small team of Nirkas, thin fast little devils, small by Katzen standards but still quite large compared to the Lykos. They were found scouting the defensive placements along the border, but that was not what was most disturbing, in their possessions the border guard found a partial copy of the defensive protocols for the capitol city of Canile. This discovery sparked outrage in the court, the Council and Parliament's decision was unanimous, and if the Kats went so far as to obtain sensitive information that could only be found in the capitol city then this wasn't just a simple border dispute.

The Kat tribes fought constantly amongst themselves for supremacy, which kept them from falling into any sort of complacency. Though each tribe of Kats governed itself for the most part, there was a loose affiliation between them, making it easier for them to work together in critical times and react quickly to attacks from outside forces. The Lykos mounted a preemptive strike; Handel, the Kat town closest to the border, was the first to fall. The Kats retaliation was fierce, with the other tribes rallying behind the Samanéra, which are the largest in both size and strength. The Samenéra even called the Furo-Sha tribe back from its northeast pilgrimage into Ryagan, while they excluded the Nirka's completely from the alliance. The Lykos assumed this was because the Nirka's had failed to keep their mission a secret and, consequently, were the cause of the war taking place on Katzen soil. Their united front proved a great challenge to the Lykos who had one advantage to keep them with the primitive Kats, their advanced large-scale military tactics, strategies that were from the days when the Erus and his Canden-Lykos united their nation. This story however, begins near the end of the war with a young Lykos operative about to leave his mark in the war and the events that followed.

Chapter 1: Dorian's Task

My name is Dorian, Dorian Vesco, from Canile. I am fighting in the war with the Kats though I am not a soldier, officially. I am a member of a task force that doesn't exist, the Kynodontes Tou Vorro or 'Kyn' as it is commonly called. That basically means that either side will kill me given the chance; it also means I can do the dirty work for the Council of Parliament and keep my government's reputation untarnished. I was activated six months ago, and since Kyn operatives rarely find themselves working together, I was right at home with the solo missions that were assigned to me. The Kats began advancing on our territory two years ago this month and now the war was coming to a head, most likely, My insertion was part of our final push to end the conflict. In regard to this, I find myself assigned to assassinate a top general of the Kat's Vikandé tribe; Andre Nyma.

I smuggled myself along supply lines, allowing me to close the distance to Nyma's stronghold. I reached the fortress with relative ease, after a few days travel. The plains of Katzen sprawl out, with an open and flat landscape as far as the eye can see, they burn hot during the day and turn bitterly cold at night, so sneaking in on foot wasn't an option. The Kats have used their landscape as an advantage many times but they let over confidence get the better of them, they became lax in their inspections. I simply found a supply crate bound for the right location, and they literally delivered me to my target. Twilight spread across the sky and I could feel the temperature begin to drop down to more comfortable levels. Out on the horizon I could see a storm brewing, I couldn't ask for better weather conditions for this operation. My only complaint was how cramped I was getting stuck in that crate for so long. This beautiful view of the sun burning down and giving way to the storm and I had to see it through the slats of a wooden box…

When I was finally dropped off with the quartermaster inside the fortress walls I started to feel anxious, one would think over the operation, but that didn't bother me, actually I was just didn't want to be stuck in this cramped box anymore. I waited, staying as still as possible to keep from arousing suspicion as to the contents of my inconspicuous hiding place. When I heard the door of the room shut and no movement outside I slowly lifted off the lid of my crate. The musty storeroom had the smell of wet hay; the room was probably converted from horse stalls. I pulled my effects from where they had been stored for the journey, two short swords, both sheathed and secured to my belt of assorted tools, which I promptly clasped around my waist. I replaced the lid quietly just in case the quartermaster returns to catalogue his shipment and finds an open empty crate and gets suspicious enough to raise the alarm. I crept out of the storeroom, which was built into the fortress wall and silently made my way to the stairs built into the wall. The general will probably be in one of the rooms higher up; the Kats are somewhat dramatic in their designs, this stronghold even had towers, and I bet Nyma is in one of them. The pathways, halls, and junctions, were crawling with patrols and from the looks of things, they were already expecting an attack. What they weren't expecting was a single infiltrator.

There were four towers in all, one for each corner of the complex; they were squared allowing for multiple rooms, however, the towers were not built very high. To my good fortune the first light to go on as the sun sank below the horizon was at the top of the tower nearest to me. Regular soldiers would have to hold up on their routine duties to light the torches, but the general would be in his office where he'd need light as soon as the sun fell. I slipped inside the tower through a window from inside the wall into a dark and empty room filled with only chairs and a large map of the area hanging on the wall that the chairs were facing; a briefing room. I cracked the door peering out into the halls of the tower.

"Least these guys were taught some discipline" I muttered observing the perfectly timed patrols in the hallways.

My best bet was to get the timing just right and skip from room to room to get to the stairs. Ten seconds, that's all I had in between each patrol, plenty of time. I waited for the right moment, dashing from one room to the next, hiding out in each one when the guards passed.

I slid into the last room before the staircase and shut the door before the patrol came around the corner and crouched low by the door waiting. It wasn't till the guard was less than six feet away I realized that the spot I had chosen was at the corner of an inside window! I couldn't move suddenly or I was sure to be heard, I also couldn't stay still or I would definitely be seen, instead I just laid down on the floor, flat under the window, face up, and remained as still as possible. I watched as the guards walked by, slowly looking into every room through the windows as they did during every pass. When he came by my room I didn't even breathe, I could look right at his face from my position on the floor. He looked in and around and then paused for a moment, my hand slowly slid down to one of the sheathed swords on my hip in preparation for the worst case, but then he moved on to the next room. I let out a muted sigh of relief as I got back up and found better cover to wait out this pass.

"Just one more run to go, those stairs should lead all the way up to the third floor"

I closed the door behind me and ran for the stairs at the corner escaping the hallway just in time. I must have been lucky, with the stairs being at the corner I didn't just have to worry about waiting for the patrol to leave my hall but also that they weren't coming down the other hall that was connected at the corner with the stairs. I dashed up the stairs past the second floor with the rush of nearly being caught still fueling me. I could see the winds picking up outside through the windows in the staircase as I ran past. When I got to the third floor I saw the stairs still kept going up.

"Guess he gets his own floor, must be nice to be a high rank" I thought to myself as I continued my ascension.

I reached the top floor and barely cracked the door at the top of the stairs open to look for any possible guard to be set. As I expected, there they were two Vikan military guards. They stood at attention in front of the door at the end of a short corridor, unlike the others I had seen so far stationed here, these guys looked like trouble. They were both at least six and a half feet tall with arms as big around as my head. The first on the right side of the door was a little taller than the other holding a spear that was about the same height. This guy looked different, all of the Vikandé that I have ever fought were very dark skinned but he was pale white, almost like he could glow in the dark. Aside from his skin the pale guard had every other typical physical trait of the average Vikan.

"A white Vikan with a spear… indoors...that's weird." I thought to myself, shrugging my shoulders as I shifted my analysis to the second obstacle.

The other guard looked to be pretty rank and file, sword and buckler, nothing I couldn't handle but, my orders were to assassinate Nyma. Everyone else in the base was to remain unharmed and unaware of an intruder's presence.

"How to do that without having to fight those guys…." I thought staring out the window for a moment."Got it!"

I went to the second floor and opened each window in the staircase all the way back up to the top. Wind gusted in howling throughout the tower stairwell, I ran up to the top floor and stood against the wall behind the door.

"I hate the cold….." I muttered shivering while I waited for the guards to take the bait.

The Kats hadn't yet installed gas lines through some of their bases so it seemed lighting here was entirely by candle or torch. By opening all the windows with the storm-winds blowing in from outside, most of the lights on this side of the tower went out instantly. Before long I could hear the footsteps of the patrols coming to check out the staircase from below and on the other side of the door I heard the Vikandé coming too. The door swung open nearly smacking me in the face as I stood silent behind it, the first Vikan that stepped into the hall yelled,

"Who left these windows open!?"

His voice resounded through the narrow staircase that served to funnel the wind into each floor of the tower, though no one had reached the staircase yet to answer him. The second Vikan turned to his fellow guard trying to placate him,

"The day cleaners probably just didn't latch them right. Let's just close em, I've been standing still so long I can't feel my legs anymore, it'll be a good excuse to move a little haha."

"Fine but we have to be quick; we're supposed to stay by that door all night, the General has the whole base on their toes. Apparently, there's a high chance the dogs will come out this way pretty soon." The first replied.

The 'Dogs' he was referring to are what the Kat tribes call anyone from the Canes. Their derogatory terms always seemed a bit generic to me personally, but I suppose that's only because their native languages aren't very complex yet. Most of the world has adopted the Lykos tongue as a trade language, due to our heavy involvement with commerce all over the world, including with the Kats before all of this started. I did find it odd that they'd speak my language even here among only their own people, or at least, that's what they thought, they must just use my language more often for its versatility, it wasn't that far of a stretch.

I held my breath and watched as they walked down the staircase closing each window they passed; as soon as they disappeared around the turn of the stairs I darted into the hall on the other side of the door and locked it tight behind me. Some open windows and a locked door would only buy me so much time though, those Vikandé were pushing seven feet tall and by the look of their muscles, weighed twice what I do. I rushed to the end of the hall; one final door stood between me the target of this mission. I placed one hand on one my swords gripping it tightly as it rested in its sheath and I put the other on the door handle slowly pushing it open.

"What was the problem?" asked an older man's voice from a writing desk in the back left corner of the room as he still sat with his back to the door.

I closed the door behind me as silently as I could, and locked it as well, in order to buy more time. Without a word I advanced toward Nyma, moving faster with each step. I drew my sword and swung for his head, since it was the only part of his body that was not blocked by the chair. At the last instant before my blade found its target he turned his head and pulled a knife and parried my strike, with the same motion he stood up straight, knocking his chair back into me.

"Not very bright are you, boy?" he said, the years of wisdom and experience earned in battle showing on his face, but his expression was one of sadness.

Electing to remain silent, I leapt back to gain some distance and charged once again, knowing I had precious little time with the Vikan guards returning and having lost the element of surprise. When I was in range I swung with the blade underhanded but as he raised his weapon to counter I dropped my sword. Grabbing his wrist above the knife I sidestepped around him, wrenching the knife from his grip I plunged it into his back. As I slid the knife out he fell with a loud thud on the hard stone floor. I stepped over him to retrieve my sword from the floor with his knife still in hand and when I passed I felt him reach up and grab my leg. I jerked it away and looked down at him, but his eyes weren't looking at me, they were fixed on his knife. I looked down at it and as the torchlight reflected off of it, the light turned blue as it bounced off of the blade. Then he looked up straight into my eyes.

"End this war, neither side has anything to gain...and..." His feeble voice trailed off as he fell back to the floor.

I looked down at the knife and cleaned the blood from it with my handkerchief.

"Guess I'll hold on to this" I said to no one in particular, then suddenly remembering the guards due to return at any moment I pulled my hood down low and went to the window.

From the tools on my belt I produced a hook and wire, securing the wire to the leather harness I wore and the hook to the window sill, I jumped up into the window and surveyed the night. The storm I had seen coming earlier had become a torrential downpour outside, I thrust open the windows to make my escape. I took Nyma's knife out looking for somewhere on my rig to secure it where I wouldn't lose it repelling out of the window, suddenly the door at the back of the room burst open.

Chapter 2: Mark's Bargain

After we finished closing the windows that'd blown open, the other guard and I thought it best to check in with the patrols on the lower floors just as a precaution. On the second floor, the guard was just turning the corner passed the stairs when my partner and I came down, he stopped and saluted before giving his report.

"Nothing out of the order, sir, just the windows blowing open."

"Blowing open? Has night maintenance been up yet?"

"Nobody has been up sin...." Before the patrolman finished his sentence I knew I had made a horrible mistake. I took off, leaving my partner behind as I ascended each flight of stairs as fast as I could. When the door on the fourth floor came into view and I saw it closed I knew something had to be wrong,

"Did you close the door when you came down?!"

My guard-mate shook his head vigorously as he came up behind me, immediately we ran up to the door, as we feared it was locked tight!

"On three?"

"One......Two......Three!"

Together we rammed the door with our shoulders, busting the lock out of the door itself. Wasting no time we moved on to the next door at the other end of the hall which was also locked, this time we didn't wait for the count to bust through. When the door swung open violently with the force of our impact, the first sight that met my eyes was Master Nyma laying face-down on the floor. The howling winds drew my attention from him to the open window where a hooded figure brandishing the knife my master always kept on him, a knife I remembered well.

"Stop! Drop the weapon and come down from the window!" I barked out the order with as much tenacity as I could muster.

The assassin's face was shrouded in the shadow from his low hood aided by the fact that the wind had extinguished nearly all of the torches in the room. In a flash of lightening all I could see were his icy cold blue eyes as though they gave off their own light from beneath the hood. He had to be a professional, my master's abilities were nothing to take lightly, he must be incredibly fast to overcome Andre Nyma.

"Heh" the assassin grunted and in the wake of the booming thunder he leapt out into the storm.

Immediately I hurtled my spear through the window in a desperate attempt to stop him; however when I ran up to the window all I saw was wind and rain in the darkness. I looked down at the sill of the window and found the wire that'd been anchored there severed and whipping in the wind.

"Damn it!"

"Mark!" my partner called from behind me as I searched in vain for the assassin, unwilling to face the reality that was right behind me.

"Mark, He's still breathing!"

At the guard's words I turned around and almost fell at my old master's side. My partner turned him over while I pulled off my service coat and folded it up for a headrest. He looked up at me and I could tell by his labored breathing and the amount of blood he lost that he didn't have long and yet there wasn't a shred of weakness in his eyes. He tried to speak, his voice cracking as he forced the words out,

"Mark…is that you?"

"It's me sir, I'm here." I tried to remain steadfast out of respect for my mentor, but I guess I wasn't doing a good job of holding it together.

"It's just war, boy….just…"

His last words gave way to the reaper as the life left his body. I closed his eyes, stood up and headed out of the room. The only other person in the room, my partner in failure, called after me,

"Where are you going?"

Without a word I kept on walking.

Two months later, I found myself in the briefing room of the Western Fortress the very same fortress where Nyma died. The war was over, last week a treaty was ratified by Canile's Parliament and our Samanéra that headed up the tribal alliance. This treaty was to ensure further incidents of this nature would not lead to another state of war, though mostly it was a formality. The treaty states that; due to this incident starting over conspiracy and espionage at the border of our two nations, heavy trade and immigration restrictions would be imposed on both sides to minimalize opportunities for any would-be instigators. In truth no immigration would be sanctioned in the foreseeable future to or from either nation, save for special circumstance, should they arise. Trade however, would continue but only in smaller, easier to inspect quantities.

Basically the war became more than it was worth, the Lykos didn't have the numbers to take us, and our defensive strategies allowed us to maintain our ground. Once they decided we weren't worth conquering they presented the Samanéra with this treaty and we were just happy they were willing to stop the fighting. Honestly if they knew our politics better they might've been able to win outright, our tribes have never been able to maintain an alliance for long and this war had strained our relations to the breaking point. The last time the tribes allied themselves was to quell the Nirkas uprising ten years ago, Nyma fought in that…

The door of the briefing room slammed shut, snapping my thoughts back to the present as three officers entered the room. They filed in and sat down at the long table in front of me. I had been through so many of these debriefings but this time was different, this was my last debriefing. I was to be discharged today. The Vikandé were scaling back their military presence in order for the tribe to be able to afford the reparations after the war, and my failure to perform my duty in protecting my senior officer put my name at the top of the discharge pile.

"For the record, please state your name, rank, and unit." The unnamed officer sitting in the middle of the other two said as he looked up from his clipboard.

"Mark Burke, Sergeant 2nd Class, 21st Specials Division." I answered plainly staring forward without looking at anything in particular.

"Sergeant Burke, we are here today for your debrief and discharge, as you know General Nyma had no family, his land and possessions are listed here as bequeathed to you in the event of his passing." This sparked my interest, now I knew why they would bother with these formal discharge procedures,

"And you're wondering if my 'failure' to protect the general was because of what I stood to gain, am I right?" I leaned back in my chair disgusted with these nameless officers and their allegation

"Straight to the point then, do you have anything to say that would convince us that this shouldn't go to the Elders?" the officer on the left in front of me said leaning forward in response. Even though the Vikandé were a military focused tribe, we were still led a council of tribal Elders like every other tribe in Katzen.

"There's nothing to say, you've seen my report, Nyma's death is my shame. I never even knew I was in the General's will." As I spoke inspiration struck with an idea that would satisfy both these investigators and my ragged pride. "Why don't you send me after the assassin? Send me after him and hold onto the property I was supposed to inherit. If I return successful then you grant me the property, if not then keep it as recompense for my failure." My proposition caused all of my accusers to hesitate for a moment. This time it was the officer's turn who sat on the right to speak.

"What would that prove? You might have no problem hunting down your accomplice to save your own skin, or you might just use the opportunity to escape conviction of the crime, should you be found guilty of allowing General Nyma to be killed."His logic was hard to question, but what he didn't see is that the prospect of finding my master's killer was more important to me than any inheritance. I had to make my intentions perfectly clear.

"Then keep the property anyway, just give me leave to go after the assassin. I'll sign over everything to the tribe and in return you let me go after the general's killer, that's all I want."

The reluctance of Katzen's tribes to form stable relations and create a unified society hindered the growth of a mature bureaucracy; this made nearly apparent bribes like this an effective means of achieving a goal.

The officer's panel thought for a moment, I could almost see the wheels in their heads turning over and over again as they processed. "Give us a moment to discuss your proposal."

The panel stood in unison and filed out of the room in the same manner in which they had entered. I sat in the empty room, that night two months ago replaying over and over in my mind. After some time, I wasn't quite sure how long, the lead officer of the panel re-entered the room.

"Sergeant Burke, your proposal is accepted under one condition, your discharge still stands. In the event that you return with evidence of the assassin's death, you will be reinstated with full honors. You should know the man you are after is the 'Wolf'." He warned.

"The Wolf?" The enemies that have caused enough damage to get the attention of the military brass are given these call signs sometimes, but I have never heard of any 'Wolf'.

The officer sighed and explained. "The Wolf is an operative that has performed numerous acts of sabotage and assassination in the east, we weren't expecting him here so far from his normal range. He always works alone and has only been seen a handful of times, be careful when you go after him." He pulled out a small envelope and handed it to me.

"What's this?" I asked

"A letter from the Furo-Sha colony where they settled in the northeast, I'm sure you know where it is." The officer left the room shutting the door behind him without even waiting for my answer to his condition. I guess he knew it was my only option, I had to take it.

My family lives in the colony, the officer must've known where I'm from. My father is a Furo-Sha pilgrim, spreading the faith of Jagćs north into Ryagan, and my mother was a Vikan relief worker when she met him on one of her disaster calls. She left him ten years ago and moved back to the Vikan tribe. I also have a younger brother Rick, and my sister Kari, they left with our mother after the divorce. That was when Rick and I met master Nyma; he was part of a guard detachment in the same colony where we decided to make our home. Nyma was a Veteran of our last war with the Nirka and after a considerable amount of begging from my brother and I, he agreed to teach us how to fight. Though when the war started Rick took Kari to the colony to live with our father, it was safer for her there than Mom's home in the country and she left to work with the Emergency Relief Corp.

Master Nyma rejoined the Vikan military and because of Nyma's special recommendation, I was placed in his personal guard. We couldn't stop mom from going back into work with the corps, she wasn't on the front lines but that didn't stop us from worrying. I held out the letter the officer brought and pulled out my combat knife, the letter was addressed to me from my sister; I guessed the postal routes are open again. I sliced it open and unfolded contents, a short letter that read,

"Dear Mark,

We've heard the war is officially over, you sent those dogs running back to their masters ha-ha! Rick and I have been doing well; Grandpa and the other Elders let us work with dad in the ministry. The word of Jagés has already spread through three towns in the area; isn't that great?! Will you be coming back soon? Another thing…I decided to write instead of waiting for you to come back because of Mom. Rick and I are worried, we haven't heard from her in about a month and she usually writes at least once every week. Last we heard, she was between the colony and where you were stationed in the west. Could you please check on her on your way home if you are coming back soon, if not, at least have her write us to let us know how she is doing. Rick almost went out alone to go look for her, but a girl that came back from Ryagan with Dad, Grandpa, and the other Elders and talked him out of it. The Rya girl seems nice; the church took her in after Dad found her out on the road alone in Ryagan.

Thank you again, May Jagés keep the ground steady beneath your feet as you return home to us.

Kari Burke"

I guess Mom wouldn't have had the opportunity to send them any letters for the last month since she got here. The Western Fortress has been on lockdown ever since the Lykos struck in the wake of our losing the general. That battle was terrible, over half the men stationed here died, but we won, barely. The only reason we survived is because we expected an attack after discovering the assassin, and were able to build up our defenses in time. My mother was part of the relief team that came to feed the men and tend to their wounds while the base underwent repairs. After Nyma's assassination I was confined to quarters for a month till the Emergency Relief Corps came, then I was assigned to guard her team during their stay. Now that I have been officially discharged and repairs have been completed, I am free to go and I just hope that I can convince her to come with me. I folded up the letter and stuck it the pocket of my service coat, after leaving the briefing room I headed straight down for the kitchen.

Mom works on the feeding end of operations for her relief unit; supervising the preparation and distribution of food on a community wide level. Ever since she came here however, she has been content to work making meals for the soldiers. I crossed the mess hall and kept going through to the back hall on the opposite side where the large sterile metal door leading into the kitchen was. When I opened the door I was met with the dense aroma of meals I had grown to love from my youth, truly my mother's cooking had no equal.

At the moment she was standing back letting her assistants prepare ingredients on the large wooden cutting tables that divided the room, while she drank water from a pitcher and observed, my mother was ever the teacher, even here. Today's dish, from the smell, was chicken and rice, probably because chicken was all there is to find out here in this side of the waste for food and rice was easy to transport.

"Hey mom, how are things going back here?"

She looked up and smiled as she walked over to me, "There's my soldier, what brings you down? Do they have you on guard duty again today?"

"Actually, I got my official discharge, now that things are pretty much done here; I can go back to the colony, and want you to come with me. Kari is worried and so is Rick, I can take you back as soon as you find a replacement for you here." I replied trying to sound as positive as possible, neither my mother nor I were very fond of my father who was also back at the colony. She looked down and over and then took a deep breath; I knew I wasn't going to like what she had to say, and she knew I wouldn't like it either.

"Mark, I can't leave yet, even if I could set this base up with a replacement chef today, there's still a week's worth of packing up equipment and paperwork. Even then, I'd have to go back to our home office and give report for the past month since I've been stuck here without any way of sending correspondence." Just as I thought, I didn't like it at all. She came in close and gave me a hug.

"I promise son, as soon as I finish up here I'll head straight back to the colony for you, your brother, and Kari, and we'll go back home together. Oh and Mark, tell your brother and sister they can start sending letters again now that the mail routes are open." She kissed my cheek and hugged me one last time, "Alright, be safe."

I nodded when I pulled away and gave a halfhearted salute before leaving her to her work in the kitchen. Kari wouldn't be happy that I left mom here, but at least I knew she would be safe surrounded by soldiers. I returned to my room in the barracks at the southern end of the base and packed my things.

One advantage of military life, you learn to stay light with your possessions in case you get orders to move out quickly. With my duffle bag thrown over my shoulder and my combat knife in its sheath on my belt, and situated behind my back, I was ready to go as soon as I turn in my spear. First I headed for the quarter master downstairs on the ground floor; he was in his office off to the side of the storeroom.

"Sir I am here to relinquish my weapon as ordered by my discharge" The old man and stood and returned my salute before taking the spear that I offered.

"I'll be sorry to see you go Sergeant Burke."

"That's just Burke now, Sir" I corrected, he just looked at me with a weary smile,

"In all my years in this military I have learned, a Vikan soldier is always a Vikan soldier, no matter what the paperwork says" I returned to attention and we saluted one another before I turned and left his office for the way out of the fortress, I had all I needed for the journey… except for a ride.

Chapter 3: Rick's Decision

"C'mon Rick! Let's go!"

My little sister and Rebecca were waiting for me to take them out hunting squirrel, not much else to do out here when you're bored. Ever since Kari and I moved out here couple years ago when the tribe got called back to help in the war, aside from the long hours working for the ministry, there was absolutely nothing to do. Rebecca has made things easier with her carefree adventurous outlook on things; she actually came back with the rest of the tribe from Ryagan. Apparently, dad found her on the road half-starved when they were on their way back to Katzen. She's a bit odd, I had never met a Rya before but she's different even compared to her people, or so she says. I just finished getting dressed throwing my shirt on and a pair of ragged pants, no need for shoes because life is more fun barefoot.

"I'm coming just hold on!" I met the two of them at the front door. Kari was a tall girl with hair that flowed like a golden waterfall and the clearest blue eyes, all the work with the ministry kept her lean and fit, she could even keep up with me now. Rebecca was thin and only a little shorter than Kari with the unmistakable vertical slit pupils in her golden eyes that gave her away as Rya. I tried to make a move on Rebecca the first time we met but...that didn't turn out so well. When I got there Kari already had my bow and arrows ready to go and Rebecca had her long knives strapped to her legs as always. When I saw her, the memory from our last hunting trip briefly flashed in my mind.

We were bored so we decided to go out hunting squirrel on our day off, just like today except it was only Rebecca and I that time. We couldn't figure out why we weren't having any luck tracking our prey. It wasn't just squirrel, we couldn't find any game at all, not even birds; the answer hit us like a herd of buffalo, very literally. The herd trampled through the wooded area we used as our hunting ground and straight for us, they came out of nowhere, the herd was too large and fast to avoid with the lack of open space in the woods.

At the last moment after we found no way out Rebecca revealed her secret, what set her apart even among other Ryas. She plucked two small scales from her shoulders and struck them together causing the air in between her hands to suddenly burst into flame. The fireball in her hands grew larger and larger, and strangely enough, turned black as she focused intently. I wouldn't have believed it if I hadn't seen it myself. She threw it at the ground directly in front of the oncoming stampede. The intense explosion divided the herd to either side of us. She blacked out shortly after the herd passed us; I had to carry her piggyback back to the compound at the colony. When she finally woke she sat down with me and explained how all Rya children have larger scales that grow on their bodies and they spark when rubbed together, even their skin is thinly weaved scale. Then there are rare times when a child is born with glands just above the wrist that secrete clean burning gases at will that can be ignited by striking the scales together. Depending on the circumstances of the child's birth, the child is either nurtured faithfully or shunned in her culture.

The closest I could use to relate is how some Kats can 'speak to the stone' a blessing from Jagés as we were raised to believe. Science says it's a combination of an acute sense of touch and an instinctual knowledge of mineral composition. Apparently in where she came from her blessing was shunned, when the Elders discover a Kat who can speak to the stone, that child is treated as a great blessing to the tribe from Jagés. Though it wasn't much of a blessing for me, I wanted to fight for my tribe in the war, we both trained under master Nyma but my brother was the only one allowed to go. I guess the Vikan, nor Furo-Sha could afford to lose one of the 'blessed children'...

"What are we waiting for? You scared we'll get run over by a wild herd or something?" Rebecca shot me a wink as she opened the door for Kari and me and my thoughts returned to the moment at hand.

We hiked out to the wood about a mile or so away from the compound the same forest we normally frequented, though we put in at a different area this time, if Kari saw the scorched earth she might have questions that we don't want to answer. She wouldn't suspect us of doing anything wrong but all the same it made things easier just to avoid it. Following the winding trails through the sandy hills covered in roots overgrown from lush trees and the sounds of life all around, we kept silent in hopes of coming across our prey…until Rebecca got bored.

"Nothing… nothing at all, I thought the Katzen wild life supposed to be really over populated?"

"Just keep quiet and look around, talking like that will scare them all off" I whispered angrily.

"Fine but…" Rebecca stopped as she poked her head through a wall of brush, Kari and I just stood still waiting for her to pull her head back through. "You guys, it's hot out here. How do you two feel about taking a swim?" she had pulled her head out and was looking over her shoulder with childish grin as she spoke. Kari and I knew this was coming since Rebecca gets easily distracted and bored, and we usually go along with her, but this time Kari had been really excited since I promised her she could do the shooting on this trip.

"I want to at least get one before we do something else alright?" Kari implored as Rebecca slowly came back to us, leaning in over Kari's shoulder to whisper,

"Then kill that rabbit over about ten yards on your left and then let's go swimming." Rebecca smiled as she pulled away.

Kari and I slowly turned our heads in the direction Rebecca mentioned, and right out in the middle of a small clearing sat a plump rabbit digging at the ground. Kari didn't think twice, she nocked an arrow in her short bow, took aim and let it fly. The thin wooden missile pierced the rabbit and carried it about three feet before it stopped; now it was Rebecca's turn. Her responsibility was to use her knife to kill whatever creatures we shoot down as quick as possible, to put them out of their misery. Rebecca shot forward with her knife at the rabbit almost before the arrow's momentum had expired. She carried back the rabbit by the ears, her knife returned to the sheath on her leg and spinning Kari's undamaged arrow in the other hand playfully.

"Now can we go swimming?" she asked with a smile

We pushed through brush Rebecca had looked through earlier to see a large creek cutting through the forest. Rebecca shoved the rabbit into my hands and ran down to the water followed closely by my sister.

I looked down at the rabbit, "Guess I'll cook it before it goes bad" I grunted under my breath as I walked down the bank to a small clearing by the water.

I have always had a knack for survivalist skills, needless to say it wasn't long before I had a campfire going and the rabbit was skinned and roasting over the fire. The girls continued playing in the water until the rabbit was finished then I called them over.

"Hey! Dinner is ready when you are!"

"Okay!!!" Kari yelled as Rebecca pulled her backwards into the water, though Kari must've told her food was involved because the next thing I heard was both girls charging the bank of the creek.

"You two are going to have fun walking back to the compound all soaked like that ha-ha!"

The girls just looked at each other and laughed for no apparent reason. I ignored them and took the rabbit off of the fire and carved the meat, handing one hind leg each to the girls and took the breast meat for myself.

"This is all we get?" Rebecca asked, looking quite unhappy with the size of her portion.

"It's only one rabbit plus we're all going to eat a real meal when we get back, now shut up and enjoy the rabbit." I said jokingly as I tore off a shred of the meat and put it in my mouth. The girls followed suit though as soon as the taste met our tongues we spat out the meat.

"What did you do to that meat...!?" Kari asked coughing off to the side.

"Nothing, that had to be a really old rabbit to be that tough." I explained

"That tasted like leather!" Rebecca spat.

"Yeah, yeah, let's just go get something actually edible, I was really looking forward to eating something."

We all got up; I pulled the burning logs apart as quickly as I could while the girls waited. Then I guess Rebecca saw something because she went running back to the water's edge.

"Guys! Look at this!"

Kari and I ran to see what she was talking about, Kari got there first and I guess she saw the same thing in the water, because she leaned over the water and stared with the same awestruck look as Rebecca. I decided to take a look so I came up between both of them and scanned the water for anything unusual.

"I don't see anything what were you two…" I turned to look at Rebecca ask her what she saw when they both grabbed my arms and shoved me down into the shallow water

"Now we all get to walk home soaked!" My sister giggled and then walked off, when Rebecca passed by on her way to follow my Kari, she stopped and glanced down at me in the water.

"Thanks for the rabbit."

With that they both disappeared back into the woods, rather than get angry I decided to let it go, I was too hungry to care. I got out of the water and jogged into the dark forest to catch up.

It was probably really late by the time we got back; dad wasn't even up waiting for us. The first thing we did was return to our rooms and change into dry clothes. I threw on a spare shirt and pants and went out to the cafeteria building where the girls were already waiting in the massive kitchen that was always kept fully stocked.

"Rick? Did something happen to the gas tanks?" My sister asked when I came in as she stared at the gas pressure gauge mounted on top of the stove.

"Not that I know of, what did pressure gauge look like?"

I read the gauge on top of the stove, the gas line pressure had bottomed out; usually the air vacuum will register on the gauge but there was nothing, like all the gas had been drained. Then I realized why,

"Rebecca, don't move! Stay as still as you can and don't freak out." I tried to sound as calm as possible.

"What? Why? What's wrong?!" she yelled, starting to freak out. I guess I sounded a bit too calm for what I noticed to be anything good.

"I think the gas was left on, if you cause a spark the whole place could go up."

She immediately went stiff as a board, gritting her teeth and not looking very happy at all.

"Kari get out of here, tell dad what happened. I'm gonna try and help her" My voice fell low almost to a whisper on the edge of a growl. Kari knew this wasn't the time to argue she ran back out the side door and off to our house.

"Alright how do we keep you from sparking?" I asked

"The scales only cause sparks when they rub together, just get some towels and wrap my arms below the sleeves and my legs."

At her word I dashed through the stainless steel kitchen and found the cupboard where the towels were stored. I grabbed four towels and returned to Rebecca who now had her eyes closed; her legs in a wide stance and her arms held out.

"I guess gas-run utilities aren't very Rya friendly are they?" I joked trying to lighten the situation.

"Shut up, don't make me laugh, I'm trying to stay still" she said stifling a smile.

I finished wrapping her arms and legs up the best I could and stood up backing away slowly. She started walking slowly towards the door. As soon as she took the last step over the threshold into the night air, Rebecca broke into a run and I took off after her. She stopped a safe distance away from the cafeteria just then we saw Kari returning with dad. We waved them over and they came running, my father looking half awake and in his bathrobe, apparently he hadn't been to sleep yet.

"Is everyone okay?" my father's generic choice of words aside, we all nodded.

"I can smell that gas from here, but I was the last one in the kitchen and I specifically remember turning everything off, we'll have to go back and open all the windows and doors and let it air out." Dad explained and then he turned and looked at Rebecca, "You should probably stay here."

She gave him a half-hearted thumbs up and sat down on one of the rocks that littered the perimeter of the colony. Kari and I started to follow dad back to the cafeteria kitchen when I heard an odd whistling noise coming from behind. Hurtling out of the darkness a spear flew passed my father, sister and I and sunk into the sand just in front of us, halting us in our tracks. In one motion all three of us spun around to look for the source of the attack, Rebecca jumped off of her rock and joined us. A lanky man with spotted skin walked steadily toward the four of us, the same pattern extended to his short hair, he was a Nirka. The Nirka carried a second spear across his left shoulder, glaring with murderous intent, staring at Rebecca, but the closer he got the more it seemed like he was looking past her and at me. But I figured it was just my imagination when he spoke directly to her,

"Ahh the Rya girl, she said you might be here."

He lifted his spear and pointed it straight at our group and took his stance. Kicking off the ground with incredible speed he sprinted at us zigzagging as he closed the distance. His speed plus the cover of night made his movements nearly impossible to track. The one thing I didn't see at all is when exactly Rebecca decided to move... Before I could react to the attacker, Rebecca had already met him five yards ahead of us; she sidestepped around his guard and slid her knife through one artery in his neck and out the other. We were all frozen in time looking at this immature girl that could never focus or restrain herself display such awesome skill and speed. I hadn't seen anyone fight like that since the days my brother and I trained with master Nyma. The scariest part were her eyes, they gave off an orange glow like they were on fire. She turned and looked straight at me with those burning eyes,

"We need to talk" was all she said, Rebecca walked by us flicking the blood from her knife and returning it to her sheath.

I followed her back to the house where my family lived and where Rebecca had been staying, leaving Dad and Kari standing out there with the body of our fallen assailant. We went back to the guest bedroom that she had taken as her own. She looked me in the eyes again, though now the fire had faded, she just looked sad.

"Your father will be safe they wouldn't have gotten a good look at him, but I can bet you they know our faces and Kari's, we have to find a safe place for you and your sister to lay low for a while, otherwise the whole colony could be hit again." The only other time I've heard her talk so seriously was the night she told me about her blessing. Though there were a couple of things she wasn't fully explaining.

"If they saw us then they definitely saw you too, if Kari and I go somewhere to wait this out then where does that leave you? While we're at it, who are 'they' exactly? Are you just talking about the Nirka or is there something else going on?"

Rebecca paused for a second like she didn't expect my response, then a kinder light showed in her eyes, and she took a deep breath letting it out slowly before continuing.

"I came back here with your father because the person I am after has been poking around Katzen looking for something but I don't know what it is yet. I am pretty sure the one I'm after has enlisted the Nirka, since they have no love for the other tribes that makes them the obvious choice for finding whatever she is after without attracting the attention of the other tribes. I'm positive the one I killed isn't the only one that made it into the colony tonight; he was probably sent in to test the waters. The next attack will be worse, since I am the one he was after, as long as I am gone the Furo-Sha shouldn't have to worry about any more attacks. When it comes to you and Kari, you have to get to safety, because they might attack the colony to take you as hostages to lure me out. I am sorry but you both have to leave the colony tonight, is there anywhere you can lay low for a while?" Rebecca sounded like a completely different person, she was calm and composed, no bouncing off the wall or getting distracted, she carried herself with grace and poise as she spoke. I thought for a moment, trying to think of a place I could take Kari where she would be safe.

"I guess we could go to the base where our mother is supposed to be working the relief kitchen for wounded soldiers after one of the last battles, but you still haven't told me, what you are going to do?" I asked, letting some frustration leak into my voice so she would know I was serious.

"I thought that was obvious, I am going to continue investigating the Nir…oh hey Kari" My little sister stepped through the open door where she had been standing with a leather bag in her hands.

"The man that you… well he had this on him, dad thought you might be able to make sense of these papers. Are we really leaving the colony Rick?" she looked me in the eye and I could see the tears she fought to hold back. Kari loved living in the colony, working in the church, the people, and the faith itself, it had become her life.

"I'm sorry but it won't be for long, Rebecca just wants to make sure that we stay safe, and by us leaving the colony won't have to worry about any more attacks. I think it's for the best right now."

"Guess I'll get my stuff then…" Kari said heading back to her room sounding miserable.

Rebecca turned back to me, "You should probably get your things together quickly too and get to bed, tomorrow is going to be a long day."

"Done, I keep a bag of essentials packed at all times, just in case." I said proudly and Rebecca let a small smile crack her lips

"Are you going to be sad leaving your forge behind?" she started, looking like a little life was coming back to her face so I thought it best to go along with it.

"Yeah I'll be devastated, but I can always come back to it, speaking of the forge I just made something a couple days ago that will be useful for the trip." She seemed a little confused so I led her back to the door of my room and ran inside for just a moment to grab my latest work.

"Here watch." I produced my latest invention, a metal rod, only two feet in length, but with a built in hidden feature. I held it out for Rebecca to look at it; she studied it for a second and then looked back up at me.

"You made a…. stick?"

"Not just any stick" I replied with a grin as I turned both halves of the pole till the internal mechanism I had rigged inside clicked into place and both sides extended two feet in either direction.

"It's a collapsible six foot pole; this was my favorite weapon that master Nyma taught me. A little bit more of her old self flashed in her eyes, and as she turned to leave she said,

"Good then maybe next time I won't have to save you." Rebecca gave another weak smile and headed back to her room.

The next morning we packed up a wagon the Elders supplied us with and headed out into the wastes for the western fortress.

Chapter 4: Rebecca's Journey

I had never killed anyone before, the memory of the attack back at the colony burned in the back of my mind. In the wake of that memory I had almost forgotten about the midday heat scorching our wagon as we rode across the open plains. We had been travelling out here for almost a month now, enough for me to know I would never settle down in Katzen. My throat was parched but water isn't exactly common out here so I was out of luck until we set up camp for tonight. Rick climbed up from the back of our wagon where Kari was resting from her shift at the reigns with a cantina in one hand and the extendible pole he was so proud of in the other; it hadn't left his side since the night he first showed it to me.

"Thought you could use a drink" he said offering the cantina to me with the lid already off. At first I thought he was just being cruel since he is the one always preaching about conserving resources, but I could see the sincerity on his face and gladly accepted.

"Thank you very much, how much further is this place?" I asked swiping the cantina from him and pouring the cool refreshing water down my throat.

"Well it's about a month's ride from the colony, give or take, since it's nearly at the western edge of Katzen; we have been on the road for a little more than three weeks so…we should get there any day now, hopefully." he said checking his compass and map to be sure.

"So that's why you're being so generous" I said with a smile raising Rick's cantina and taking another drink.

"So what's that thing even made from?" I asked looking over at his weapon, remembering the occasional scuffles we've had with the raiders that live out here in the waste. When he fought, his weapon seemed to shrug off the impact of other weapons and the force of each strike seemed to be amplified by the weapon itself, I had never seen anything like it and that made me curious.

"We have some pretty advanced metallurgy back in Ryagan and I have never heard of anything like that." I took up his retracted staff and spun it in the palm of my hand while waiting for his answer. He donned a cocky grin and began his explanation,

"Remember how I told you about the blessed children and how they can 'speak to the stone'? I am one of them, that's the same reason the tribe wouldn't let me fight in the war with the Lykos." His arrogant voice reminded me of the entitled nobles back home.

"What does that have to do with the staff?" I was getting impatient still waiting for him to make sense,

"Metal is mineral, just like the earth so I can feel it, my blessing helps me understand how to use this type metal to make things. I call it, Luminore, because when I found the raw deposits in the caves down by that oasis, the ore-veins were glowing. At first I thought it was a stream flowing from underground reflecting the moonlight but it turned out to be a large deposit of ore that I had never seen before" The genuine excitement that flooded his words as he spoke showed me a side of him I had never seen before. In the year since I met him, he's always kept up the façade of an overconfident and brash young man. However, right now he sounds more like a starry-eyed schoolboy.

"This…'Luminore' is pretty impressive, not a dent or a scratch anywhere, why don't more smiths and engineers use it?" I wanted to keep him talking about his work because I knew, at least for the moment, I could distract him from the drastic change his life was taking.

"Actually I thought the same thing, so I went to one of the engineers in the colony, an old scruffy man that maintains the gas lines and such to find out if he had ever seen it before. He told me that ore is really rare, even asked me where I found it, apparently its worth a lot. I just told him I bought the sample off of a merchant that came to visit the colony. He also said it's incredibly difficult to work because of the density so most smiths can't do much with it." Rick explained as his eyes lit up with pride, because somehow he had found a way to get the metal to work for him when most couldn't, so I indulged him,

"I'm guessing you found a way to make it work?" I asked with embellished interest.

"That's what it means to speak to the stone; it's not about knowing, it's about feeling, I could tell what to do just by working with it. This staff is just the first thing I made, but I stocked plenty of ore back at the colony. I left it in the warehouse with the crates marked, I could even have dad send it out here depending on how long we are stay. I really wanna try and do more complicated projects with it."

My thoughts drifted for a moment while I listened to him go on into even more detail about how he designed the mechanism that automatically extended and retracted his staff and how that sort of construct was only possible with that special metal and that's when it hit me. What if *she* sent those Nirka after Rick's Luminore? Of course, then why would she have us attacked instead of captured and questioned to find out where it was when she had the chance? That trap in the kitchen was specifically designed to kill…

"There it is!! Kari get up here, we're almost there!" Rick shouted back at his sister who stuck her head out from under the sheet we used as a barrier into the back of the wagon.

"Finally!" she almost screamed as she jumped out of the back and sat on the driver's bench between Rick and me.

We approached the great stone fortress in the west, it looked like a large stone cube with four towers, one built at each corner. The whole building looked stunted from the kinds of things Kats normally build, though the war was sprung on them from the outside, and installations like this aren't needed with the way they fight against the other tribes. Rick took us up to the dock where the soldiers and merchants loaded and unloaded supplies. One of the guardsmen approached, obviously cooking out in this heat and in no mood to be bothered.

"State your business." he demanded with every bit of military bearing a rank and file soldier should display. Rick spoke for our trio as usual,

"We came by permission of the Elders in the Furo-Sha colony. They sent us with this letter to deliver to your commander." Rick explained holding out the letter for the guardsman to see his Grandfather's seal.

"This way." He led us into an alcove where we could tie up our wagon and then opened a door and waited for all three of us to enter. "Just down this hallway take a left at the end and his office is on the right"

We followed his directions through the stone corridor and when we came to the end of the hall I looked into the office on the right, and all I saw were stacks and stacks of files strewn all over the cramped little room. The man I assumed to be the commander by the steel chips sewn into his leather service jacket, was at the desk in the back of the room surrounded by even more files. He kept rifling through a mound of paper talking to himself…very loudly, I guess something big happened here recently.

"Excuse me, my name is Rick Burke, we've come from the Furo-Sha colony up in the northeast." Rick then just repeated the same words he had given the guard a moment ago and produced the letter.

The commander looked over the top of his ever growing stack of papers quizzically but when he saw the seal on Rick's letter, he snatched it and tore it open without a word. He flicked his wrist throwing the letter to his desk. The commander looked at each of us in turn like he was sizing up our story, then his attention returned to Rick.

"Young man, I'm surprised you didn't join the military. A man capable of taking care of two women and bringing them through the wastes without harm would've been welcome in my command." The pompous commander seemed to imply Kari and I couldn't take care of ourselves because we are female. He should've been glad I wasn't sticking around, one spark and I could fix his surplus of paperwork. I shot Rick a mischievous glance but the brief sadness that flashed across his face stalled my quip, though the commander didn't seem to notice. "You might have even given your brother a run for his money ha-ha. Now follow me I'll show you were you will be staying." he laughed as he pulled his large frame from his chair and led us back out of his cramped little office. Rick stopped in his tracks, just for a moment, a look of surprise plastered on his face at the mention of his brother. Kari who had been very quiet ever since we got here answered his unspoken question first.

"Didn't you know? That's how we knew where Mom was, I wrote Mark to ask if he had heard from her but that merchant that came through a few days before we left had a letter from her saying she was here with Mark helping out after one of the battles."

"What was so funny?" Rick's question was directed at the commander walking ahead of us because his chuckling kept echoing through the stone halls of the stronghold.

"Oh uh, I guess you wouldn't know since you haven't heard from him in a while, he was discharged at the end of the war for failure to perform his duty" The commander explained casually, but Rick wasn't through with his interrogation.

"What was his duty?" Rick's aggravation at the commander for laughing at his brother's failure was apparent, but the commander answered him, not paying any attention at all to the angry young man only a few paces behind.

"He was assigned to the general's guard while he was stationed here, on his watch an assassin came in and murdered the general right under his nose. You must have just missed him on the road; he left for the colony not too long ago." When the commander said this I heard Rick grunt under his breath before recomposing himself and resuming his pace behind our guide.

The commander left us after we got to the barracks under the southern tower but he did tell us where the mess hall was so we could find Ms. Burke. Kari ran off for the mess hall as soon as she could but Rick caught me as I was about to follow her and asked me to stay behind,

"Hey could you hold on a minute Rebecca?"

"Sure, what's up?"

"I noticed that you've spent most of the trip here trying to figure out those papers dad found on that Nirka, have you had any luck figuring anything out?" Rick was usually too preoccupied with what is going on in his own mind to actually care about what was going on in someone else's so this type of question was really out of the ordinary for him.

"Not much unfortunately, your languages are so diverse; it makes it hard to translate. What I have been able to figure out is that his squad was on their way to Crown Lykou, but it doesn't say why." I explained, I could hear some of the frustration I felt trying to decipher those papers come out as I spoke.

"So that is where you are headed next?

"Yes" I answered flatly, not willing to explain my motivations to him just yet.

"Then I want to come with you, Kari has every soldier here and mom to look out for her and I want to find out why we were attacked. Whatever is going on with you and this person you keep referring to aside; the Nirka were responsible for inciting the war with the Lykos, if they are going back into Canile I have to do something stop them, before they cause another war." The conviction in his voice was unmistakable, but I knew him. Richard Burke loves to fight and since he couldn't fight in the war, now he's found a perfect excuse.

"You just want the danger; they didn't let you fight against the Lykos so now you've found a battle of your own that the Elders can't interfere with!" I scolded

"I just want to do my part! Yes I wanted to fight in the war, fighting is something I am good at, Mark and I both trained with Master Nyma, and you know what? I won every match against my brother yet when real danger came around I was isolated because of this 'blessing'! Now it's my turn, I couldn't fight in the war but I can help stop another one." Rick's conviction didn't waiver but I couldn't help feeling uneasy about taking him with me. Still, it's not like I could stop him from following me…at least not without hurting him.

"Do whatever you want, just don't screw this up for me" I left the barracks headed for the alcove where we left the wagon with Rick close behind, thinking that if there was a chance that *she* was after Rick, I would have to keep him close.

"The wagon is too slow so we're just taking the horses, do you know of a way into Canile without having to deal with border patrol?" I asked as he and I worked to detach the wagon from the horses and saddle them up.

"Yeah there's a town right on the border, Handel, but it's kinda far, maybe two months, if we push it."

"Well then, we better move out" I jumped up into the saddle and turned my horse around and galloped out towards the entrance Rick followed as we sped past the gate guard and onto the road for Handel and from there straight on to the Lykos' capitol city, Crown Lykou.

Chapter 5: Dorian's New Assignment

"Hurry up! Those men need their pay delivered on time!"

Those are the words I heard while dashing out of my father's office with his briefcase under my arm and headed for the work house commons.

My father, Andrew Vesco, is a supervisor for a few of the local construction crews in Crown Lykou. He worked his way up from a ditch digger all the way to where he is now, it was difficult watching him come home exhausted every night but now he says his position was worth it …except for the paperwork.

"I'm going, I'm going!!" I yelled back through the door I left open while rushing out to the commons to drop off this month's payroll.

My family moved here to the capitol about ten or so years ago, it was my father's job that brought us here. Dad had leadership training to go through and when the company had a look at his skills first hand they offered to set us up here in the city. Business took a bad turn when the war began; mom and dad were considering leaving the city but at the time both of my brothers and their families were here, so they decided to stay. I have two older brothers; the eldest is Wayne, he has a decade on me and lives in the Garrison, which is the city's military district along with his wife and child. My other brother's name is Hod, he is only a year older and also lives here in the Mill with us, though he and his family live close to the district wall, I guess they prefer being closer to civilization.

Crown Lykou is a marvel of the modern world, the city was finished only twenty-five years ago in a cradle valley halfway up the side of one of the largest mountains in Canile. It was built as a perfect hexagon with each section covering a specific requirement for the nation's capital.

The Mill is the city's industrial district and where my family has made their home, most of the city's production and labor force works lives out here as well. A dense forest makes up over half of the industrial district; few know the reason for this is because the Kyn are given the orders from the Council through individual locations hidden in the forest and unique to each operative for the sake of subtlety. In the Trade District they have the trader's hall where commodities are bought and sold. There are also a large number of civilian businesses there such as restaurants, farmers markets and crafters. I usually go there when I have nothing better to do and look around. The Garrison and the Consilium are our training districts, the Garrison trains our soldiers and is the headquarters for Canile's military operations, while the Consilium trains the brightest minds the nation has to offer, and new innovations churn out of this center of knowledge every day. Then we have the urban living districts which couldn't be more different, Everest and the Pit, as their names suggest Everest is for the higher social class, nobles and the like, whereas the Pit is for the lower class and the poor. Anybody that falls somewhere in the middle of these two classes lives out of the same district they work. My family isn't the richest but the noble that governs The Mill respected my father's skills enough to have a house built for him on the condition that he take the job supervising operations just down the road from the workhouse and right on the edge of the forest.

I ran past the crowd outside of the large brick workhouse and into the main office where the crew representatives were waiting and not too happy about it. I immediately got to business laying the briefcase on the table and popping open the clasps.

"Here, I have all of your payment packages; inside each amount is labeled for every employee, my father wanted me to thank you all for another good month. I'll see you all again the next couple of weeks." After handing out the packages to the ten crew reps, I closed the case and went on my way up to the main road.

It's been almost six months since I was recalled to the capitol after my mission to assassinate that Kat general. I've been grounded ever since I got back because the assault on that fortress that followed my mission failed since they were ready after those two guards caught me before I could escape. The plan was to kill the general and get rid of the body so that assassination wouldn't be suspected and instead our military could take advantage and strike in their moment of confusion while they searched for their lost general. Though, if I had taken any more time those guards may have killed me in the process, so it couldn't really be helped.

The rush of those infiltration missions is just so incredible, and the look on that guard's face when he tried to stop me was priceless; but the joke is on me, I got caught and I have to face the consequences. The problem now is the waiting, the whole point of the Kyn is to undertake missions that parliament can't be connected to and waiting to see what the politician's will do with me is driving me crazy.

In the meantime I've been keeping my head low working with my father's crews on the roadways and other labor intensive projects for the city. The job isn't so bad, the hours are long and the work is hard, but I guess this is what most people do with their lives. I still have some excitement in my life though; the last thing I have to do today is check on the two refugees I caught sneaking into the city a couple months ago. I was working with one of the crews down in the canals at the foot of the mountain our city sits on, where the water collects from springs further up the mountain. We were trying to install hydraulic powered pumps that send water to various parts of the city when something big floating in the water caught my eye. A half drowned pair; a Kat and Rya were treading water in the canal. I pulled them out and when they came to they told me that they were stuck on our side of the border when the war ended and with the restrictions that were imposed, they couldn't get back to Katzen so they thought they'd come here and try and blend in with the crowd until the restrictions eased up. They both couldn't have been much younger than I and after everything I did during my small stint in the war; the least I could do was try to help them out.

The Kat's name is Richard though he goes by Rick, a Furo-Sha by the looks of him, kinda tall and lean with a pale tone to his skin that seemed familiar for some reason. His most notable features were the large tiger stripes he had tattooed across both shoulders that could always be seen because of the blue sleeveless hooded shirt he wore constantly. Rick was always honest if nothing else. He set up a small forge and opened for business in the Trade District almost immediately after I brought them into the city with my crew. The Rya girl seems nice but I can tell she is hiding something; it's probably just how she and Rick ended up in the canal but she always seems like she's playing the part of an immature teenage girl. Rebecca is a little shorter than me, her jet black hair streaked with crimson is about shoulder length and she is surprisingly strong for her small build. She can be a bit childish at times but she sticks with Rick, and together they've made a good start for themselves here.

I've always been a little wary around the Rya, only because aside from the ones in the city I know relatively little about their race or culture. The nobility import Rya engineers to design all sorts of luxuries, and every time I see one in the Trade District they're setting off sparks constantly when their scales rub together.

A Rya's scales have always freaked me out personally, from I'm told, the scales grow thick like calluses so a Rya that is used to manual labor will spark more often. Rebecca doesn't seem like the heavy-lifter type, but I've never actually seen her spark at all, which is abnormal for a Rya as far as I know.

I visit Rick's shop a couple times a week to check in and make sure they are doing alright it's hit or miss whether Rebecca will be there, even Rick doesn't know where she goes most of the time. Today I'm headed down there to make the final payment on a sword Rick offered to make for me after hearing that swordplay is a specialty of mine. He didn't ask for any money but I figured I would give him what I could. I also took him up on his offer because if my luck turns south with the council I'll need a good weapon to fight my way out of the city. All Rick said when starting this project was that this weapon would be unlike anything I had ever seen, but he also said it still won't be finished for another week or so, which makes the sword just one more thing to wait on...

The Trade District was right next to our district so it didn't take very long for me to walk over. Today wasn't just payday for the work crews; the briefcase also contained my pay for the last work period. Rick's shop was just south of the main crossroad of the district, not far from the main road that circled the Royal Quarter, the same road let out at the main entrance of every district in the city. I found my way there quickly, the sound of countless artisans from all over the world plying their trades, hammers pounding, metal grinding, and fires roaring, reverberated through the city streets as I drew closer to my destination. When I turned the corner I saw a crowd of at least twenty people outside one particular shop. When I ran up to see what was going on I was not surprised to hear Rick, calling out over the mass of people.

"Open for new orders! Take a look at our list of designs and it will be ready for you in a week or less, and at half the price of any other smith!"

I sighed and shook my head as I walked around to the side door and pulled the key from the hollowed rock in the wall. I slid the key in a lock Rick designed himself to get through the back door to the shop. No one was around the forge just, old style armored breastplates, helmets, and greaves hung from various hooks in one corner. I suppose Rick was in high demand for this old style armor, on the other side of the room there were stacks of crates designated either incoming or outgoing. I walked up to one crate that had come in a few days ago according to the shipping label; the top had already been pried off and I could see a faint glow coming from inside that drew my curiosity. I dug through the hay filler and pulled out a chunk of ore with a soft blue tinge to its glow.

"Find anything interesting?"

I spun around and my hand went for the knife I kept lashed to the small of my back but Rick already had his pole extended and pressed it against my throat."You really should be more careful snooping around other people's things." He rotated the shaft of his staff forcing both ends to retract back into the center.

"You're gonna have to show me how you rigged that thing to do that one of these days" I laughed removing my hand from my knife and returning the chunk of ore to its crate. Rick just shook his head and walked up to the crates.

"Sorry, but that's a trade secret" He said with a smirk as he replaced the retracted pole into his belt and reached into the open crate to pull out the piece of ore I had just put back.

"Where did you find that? I've never seen metal like that before." I inquired since Rick's crowd seemed to have dispersed; either that or he was just tired of dealing with them.

"This is what I'm going to make your sword out of; it's from my home, and the same metal I used to make this pole, with any luck a blade forged from it will be pretty amazing. I used the money you gave me to have it shipped here, wasn't easy with the trade restrictions still in place but I figured it was worth it to make a weapon truly excellent. Don't worry; any sword I forge will stay by your side till the day you die." The indomitable pride Rick always seemed to have had no lack for impact, since I was getting excited about my new weapon too.

"How long will it take to finish?" I asked as the anxiousness got the better of me for a second.

"Hopefully if I get started today it'll be done at the latest by the day after tomorrow. If Rebecca gets back to help me, then I may be done even sooner. I know I told you a week, but that was because I needed another shipment of the ore to complete the sword but as you can see, it got here ahead of schedule." He answered looking out the window at the busy streets.

"Here, this is the last of what I promised you, you can use it to cover the delivery fee for the last shipment; and give Rebecca my best when you see her, please?" I handed him a roll of cash from the side pocket of the briefcase and shook his hand, before leaving him to his work.

The sun was starting to fall beneath the horizon creating the orange glow of twilight that seemed to envelop the entire city. This was my favorite time of day, the air gets a little cooler and everything reflects the eerie glow of the retreating sun, making the whole world seem to run away, you can't catch it you can only watch and enjoy the precious moments of light you have left before the darkness descends. A child bumped into me bringing back from my daze, I always had a habit of getting lost in my own mind from time to time. When I was growing up my grandfather always said people like that saw further than most, I just thought it made me strange. I had been staring at the waters of the fountain that sat in the middle of the Trade District crossroad as the light reflected off of the cascading streams for a good few minutes apparently.

"Time to go home, gotta be up bright and early for work tomorrow morning" I groaned sarcastically under my breath, genuinely disgusted with this life in the city. My walk home after I left the Trade District was slow and uneventful; each district has its own form of nightlife…except for the Mill. The Trade District has late night shopping events, Everest has ritzy parties, even the Pit has gambling and nightclubs, (from what I hear those establishments bring in much needed outside money). But for whatever reason, the district I live in seems to shut down squarely at sundown, perhaps because all of its inhabitants are too tired from the day's work to care about doing anything fun, and I guess for now, I am one of them. Today was a long day at work and I was tired, though I still couldn't help but feel a little restless. The feeling increased the closer I got to the house, and by the time I got home I wasn't ready to go inside. I trudged toward the front door, more weary from the realization that this life is the one I am stuck with than actually being tired, when out of the corner of my eye I saw the dim light of a torch in the middle of the dark forest next to my parent's house.

"Finally" I thought to myself with a sigh of relief as I poked my head through the door of the house and told Mum and Dad that I was going for a run, it was mostly true.

I took off into the forest with the speed of a prisoner given the promise of freedom. The torch is the signal I was designated with, since I live so close to the forest. The signal lets me know when I am required to report in by the Kyn. I ran as fast as I could, leaping over bushes and swinging around trees, anything that could get me where I was going just a little faster. The sun, which was burning bright at twilight, had since given way to the cold light of the full moon that bathed the small clearing we use as a gathering place in the middle of the forest. I slid into the clearing to see only one man standing up on a small cliff with a tree at its tip, and a stream that ran off the edge into a small pond in the center of the clearing, the man's name was Alexander Fox.

Fox is a member of the Parliament's primary council and the overseer of the Kynodontes Tou Vorro, an old Canden-breed with greying scruff and short unkempt hair; every time I ever saw him, he seemed to be wearing the same old red robe and was always smoking his large-bowl pipe. I knew when it came time for my fate to be decided, Fox would be the one to deliver the news. The fact that there were no soldiers here with him at least, was a good sign. Though, Fox could easily take me by himself, he didn't make it all the way to the top of the Kyn by being lazy, some say he was even granted his rights back as a full citizen. Fox's achievements are the stuff of fairytales to most of us in the Kyn.

"You came quickly; I suppose you want to know what we have decided to do as far as your failure during your last mission is concerned?" the tall old Canden asked while he packed his pipe and lit a match. I just nodded silently, anxious to hear what the he had to say. "Even though you were discovered and that resulted in the failed attack on the Kat's western fortress the fact of the matter is, you have been very useful, and we have still have use for you. Some time ago you found a pair of foreigners in the city canal system. The Kat has been diligently working his forge, but the Rya… she has been seen in every city district over the past couple of months, this makes us suspicious, especially since the girl has been spotted numerous times around the Albedo's estate in Everest. You are to continue as you have been, keep up your family job and stay in contact with those two, find out what they are up to, and if you have any reason to think their purpose is to do any harm to the people of this city then eliminate both of them." Fox' orders were prudent under the circumstances and it was no surprise that he knew about our city's newest immigrants. The Kyn aren't only deployed on assignment to faraway lands, some are planted all over our own country, and even inside this city to keep an eye on things at home. He probably has spies in every district of the city and apparently, now I am one of them.

"I accept the assignment; I will figure out what the girl has been up to and make my report." I stated clearly, straightening up, holding myself properly as any soldier would, unlike some of my comrades I try to be serious about my duties.

"When you succeed, whether there is any danger to be found or not, your status within the Kynodontes Tou Vorro will be reinstated along with your privileges." Fox was stern but I knew he had been on my side, in truth there are a few times I probably would have been executed if not for him.

"Understood" I gave a slight bow and he responded in kind before disappearing into the dark forest, leaving me alone in the clearing, a trail of smoke and the lingering smell of his pipe tobacco was the only evidence that I had not been alone talking to myself in the middle of the woods.

Before taking my leave as well, I walked up to the thin curtain falling over Fox's little cliff and looked through the water. There standing just the way they were six months ago when I thrust them into the gnarled tree root that had grown down below the cliff, were my twin fangs, the swords that saw me through every mission I took since joining the Kyn. I hid them here after being called back from the front. I would be instantly recognized as Kyn if I carried these swords in the city where the only ones who are legally armed are the soldiers.

"If I can prove my worth to Fox, I can take up these swords again and life can go back to the way it was, I may even start getting missions outside of the country again! All I have to do is make sure Rebecca isn't a threat to the city, and if she is…, I have to end her myself." My words trailed off in the cool night breeze like a whisper to the dead as I raised my eyes to the glow of the full moon shining down on me.

Chapter 6: Mark Arrives in the City

"Your brother and sister left for the Western Fortress to stay with your mother. Someone tried to blow up the gas system and I suppose Rebecca knew something about it because the next morning the three of them had decided to leave the colony. Rick isn't with your sister anymore though, we received a few delivery requests from him concerning some of his marked crates he kept in storage, the last one is set to go out as soon as I can get a special permit. All of the requests have been to send the shipments to Crown Lykou... in Canile. I don't know what kind of trouble he's gotten himself into, going there of all places, but you know your brother..."My father's words echoed in my memory as I rode in the back of the covered delivery cart along inside of Rick's emptied crate in the dead of night. I had stayed a little while in the colony with my father and grandfather and lost valuable time because of their insistence, though with their help I was able to use Rick's delivery request as a way to pass the border undetected.

Six weeks I have been travelling with this delivery man and neither of us knows the other's name. My driver was a quiet man that even kept his face covered with a low hood in the heat of the day. However at the moment, all I was concerned with is getting to the city so I can kill two birds with one bone. I have to find Rick and bring him back home; I will also have the opportunity to at least learn something about the 'Wolf' my debriefing officer spoke of, if he is the one who killed Nyma, I'll kill him myself.

"We're coming up on the city now, get into that box. Now!" my companion hissed with uncharacteristic urgency. At once I grabbed the lid to a large empty crate that I used to hide in when we crossed the border into Canile and laid down pulling the wooden panel over the top of the box. I was surprised that a postal worker could be so easily bought, or at least dad made it look easy, he and Rick have a gift for charisma that would put most politicians to shame.

I could feel our cart stop short and the crunch of dirt beneath the boots of at least six men surrounding us. "What are you carrying?" the strong voice of the Lykos gate guard carried over the night wind.

"Just some ore from the local mines for the city smiths, you can take a look if you want?" I could hear my driver start to leave his perch when the guard stopped him.

"Why is your delivery so late? You know the gates are closed down after sunset." There was an unmistakable hint of suspicion in the guard's voice, but without missing a beat the driver answered,

"I had a stop off where I picked up a few extra deliveries that I didn't expect. The extra weight slowed me down quite a bit." Surprisingly enough he really wasn't lying.

"Don't make a habit of this old man." After the guard fell silent the cart lurched forward as the horses struggled against its weight.

Once I heard the horse's hooves hit cobblestone I knew we had made it inside. I stayed in my box for a good twenty minutes or so before the driver gave the all clear for me to get out. It occurred to me when I slipped out of the back of the cart that I had never gotten a good look at his face during the entire trip, I don't know why I even cared to be honest. I walked around the front of the cart where he still sat in the driver's perch; all I could make out in the light of the lamp that hung on a pole next to him was the grey scruff covering the lower half of his face.

"Watch where you're staring boy, Do you have your things?"

I gave a quick nod since all I had brought with me was my old combat knife and the clothes on my back. Without saying anything else the driver cracked the reigns and headed off into the city. Forgetting my suspicions of my driver, I turned my attention back to my reasons for being here. I figured the best way to get information was to take some time looking around the city before dropping in on Rick. I wandered around for hours looking at each entrance to the different sections of the city that were just off of a main road that circled an inner wall that protected a large dome and a gigantic castle of some sort. Every entrance off of the main road except for one was under guard, the guards were rigid, they didn't talk or move, but it was their strange weapons that caught my eye.

Every guard was armed with short spears, that had blades attached to a pipe on one end, the pipe seemed set inside the wooden handle that extended and curved at the end to form a large flat club shape. The guards held the spears at the curve above the club end and rested them against their shoulders. I couldn't risk being asked any questions by these guards. I spent at least an hour after my self-hosted tour of the city searching for a place to bunk down for the night, without having any luck. It was beginning to look like I would have to sleep on the street and there again risk being caught by a patrol in some back alley.

The only entrance that I had found without any guards led into the city slums, that entrance was completely open. Night clubs and parties raged all over just inside the threshold of the dirty sector. There were people running around like lunatics all through the streets, some looked different from any Lykos I had ever seen. I had thought all Lykos were like the large soldiers with jet black hair and bronzed skin that I had fought against in the war but these people were different, some were pale, some were small, and most had bright red hair. It must be true what they say, just like we have our different tribes, the Lykos have different breeds of their own, but for them all to live in the same city together…that, is kinda weird. There were also the assorted smells of alcohol and the burning wood of the various bonfires that could be seen right off of the street that filled the night air as well.

I was slightly impressed with how well this lunacy was kept under control, when I was outside of the inner walls that surrounded this section of the city I could not see, hear, or smell a hint of the craziness going on inside. Now it made sense why there was no guard at the entrance, i guess as long as they restrict their partying to the inside of these walls there's no need for a guard, and I'm sure quite a bit of money changed hands to make it this way.

When walking down the dirt road of the slums it became clear, staying here till morning was probably the best idea, considering I am…, was… an enemy soldier and am now inside the walls of my enemy's capitol city. No one in this part of the city would notice or care about an unassuming stranger, now I just needed to find an abandoned building to crash in until morning.

One building stuck out compared to the others, tactically sound, built against the inner wall that separated the district from the main road, and far enough away from the bigger parties so I didn't have to worry about any unwanted visitors. Like most of the buildings in the area, this one was built almost entirely out of wood and very poorly designed by the look of it. The floors were cracked and broken in some areas, the full moon was visible through the rather large holes in the ceiling, and from the sound of the whistling wind I would say the walls were probably falling apart as well, as good a place as any for me to wait for the sun to rise I guess. I took a seat in the far corner of the second floor of the house, on the side that leaned against the city wall, resting a hand on the knife at my side and almost immediately, I started to drift off.

I woke to a burning beam of sunlight that had pierced the holey roof of my resting place. As soon as my eyes opened I heard the door to the room bust off its hinges, I leapt to my feet and pulled my combat knife. Four guards flooded into the room pointing those odd short spears I had seen them carrying the night before.

"Drop your knife Mark" a familiar voice ordered from behind the guards.

The two guards in the center stepped to either side to make way for a young man I knew well with tiger striped tattoos on his shoulders and that same cocky grin he always wore that made my blood boil. Rick wasn't alone however, another person I had seen before entered the room with him, sword in hand and a hood pulled low so as to darken his face, the Wolf.

"Well this saves me the trouble of hunting down both of you separately." I snarled, my only weapon ready to strike.

"He told me what happened in the war, when he killed master Nyma. (Rick motioned to the hooded figure) He is the reason you came here right? You probably told Mom or Dad that you wanted to bring me back but, all you really want is to kill him, well now's your chance." Rick's cocky tone did not falter as he stepped aside to make room for the assassin to take a fighting stance.

When Rick stepped away from my opponent however, the light from the sun shot through the open door behind him, blinding me. I raised my hand to shield my eyes from the burning light when I realized, my knife was no longer in it. I looked around to see all of the guards, my brother, and the assassin, were gone and I was back on the floor in my corner with the sun shining in my eyes.

"A dream, just what I need right now…" I sighed, standing up and checking my gear before making my way back into the sprawling enemy city to look for my brother, and Nyma's killer.

I had never been to a city this size, my people always lived in harmony with the stone. The way the Lykos cut every stone exactly the same and pile them together is…boring. I started on my way to their market center as quickly as I could, the faster I find Rick, the faster I can send him home and get to work on finding that assassin. Then I thought for a moment, the military base I passed by last night would have mission reports from the war, a look might give me a good start at finding the Wolf.

As I walked down the main street towards the base I heard an alarm break out through the streets, a sound that I knew all too well, it was a military alert. I went running, half out of the instinct that the military bred into me, towards the sound of the alarm to see what had happened.

This could be my chance to sneak into the base if they are in disarray for whatever reason the alarm was sounded. When I got to the main gate of the base, the guards that were posted there last night with the odd spears were gone and looking through the empty archway I could see at least two squads searching the left side of the base. I slid up to the edge of the arch ready to sprint over to the right side that was left completely open when someone grabbed my arm and pulled me back. I jerked away and turned around to see a young girl, around seventeen-eighteen years old, standing behind me smiling.

"I wouldn't do that now, if they catch you, you'll go away for a very long time. See you around." She gave another big grin and took off into the crowd that was moving up and down the circular main street. Sure enough when I looked back inside the arch a third squad came up from behind the right side of the base, still searching.

"Could she have been the one they were looking for? Whatever, I'll get Rick and worry about this later." I muttered to myself.

I made it into the center of the Market just in time for the morning rush, asking around may draw too much attention so I just wandered instead. Since Rick had sent for his forge materials according to Dad, I followed the sound of pounding metal to the district quarter where the smiths made their homes. I finally found his shop just off of the road that ran straight down the center of the district, it had to be Rick's, there was a large tiger on the sign working the forge with a red and black dragon, my brother liked to paint to relax and I recognized his style of brush work instantly.

Rick's set up was impressive, he couldn't have been here for more than a month or two and already he was running his own business, though I could never tell him that. He wasn't out front but I guess no customers would come out this early to make an order. At the very least, someone was up and working in the back; I could hear the smith's hammer banging away from out on the street.

I walked around to the side gate that led into the open area in the back where I could hear the smith working his forge. Since the wooden gate was unlocked I let myself in, and there stood my brother, over the large anvil holding a red hot strip of metal in a pair of tongs, hammering it flat as green sparks showered with every strike. I stood and watched for a moment, having seen the craftsmen in the colony work; I knew how dangerous it could be to surprise him while he was working. Once the metal started to cool off he thrust it back under the coals.

"How's business, is this what you abandoned Kari for?" I made no attempt to hide the contempt in my voice as Rick's head jerked up and he dropped the tongs.

"What're you doing here?!" his hand went instinctively for what looked like a short pipe that was stuck in his belt behind his back.

"Answer the question, did you want to be free so badly that you'd just leave Kari and Mom at the Western Fortress to live here, with the enemy?" I made the threat of violence evident in my tone; he would answer for leaving our sister so far from home and so soon after the war.

"You came all this way just to start a fight?" He shot back.

"No, I came all this way to take you back, how that happens is up to you." I responded only letting a little anger show now, since Rick wasn't really the only reason I came. I knew my brother wasn't beyond getting into a brawl right here. Instead of anger a slightly disgusted expression tightened his face.

"Don't lie, we both know I am just a convenient excuse, if you really cared that much about Kari and Mom being left at that fortress, you would have stayed back, instead you came out here. I talked to your base commander told me what happened when I dropped off Kari; he told me why you were discharged. You're after that assassin, the one who killed Nyma so don't try and act all righteous!" His defensive stance had turned into an accusatory one.

"You're right! I did come out here after him! But Mom wouldn't forgive me if I just left you here, so you are coming back with me whether you like it or not!" At this moment we both had our hands glued to our weapons but they still hadn't been drawn... yet.

"Hey Rick! You've got a new order, this guy wants a custom dueling gauntlet, I took his measurements and did the rough sketch he said you could do the..." The voice of a familiar young woman rang from the back door to the shop as she stood with a familiar grin. "Hey I know you, you're the big guy that was snooping around outside the Garrison. Rick, do you know him?" It was really strange how her voice stayed cheerful despite the scene she walked in on, could she really be that oblivious?

"That's my brother, Mark. He wants to take me home" Rick answered her without removing his menacing glare, as she heard my brother speak her warm smile turned into a cold grimace.

"Well then Mark, you should really let go of that knife on your back. Rick might have a problem causing you any real pain because you're his brother. I on the other hand, do not have any problem killing you if I have to, I need him." Her eyes burned darkly and her words made it sound like I had no choice in my own actions. She was serious. At this point it seemed like this girl was going to be more of a problem than Rick but before I could respond to her threat Rick stepped right between us.

"Rebecca, calm down, and Mark, we are here looking into why a Nirka with orders to come to this city attacked the colony. Rebecca thinks there's something bigger going on than the Nirka just going too far to cause trouble like they did when they started the war with the Lykos. Since we've been here Rebecca has been investigating while I keep this shop to cover any suspicion." For once Rick was the voice of reason, I guess he knew her well enough to know she wasn't bluffing when she said she would kill me, and if what he said was true about the Nirka, then he did the right thing coming here. The Nirka could start another war if they are poking the Lykos so close to home and this soon after the last conflict. The girl's face immediately returned to her usual cheery grin, and came up to me with a bow.

"I think we got off on the wrong foot. My name is Rebecca, and if you really can't leave without Rick then stay here and help us figure out this Nirka problem." Even when she was being all bubbly and smiling, she still made it sound like I had no choice in the matter. I looked up at Rick who shrugged his shoulders as the tension left his face looking tired.

"Fine, but I am still after the Wolf, don't get in my way again." I grunted at Rebecca who trotted over to a bench next to the forge, her smile now bathed in firelight.

"Is that what the military is calling that assassin?" Rick asked picking up his tongs and pulling another metal strip back out of the fire and carefully striking one side with the hammer.

"Yeah, he apparently works alone and has caused a lot of trouble for the Asker tribe in the east near the end of the war. Is that supposed to spark like that? I asked pointing to the random green embers flying with each swing of Rick's hammer.

"Sounds like a tough guy, and yeah it's part of my secret forging technique." he explained with his usual cocky tone. Then he turned to Rebecca, "So what'd you find out?"

The girl seemed to be thoroughly enjoying the heat of the forge, I couldn't see how, it felt blistering to me and I was in the shade at least six feet away."We were right; the Garrison warehouse they hit was for weapons storage. They made off with at least one hundred and three hundred of those new rifles and enough ammunition to keep them well stocked." She gave her report with grave enthusiasm though I had no idea what she was talking about.

"Excuse me, what are 'rifles'?" I asked, I figured if I was getting dragged into this I should actually know what is going on.

"The rifles are a big reason why we are working so hard to stop whatever the Nirka are doing here. You've seen those odd-shaped weapons the city guards carry?" Rick stopped his explanation and looked at me expectantly.

"Yeah those stunted spear looking weapons, those are rifles?"

"Yeah…, the Consilium University developed them near the end of the war to secure Canile's victory, but the Council opted for a more peaceful solution and proposed the treaty instead. If the Nirka get their hands on enough of those rifles to make a difference, they'll be a real threat to the Lykos or even the other tribes back home." Rick continued without actually telling me what I wanted to know, he sounded like he was trying to avoid details about the weapon itself.

"What's so dangerous about these new weapons? Or is it how they use it?" I asked wanting him to just get to the point. But Rebecca decided to cut in,

"They fire small metal cones called 'bullets', the bullets travel so fast they can even pierce armor plating at two hundred yards. The blades attached to the ends are used to fight an enemy in close quarters just in case anyone can get close enough. These weapons are going to change the face of war on a global scale, and right now the last thing we need is to give the Lykos a reason to test them. Not to mention what the Nirka would do if they had enough of them, either way nobody is safe unless we figure out what is going on." She stood up and disappeared back into the shop, I turned back to my brother who was wearing her same grave expression she had taken during her explanation before he began to speak.

"Right now we have bigger problems than the Wolf, I am sorry about what happened to Master Nyma but we need to deal with the bigger picture first. Are you in?" I nodded and let myself relax a little bit as the tense situation began to dissipate.

"Good, now grab that hammer, I need this sword to be finished by tomorrow." Rick took the flat piece of metal back from the fire again and laid it on the anvil, holding it firm with the tongs. I picked up the hammer and took a few shots smoothing out the rough areas. Then I looked over at my brother as curiosity welled up in me, I just had to ask,

"So...are you and Rebecca...together?"

Chapter 7: Rick's New Friend

"Hey Mark, I need you to watch the shop for a little while, I have some errands to run and Rebecca ran off again, would you mind?" I asked as I threw on my hooded shirt and laced up my boots to leave. I passed my brother on the way out; he just gave a grunt that I took to mean he could handle the shop while I was gone. He and I never really got along well, he didn't like my free spirit and I didn't like his attitude, but we could still get the job done when the situation called for it.

Today I had an investigation of my own to go on before it got too late in the day; I had to be back for when Dorian comes by to check on the sword. Of course I finished the Luminore sword last night, a new design I was quite proud of, but since I had some spare time this morning, I thought I would go make a new friend. My destination was the Consilium University on the other side of the city. Rebecca found out that the two who designed the Lykos' rifles were a professor and student at the university which piqued my interest.

The main road was packed today; Rebecca said traffic is always gets pretty heavy toward the middle of the day which made me think I should've left earlier. I haven't left the Trade District since we came to the city to avoid raising questions, but from what I can tell there is a surprising amount of racial diversity here. One exception was the university district, when I got there the place was filled with Candor, and only Candor.

The Candor are breed of Lykos known for their higher-than-average intellect, which made it no surprise that the university was full of them, from what I have been told you have to be a Candor just to be admitted to the college. The front courtyard was alive with activity when I arrived, groups of students scattered all over the yard, either discussing classes or on break eating lunch. In one area off to the far side of the yard, three students were constructing a strange looking apparatus that looked like a metal cart with some sort of mechanical workings all compacted in the front end that I thought looked interesting. For a second I considered going and talking to them but since I wanted to make it back to the shop on time so I opted to keep to my original goal.

I had to find Albert Vel, Rebecca mentioned him earlier, saying he is the student responsible for the original rifle designs, and as a student he would be easier to get information from than the professor, regarding the matter. Something else she said made my job a bit easier, Vel happens to be the only Kokin-breed Lykos ever admitted to the Consilium. According to Rebecca's information the 'Grau Rot', Alexander Fox, pulled the strings to get him into the Consilium. Fox holds a seat on the Council as the representative of the Kokin; which are the servant class breed of Lykos, though Fox isn't a Kokin himself. There is also a parliament made up of nobles and headed by the overseers of each city district. Unlike this larger group, the Council consists of representatives for each Lykos breed, and the current 'king' which is more of an honorary position than one of real power. The Councilors are the real governors of Canile.

Being a different breed will make Vel pretty easy to spot here, the Candor breed has snowy white hair while a Kokin's hair comes in varying shades of red, he should stick out like a sore thumb among the pale masses. I searched the courtyard but tried to avoid talking to any of the students, because I would be tempted to discuss their work more than the obvious benefit of not drawing any more attention that I already had just by being here. Vel being the exception, I was sure that the Candor students had never seen another Lykos breed set foot in this part of the city much less a foreigner. If nothing else, simply by the way they all stared as I walked through.

Though after a little while one girl must have noticed I was looking for someone because she came up to me and told me if I needed to find a student I could ask inside at the front desk for the student's current class schedule. I decided to take the girl's advice and headed straight into the Consilium main hall where an elderly receptionist greeted me from behind a large desk off to the right of the doorway.

"May I help you… sir?" She seemed a little unsettled and kept staring at the tattoos on my shoulders, but I figured I should just ignore it and ask about Vel.

"Yes, I am looking for a student that made an order at my fabrication shop in the Trade District last week, a problem has come up and I wanted to let him know right away." I said with a confident grin, people always respond better to confidence.

"I see, and who is your friend?" she asked looking back down to the filing drawer on the underside of her desk.

"His name is…Vel, Albert Vel. I am at the right place aren't I?" I did my best impression of a professional just doing his job, and it seemed to work.

"Ahh yes, Albert, he's a good kid. Let's see…Professor Rayburn has him helping out with a project in Garage A, in the east wing. Go down the hall on your right and just keep going until it turns right and the door will be at the end of that hallway on the left." The receptionist went back to her work after dispensing the directions, nervously pushing papers. For all the diversity in the city I guess 'proper' citizens are still put off whenever someone steps outside of the rigid social class rules they have.

I left down the hall for the professor's garage at a brisk pace, keeping in mind that I was still on a time schedule, though I was distracted by the strange lighting fixtures. Hanging from the ceiling throughout the building were these odd glass tubes that radiated white light, yet there was no heat coming from them. I had heard the Lykos had developed a phosphorous substance that they used instead of gas lamps or torches as an alternate form of lighting. Though I also heard it's expensive to manufacture, so only the more affluent establishments can afford the modern lighting. Since the university developed it I wasn't surprised to see that every room I passed was lit with these 'bulbs'. I was just within sight of the door that the receptionist had mentioned when I heard what sounded like a loud explosion coming from inside. I ran as fast as I could to the door, throwing it open only to see nothing but the thick white smoke which blanketed the entire room.

"Is everyone okay!!?"

"Cough...cough...We're fine, just a blowback in the system...Albert could you get the fans?" a somewhat weary voice came from inside the smoke sounding like a middle-aged man whom I assumed was the professor. I heard the sound of a pump being worked from the wall with the windows to the outside and fans slowly coming to life, pulling the smoke out of the room.

A stout elder Candor man wearing glasses in a long white coat came into view as the smoke dispersed, and over by the wall was a Kokin, no older than myself, though he was thin and frail-looking. He was wearing a coat similar to the professor's but that was where the similarities ended, in stark contrast to Rayburn's clean white hair, his hair was fiery red, and he had to be at least six inches taller. Both however, were clean cut both in the way they held themselves and in their appearance.

"Good afternoon, I'm Professor Rayburn, and this is my assistant Albert. Sorry about the mishap, we let the experiment get away from us, come over here Albert." Albert came up to stand beside Rayburn and they both shook my hand in turns, then the professor turned and gestured to the mechanical apparatus that sat in the middle of the room, there were actually two side by side.

"What do you think; this is a steam powered engine the boy and I are working on. That explosion you heard was because we miscalculated our chemical ratios. I am sorry to have caused you any trouble Mr....?"

"Burke, I own a fabrication shop in the Trade District and I was just going to take a tour of the campus but no one was available to show me around so the receptionist said I could just look around by myself as long as I didn't cause any problems." I explained sounding as innocent as possible.

"Ahh well, in that case Albert can show you around. I have a lunch-meeting with the dean that I'm already late for anyway. I am glad to see a Kat show interest in higher learning, it's really a shame the school doesn't admit other breeds or races. Albert, be sure to look after Mr. Burke, I'll be back in an hour." Rayburn hung his lab coat on the rack next to the door and left shutting the door behind him.

"I'm sorry, he can be a bit absent minded, but he is a good man when it comes down to it. Come with me, you've already been through this wing so we'll go over to the west side." Albert opened the door once more to show me out.

"Actually I am interested in what you're working on here. The professor said your chemical ratio was off? I thought engines like the ones in the city for plumbing only ran off of hydraulic pressure." I left Albert by the door to look at the engine. He came up beside me with an excited look on his face as he began to explain,

"Well actually the city water pumps do work off of perpetual motion hydraulic energy. The system is sort of like a two-stage waterwheels, the first is turned by the water flowing into the canal and operates the city pump system, the second is turned by the same flowing water, further down the canal, which operates another pump, the second pump sends the water collected at the end of the canal back up the mountain through pressurized hoses allowing it to flow back down and through the first wheel in a cycle." As I listened I thought, if I didn't know better I would have thought Albert was the professor by the way his explanation seemed to roll off of his tongue as though he had it perfectly rehearsed.

"So what is this steam engine then?" I asked bending down to get a closer look at the machinery.

"The Consilium looked at steam energy once before, but it wasn't a viable solution at the time, seeing as it would require a boiler that would either take gas or coal as secondary fuel. That being the case, Ryagan's engineers are working on a system for internal combustion using only coal or gas, but their problem is they can't find the right fuel composition for their designs. Originally, the Consilium's policy was simply to emulate Ryagan's research and discover the right combination ahead of them, but now things are a bit different.

The current system that the Professor and I are working on requires no such expense, now that we have something else as fuel. The new fuel is a simple chemical that, when mixed with water, causes immediate, rapid expansion and vaporization. The water vapor expands at such a high rate that it can be used to power most modern pump systems and machinery with only minor adaptations, as well as opening up a wide new range of technological innovations. It's really an exciting time here at the university." As Albert recited his explanation his eyes shined with ambition. He walked over to a tank containing a thick dark blue substance and placing his hand on top as he finished.

"Then you are trying to find the right ratio of that chemical to a certain amount of water to run the engine." I stated, as I began to understand the theory behind the student's work.

"That's the thing, I have actually already discovered the proper ratio, but I can't tell the professor, his pride wouldn't allow him to accept that I found it first. The professor is a kind man but he was still raised to be proud of his breed and in the back of his mind he still sees me as an inferior for being a Kokin, even though he'd never say it out loud. Instead, he would do whatever it took to find another way, even if it meant adding months to the project." The young prodigy walked solemnly around the steam engine as he spoke, which gave me an idea.

"I don't see any professor now, let's start her up." I walked over and slapped him on the shoulder though by the way he shuddered I could tell that wasn't the best idea.

"If Rayburn finds out…" He began to protest.

"Rayburn will find out, but there isn't much he can say if you already have the machine working. Let's do it." A smile cracked along his face as he started to realize what this success would mean for him, though there was still a little apprehension in his expression, but I could tell the temptation outweighed his anxiety.

"Alright, pump that lever by the engine five times, and let me know when you have it primed." I found the lever he mentioned and did as he said.

Albert went over to the unit containing the blue liquid and waited for my signal to begin turning the crank. Once I gave him the go-ahead he turned the crank, slowly counting the ticks, which let the chemical flow through a pressurized tube and into the engine. A loud hiss came from the exhaust port on the side followed by a low hum, the outside gears turned, rotating the rubber belts and began to pick up speed. Albert let go of the crank and stepped back, I followed him and we both stared down at the mechanical marvel at work. With a low hum the engine began to kick into gear, the internal steam reaction stabilized perfectly as the engine started pulling fuel from the tank and water from the pump on its own.

"This is amazing! Even with how small it is, I wonder how much power it can generate." I mused as the possibilities for such a machine piled up in my head.

"What is going on in here!?" The door behind us had burst open and Professor Rayburn stood in its threshold, his face was beet red and contorted in anger. I thought he might explode as his eyes darted from Albert to me then to the engine and back to Albert, as his slightly plump face grew an even darker shade of red

"I thought I would try a different ratio while you were gone, since the water pressure is half of what we tried last time I was sure there wouldn't be any blowback this time. If anything there wouldn't be enough pressure for any negative reaction." Albert frantically explained as he stepped away from the machine that was humming away. Rayburn's eyes slid slowly away from Albert to the engine and fixed themselves there while he paused for a good ten seconds.

"It's working…you did it…?" He turned to his student as the color in his face began to even out. He ran over and grabbed

Albert by his shoulders and yelled once more, "You did it! Do you know what this means?!" Albert just shook his head, as I am sure we both still couldn't tell whether we were in trouble or not.

"This means you'll finally have the attention of the Council, this is it!!" Rayburn turned around and shook my hand, and then he ran for the door.

"Be sure to record that exact ratio, I have to report this to the Dean! Mr. Vel, you will be hearing from the Consilium board as soon as tomorrow if I have anything to say about it. I hope you are ready to stand beside me as we present our work!" With that the professor shot into the hallway leaving the door wide open and a gust of wind in his wake.

"Well I guess you're gonna be famous" I said turning to Albert who was still standing stiff as a board, exactly the way he was when the professor grabbed him.

"Uh yeah... I think I need some air" Albert's voice fell low as he walked over to a door below the windows with the large fans and stepped outside.

When I followed him outside the bright afternoon sun blinded me for a moment, once my eyes adjusted I saw Albert sitting on a bench against the wall just staring out at the other students in the yard.

"Cheer up bro, the professor wasn't even mad."

"It's not that, I spent so long just trying to get into this school, when Fox told me that I had gotten in I knew I was one step closer to my goal. Now I'm right here on the edge and it's just a lot to take in." His halfhearted reply came through almost like a whisper through the autumn wind.

"What is your reason goal?" I asked taking a seat beside him in the shade of the wall.

"It was something my brother and I promised we would accomplish. He and I are Kokin, the lowest breed, and when we were kids we promised we would find a way to prove whether you were born Kokin or even a noble Canden, anyone should be able to do whatever they want with their lives. My breed are treated like trash, barely tolerated, and even despised by some of the other breeds. At least the Ater have the right to serve in the military, we aren't even allowed to defend our homes unless they run out of options. All Kokin are resigned at birth to live out our lives in subjugation to the higher breeds, it's maddening! Growing up in the Pit, knowing the closest you'll get to any recognition in this society, is when a Canden might tip you for an exceptional job cleaning their house or tending their lawn… That's no way to live." I could tell by the frustration in his voice just what he was feeling. He had clawed his way up all the way to this success from the back alley streets of the Pit, but something was still missing from his life, the one he made the promise to that had gotten him this far.

"Where's your brother now?"

"He's gone; he gave up, saying that the other breeds would never accept us no matter how hard we worked or how much we sacrificed." Anger now surfaced in the young man's voice.

"Screw him, you earned your place here, and with that engine in there, you've shown the people in this city that Kokin are just as capable as any other breed." I stood up in an effort to inspire him, though at that moment he looked more like he was in shock.

"The engine!!" He jumped up from his seat and ran back through the door. A couple seconds later he poked his head back outside. "Thanks for the help Mr. Burke, I have to shut down the engine so it doesn't overheat, we haven't added a cooling system yet."

"It's Rick and you should come by my shop in the Trade District sometime, just look for the sign with a tiger and dragon on it."

"You got it." He answered with a nod before jerking his head back inside and shut the door.

"Whew..." Today had turned out to be very interesting, I witnessed new technology that could affect the whole world, but somehow I felt like I was forgetting something... Dorian! I looked onto the horizon to see the sun falling ever closer to the line. I shot out through the east yard into the university central courtyard. I flew as fast as my feet would carry me across the cobblestone pavement when a sound stopped me in my tracks. A familiar laugh had broken out from one group of students off to my right.

Rebecca sat at a table close to the inner wall of the school with three Candor boys and a large chemistry set…, this wasn't going to end well. She looked up and waved with a fake angelic smile and the guys with her turned to look for who she was waving at, the moment they looked away from her I knew something was wrong. Her smile took a devilish turn and I could make out a small fire in the palm of her hand, as she held it under one of the vials with a dark green colored liquid in it. Before they could turn around there was a loud pop as if a large balloon had been punctured and green smoke rushed out in a gigantic wave across the side yard of the school. A small hand grabbed mine in the confusion of the smokescreen and yanked me towards the exit. Rebecca and I erupted from the smoke, through the main archway, and out into the main road where a small crowd of pedestrians stood on the street staring right at us as we emerged.

"I guess one of the student's experiments went wrong, haha-ha…" Rebecca laughed awkwardly, rubbing the back of her neck. I looked down at her urgently, having a more important matter to deal with than her antics at the moment.

"We have to go! Mark is watching the shop and Dorian will be there for his sword any minute!" I resumed my pace running back for the Trade District when I heard Rebecca call out from the opposite direction.

"I'll have to catch up with you later! I have a lead to follow!!" Without looking back I kept going at full speed back to the shop.

Chapter 8: Rebecca Goes Undercover

"Yes!!"

I leapt through the air out of excitement as I dashed across the stone paved streets of the gigantic city. Rick thought he was being clever sneaking off while I was gone and talking to Vel, though he did get further than any of my attempts. I wonder if he knew I had already tried to find Albert, I just never thought of walking right in through the front door. I was at least able to eavesdrop around the outside corner of that garage while they were talking, but I will have to ask Rick what happened while they were inside when I get back. Judging by what Vel said to Rick about his intentions, he will be a good ally to have in the coming days. What he said about his brother on the other hand…something about it doesn't sit well with me, if I'm right it could mean some trouble for us in the long run.

I did learn something interesting from the other students while waiting for Rick to finish up inside; the man responsible for weaponizing Professor Rayburn and Vel's work is none other than Neil Canaan. I also heard a rumor that the vaporizing chemical was actually Vel's theory that Rayburn took advantage of, not that it would have ever seen the light of day without Rayburn because of Vel's breed, but still I like for credit to go where it's due. Right now however, I am more concerned with how often Canaan's name keeps popping up in recent events.

Canaan is the current 'Albedo', the Candor's highest official and representative on the council. Using his political powers, the Albedo enlisted Colonel Vesco of the Capitol Garrison to find a way to use Vel's chemical as a weapon, and their answer was the rifle, or to be more specific, the 'bullet' it fires. The concept is genius; the problem is Canaan, he's been at the heart of a few too many events surrounding the war, and now it turns out he is behind the new weapon development too? All of this is bit too much of a coincidence not to investigate, so I've decided the best way to know for sure if Canaan is involved with the Nirka's activity in the city is to infiltrate the his estate in Everest, the district where all of the state officials reside. Canaan is throwing an outdoor party this afternoon for the Everest nobles to kick off his campaign for another term in office, giving me the chance to take a look around inside without being noticed.

Canaan will be overseeing preparations outside, between that and with the cover I've prearranged, there will be no one else to question why I'm there. This opportunity was just too good to pass up, not to mention I can't think of a more fun way to spend an afternoon trapped in this walled city than to break into a dignitary's mansion looking for suspicious evidence. I loved these kinds of escapades, the adrenaline is what I live for, never knowing whether I'll be caught or how I'm gonna get out of a tight spot, made any normal problem seem so trivial.

"Hmm...ha-ha...haha-ha!" I couldn't help but giggle to myself as I passed through throngs of citizens drawing closer on my way to meet with my contact. I passed through the gate into Everest without even noticing and found myself standing in the middle of the street staring out at the beautiful scene that laid out before me. The white stone roads and enormous houses, outdoor gas lampposts and small pavilions dotted across small grassy fields that separated the privately owned land. The smaller properties closer to the entrance, but even those houses were built three floors high and all varied greatly in grand style and architecture. Some were stucco or brick and even obsidian towering on either side of the street with grand arches, a few seemed like they were built as cathedrals.

"Now if all this were all metal it would be just like home." I thought to myself as I continued to my destination.

The deeper I went in the bigger and more extravagant the homes became until I finally reached the Albedo's estate. The enormous mansion, set behind a lush courtyard filled with statues of stone and bronze, was made entirely of polished marble with four large columns in front. I could smell the comforting fragrance of flowers coming from beyond the fence, it came from the elation flowers that some nobles had planted around their mansions. The elation flowers have a euphoric effect on people so they are quite popular though they are a bit expensive to grow and maintain. My eyes followed the trail of the wrought iron fence as I refocused on the task at hand, there all the way up at the gate leading into the estate stood my contact next to the rather large Ater guards. A young redheaded lykos girl in a modest dress with a cheery smile was waiting for me, Margot.

"Hey!!! You came!" She ran up to me carrying a small canvas bag and looking quite pleased with herself. "I have your change of clothes right here, thanks so much for covering for me tonight. I really didn't want to have to cancel on my boyfriend again..." She smiled with only a twinge of guilt in her face from passing on her responsibilities to someone else before handing me the bag.

What she didn't know is that I had fostered our 'friendship' for this exact purpose. After reading what I could of the Nirka's orders I had guessed they were working with a city noble and once I decided on one to investigate, it wasn't difficult to find an oppressed house maid that wouldn't ask questions when I offered to take her shift for one night.

"No problem, I'm glad I could help. So... what do I do exactly?" I asked, while taking a reluctant look inside to see what I would have to wear to pass as a house maid.

"Be sure to wear the uniform, no one will question you if you do, they'll barely even notice you're there. Just try and look like you're busy if anyone comes inside, you won't have any cleaning I've already taken care of that, you may have to deal with a guest or two but that shouldn't be difficult, and I'll be back in a few hours. Thanks again!" She rushed passed me and on down the street, disappearing around the corner.

I passed through the gate without hearing a word from either guard and slowly strolled through the forest of statues that formed a barrier between the front gate and the colossal mansion of marble. Small engraved plaques at the bottom of every statue bore the names and a short description of each image portrayed in epic proportion as they lined the wide road leading up to the front door of the house.

I reached the large wooden doors lacquered and painted white, adorned with brass embellishments with prayers in ancient Candor if I remember right, inscribed into the metal. I let myself in, slowly pushing the doors open, the smooth motion of the well-oiled hinges didn't make the slightest sound as they opened, and as I figured the inside was almost completely deserted when I peered into the sparsely lit home. The sunlight filtered through the silk curtains splayed out on the imported high quality wooden floor, I could hear the hydraulic pumps that only the most affluent could afford churning as they worked the fans that kept the house cooled by circulating the air which created a constant light breeze inside. Now I just needed to find a place to change...

I found privacy in the form of the most beautiful bathroom had ever seen before, it was a shame I didn't have room in the bag Margot gave me for some of these amazingly soft towels. The bathroom was done in black marble, with white ceramics for the facilities, and brass fixtures. The towels hanging on the three racks in the bathroom really did feel amazing, as I felt one in my hand I seriously considered leaving Margot's uniform here when I left so I could pack the canvas bag with these towels.

Living with Rick isn't all bad but sometimes places like this take me back and I still miss the little comforts of home. When I still lived in the empire, I had luxuries like this to call on at any time, now I had to wait my turn to 'shower' using a hanging bucket of water with tiny holes in the bottom… I let out a sigh as I looked in the mirror at myself holding up this absurd maid's outfit and felt a little sorry for Margot, why she would degrade herself by working a job like this is beyond me. After a few adjustments to the fitted black and white traditional outfit for this profession and tying up my hair I stepped out of the gleaming bathroom and set to work looking all over for signs of anything out of the ordinary, most side rooms were for sitting, dark and unused with covers over all the furniture.

I could hear the party already getting underway outside, glasses tinkling as the champagne was poured and the hoard of guests all talking at once over the background music, I heard them all the way in here though through the walls it just sounded like a jumble of collective murmurs. The Albedo had spared no expense for this event, even hiring a small orchestra to serenade his guests while they took advantage of the exquisite service and cuisine. All the while they would half listen to Canaan's new and well-scripted campaign speech.

I looked up the dark cherry-wood grand staircase in the main hall of the large mansion as it split off in two directions leading up to a terrace that connected the two wings on either side of the second floor that I would need to search. I decided to start with the east side; I ran to the top of the staircase and shot down the hallway on the right. Twelve rooms on each side and every one more boring and dreary than the last, though at least every other one of the outer rooms had balconies. If not for being able to see out from those balconies, I would have forgotten I was in the east wing of the mansion because every room was so identical. They looked more like they had been stripped of all the refinements that were all over the rest of the house.

"Nothing, does this guy even live in his own house?" I whispered, a little out of breath. It seemed so odd, all these rooms, in contrast to the lavish décor in the rest of the house, were almost too dull like they were purposely furnished with cheap beds and faded black curtains which gave it this weird feeling, especially because there were clear signs that the rooms were being inhabited. Half opened boxes all filled with identical commoner's clothing and unmade beds were in behind every door. "Whatever, the master bedroom must be in the west wing" I thought as I reached the end of the east wing hall.

I bolted back down the hallway quickly glancing at each door along the way to be sure I had returned them to the way I had found them. Once I reached the grand staircase just as I was about to rush across the terrace for the west wing, I heard footsteps at the bottom of the stairs, immediately I snapped into character. A tall man, too tall to be any Lykos breed except maybe a really tall Ater wearing a fine suit and holding a top hat to his stomach in a very formal pose, stepped out at the bottom of the stairs and stood still looking straight up at me.

"Was that you running about upstairs? Why aren't you outside attending to the master's guests?" The arrogant condescension in his voice nearly made me sick, but I knew with the red and black in my hair as long as I didn't look him in the eye that maybe I could pass for a half-breed.

"Sir, I was just checking for my missing bag, I dropped it in one of the east wing rooms while I was checking the linens to see if they might need laundering. I'm really sorry, I am new here. The Albedo hired me to tidy up inside during his party in case any guests might need to come indoors." I did my best impression of a downtrodden servant girl, and did an even better job not gagging on the words.

"You're new, then you should know Master Canaan does not allow the help into the east wing, be glad it was me that caught you and not the master, he does not take kindly to servants who don't follow his rules…, whether they know them or not." The man raised his hat to his head and tipped it, that's when I saw, the sleeve of his suit jacket and shirt pulled down ever so slightly revealing a distinct spotted pattern on his skin.

Until that moment I avoided eye contact, but I couldn't help but look up to confirm what I saw when his eyes caught mine. He gave an arrogant grin as his hand dropped from his hat's tilted brim. He was one of 'them'… I watched him turn and saunter down a dark hall that ran straight back behind the stairs and disappear into the black, looking over his shoulder at me with that smirk still on his face.

This situation just got bigger than just Rick and I, the Albedo is definitely using the Nirka for something, now we are going to have to alter our strategy. The worst part was, I just knew by the way the man with the top hat was acting, any evidence I could have found was down that dark hall. If only I had just gone for it, but I couldn't run the risk of being caught in whatever trap the Nirka in the top hat was daring me to spring. After catching me snooping around there was no chance he would have left anything important unguarded. In the second I saw the eyes of the man in the suit, and he saw mine I was sure he suspected I was more than I appeared.

Normally I wouldn't care about the risk of him pegging me as a Rya, I had the firepower to at least give myself an opening to escape, but Margot would face punishment too and I couldn't let that happen."Ugh…Sometimes I hate being a good guy…" I groaned and went back to the bathroom to change and get out of there. "Guess I'll just tell Margot I was fired for going into the east wing."

I finished getting back into my normal clothes and gladly put the maid's uniform back in the bag. Thankfully the party in the side yard kept the courtyard clear of people so I could leave without being noticed. When I was close to the exit gate I passed a statue that looked vaguely familiar, after looking around and seeing no one close enough to worry about, I squatted down to read the plaque at the bottom. Unlike the other statues there wasn't a description only the name 'Alistair V.' inscribed on the brass plate.

"Hey, what are you doing out here?" My hand slid down the knife on my leg as I turned to see where the voice had come from, Margot stood above me with a slight look of disappointment on her otherwise cheerful face. I let go of the knife and stood up, offering her the bag containing her uniform.

"Uh sorry, I didn't know servants weren't allowed upstairs and I was asked to leave. Don't worry though, I just told the man in the suit that Canaan hired me as extra help so you wouldn't get into trouble" I explained with a fake smile.

"Oh well I guess no harm done, it's a good thing my boyfriend got called in to work so I could make it back early. What were you doing with this statue?" She looked up at the robed figure chiseled out of modest granite that stood before us and then back to me looking a little confused.

"This one is just different from the other statues, they all look like epic heroes, villains, and even monsters but this guy… he just looks like an ordinary man and all it says is his name." I said pointing down at the plaque.

"Ha-ha. That's the prophet Alistair; the old church says he is the one responsible for convincing Erus to gather the Lykos breeds from the warring provinces and form us into a nation. No one knows what the 'V' stands for, probably some title from the old world or something." I looked up at the statue as she spoke, unable to shake this awfully familiar feeling seeing it gave me, when I noticed the sun dipping below the horizon.

"Ah great, hey I gotta run Margot, stop by the shop sometime alright?" Without waiting for her answer I rushed out through the gate and back towards the Trade District, Rick would want to know what I've learned.

I flew by gate after gate of city districts, running around the circular main street looking and listening for the signs of the evening crowd that always flocked to the markets in the Trade District during the late afternoon. The night air was the rich smell of cooking food from the various dinner restaurants Rick and I would frequent when we didn't feel like making anything ourselves that let me know I was getting close. I cut left into the main gate of the Trade District and avoided getting caught in the masses of people by taking a couple of back alleys I knew would drop me right at the wooden fence at the back of Rick's shop. I opened the old wooden door in the slatted fence and stepped into the back yard of the shop, already the evening dew had dampened the ground.

The orange light of sunset fell on the second confrontation I've unknowingly walked in on back here. Mark stood with gritted teeth and animalistic fury on his face, with his combat knife in hand. He faced a young Lykos male holding a gilded silver dagger defensively, wearing the look of cold indifference, and Rick standing with his staff extended, squarely in between the two.

"I have to learn to knock before coming back here…"

Chapter 9: A Sword for Dorian

"Finally!"

For a moment I considered just what it said about me that I was so excited at the prospect of getting a new weapon, but I just shrugged it off as I signed my time card on my father's desk at the end of the day's shift. My father looked up at me with that same blank expression he always had when he wasn't telling me what to do as I put his pen back in the stand on his desk. My induction into the Kynodontes Tou Vorro was only known to my immediate family and military personnel for the sake of secrecy, since members of the Kyn are basically disowned by our society. My father was kind enough to let me work for him when I came back from the war but the fact that I joined would bring shame to the family if it ever got out. So maybe he was just protecting the family name by hiding me away in this little corner of the city.

I left Dad's office and headed out for the Trade District, wanting to get there before sunset so I could see my new sword in the light of day. I got to Rick's shop fairly quickly, though the shutters in the front were already closed up, I guess he decided to close up early today. I checked the front door and found it was unlocked, figuring Rick was inside waiting for me, I went ahead and let myself in. I heard people out back, sounded like they were fighting so I rushed to the back door. I found Rick sparring against another Kat, even taller than he was, but with the same pale skin.

He looked familiar, like I had seen him before, but I couldn't quite place him.

"Hey, you're back. I wasn't sure if I was going to catch you, I've been out on errands most of today. This is my brother by the way." Rick had noticed me at the back door and walked away from his match as he spoke, and cocked his head back to indicate the one he was fighting as his brother.

"So you came to the city for your brother. There aren't many that would come so far. I'm Dorian, a friend of your brother's." I shook the other Kat's hand as Rick walked over to a box leaning against the wall of the shop. "So were you able to finish the sword?" I turned to watch Rick pull the lid off of the box and that's when I heard the scraping of metal, a blade sliding out from its sheath, and coming from behind me.

I ducked low to avoid his strike and thrust my foot straight into the other Kat's stomach knocking him back a good five feet. I drew the gilded knife at my back as I slowly stood up watching him do the same.

"Should I know why you're attacking me?" I asked a little annoyed at being interrupted after waiting for so long to get my sword, more than having a weapon drawn on me.

"You're the one that killed master Nyma; that's his stolen knife!" The tall Kat snarled.

When I heard him say the name 'Nyma' it dawned on me, this was one of those guards that caught me the night I assassinated the general on my last mission. Instantly, it all clicked, he was here for revenge and judging by the shoddy attempt he had just made to stab me in the back, I decided this Kat wouldn't be much of a threat. Rick jumped between us extending his weapon to keep us apart. Just then, the door in the back fence swung open to reveal the Rya girl I rescued from the canal.

It was a standoff; Rick acted quickly to keep us apart, and now there was another player, things had escalated quickly. Rebecca paused for a moment then a dark anger spread into her face, she leaned forward letting both hands drift down to the handles of the long knives strapped to her thighs. In one fluid motion she made the first move, she shot forward drawing her weapons. Both the Kat who attacked me and I raised our knives to defend against her attack, but she wasn't after us... She leapt and caught Rick off guard hooking her arm around his neck and swinging around behind him, kicking his legs out from under him she held him up by his neck and pulled him back towards the forge with her blade at his throat.

"Let him go." The tall Kat growled, though I could see him watching me out of his peripheral.

Apparently killing his superior had gotten me so far on his bad side, even his brother's life being in danger wasn't enough to fully distract him. I had more pressing issues at the moment though, since Rebecca had shown her true colors. Now I'd have to kill her like Fox said earlier. I changed my grip on the gilded knife from a defensive position to an offensive one; no matter who makes the first move in this stand-off, it would end up a free for all with Rick getting the shortest end of the stick.

"Rebecca, why don't you let Rick go and we can talk about your problem, no one needs to get hurt." I said trying to sound as friendly as possible.

"Ha! That's funny coming from an assassin, 'Dorian', or maybe you prefer your other name, Wolf?" Somehow she knew who I was, and then she looked over at the other Kat. "As for you, soldier boy, I've already had enough of the way you act, pissed off all the time like the world owes you a favor." Her words shut both of us down. (Was she really holding Rick hostage just to get a point across?)

Rebecca kept her knife at Rick's throat and I could see steam rise off of the blade as it began to heat up. The other Kat and I looked at each other and back to her, she donned a sly grin and began to speak again.

"Mark, you and Dorian here, are exactly what I need. Right now Neil Canaan, one of this city's government officials is working together with the same Kats that caused the last war" Slight desperation worked its way into her words as she spoke

"The Nirka aren't that stupid, after what happened the last time they came after the Lykos, they wouldn't dare risk angering the other tribes again." The Kat she called 'Mark' growled.

"Then maybe you can explain the entire wing of Canaan's mansion he has cleared out and turned into a makeshift barracks, or his Nirka butler. I was just there, I saw it all myself!" Rebecca growled back.

"Hold on, let's say you're right. What do you want us to do about it?" I asked lowering my knife. Her expression softened a little as she looked over at me.

"We need to find out what Canaan and the Nirka are planning and stop them before they start another war. You are one of those assassins the Lykos council uses when they can't be attached to an incident, as for these two and myself, we shouldn't even be here, which means the four of us can investigate without attracting too much attention. I don't know what the issue is with you and Mark, but right now we have bigger problems. I'm sure neither of you wants another war, and after we fix this problem, then you two can kill each other for all I care." Rebecca's desperation turned to resolve as she explained the situation to us.

I looked away from Rebecca over to Mark who met my eyes with that same animalistic ferocity he held ever since he took that shot at me only a few moments ago.

"You said the name Nyma, I guess you were one of the guards that caught me the night I was ordered to kill the general? Well I think we should listen to the lady, you have others you care about back home, and from the sound of things if we don't deal with this Nirka problem they might be caught up in another war." He couldn't deny the truth in my words, with a loud grunt he sheathed his knife

"When this is over, you're dead." The colossal Kat spat and walked over to the far wall and leaned up against it staring intently at the three of us.

Rebecca released Rick from her grip and stepped back as he got to his feet. He rubbed his neck as he looked at her a little frustrated, but I could tell he knew she did the right thing to diffuse the situation. I was actually kind of impressed. In the span of only a few minutes, that girl turned three people who were at each other's throats into something resembling allies. I sheathed my knife and looked over at Rick who was walking back towards the wooden box where my sword rested when I heard Mark speak out behind me.

"You, that's master Nyma's knife that you stole, I want it back." I was beginning to think the only way this guy could talk was in growls. I turned to look at him over my shoulder as I drew the knife.

"I'm guessing you saw this, and that's how you knew who I was? You're such a devoted student. Catch." I spun the knife through my fingers and let it fly, aiming just above Mark's right shoulder, he caught it without so much as blinking.

"You'll be needing this then, I think we'll all probably have to fight before this is over" I heard Rick from behind me as he pulled the sword from the box and threw it to me.

Without looking away from Mark just in case he decided to take another shot at me with my back turned, I simply stretched out one hand in the direction that the sound of the sword came from as it flew through the air. The weapon landed perfectly in my palm and even without seeing it, I could already feel something different about this weapon. I looked down at the sword in a polished metal sheath which rested in my hand. I had never seen a sheath made of metal, I've only ever seen them in hardened leather. The next oddity that caught my notice was the shape of the weapon; this sword was not a straight blade as is common in this day and age, from where the hilt ended at the hand-guard, the blade extended in an elegant arc with the sheath shaped to match.

I looked over at Rick who nodded with his usual cocky smirk "I took some inspiration from what my father told me about the kinds of swords they use where you are from, Rebecca." Rick directed his smooth tone towards Rebecca, though she just rolled her eyes and walked away.

My eyes returned to my new sword that could be seen as more a work of art than a weapon, not for its glamour, but because of the simple beauty in its design. I placed my hand on the hilt wrapped by interwoven black leather strips and began to slide the blade out from its resting place, the light that reflected off of the blade was silver at first, but as I drew it all the way out it took on a sharp blue hue that was almost white. For a moment I was entranced by the single edged sword until I heard the roar of fire. I turned around and saw Rebecca, holding fire in her bare hand as she and Rick exchanged an affirming glance.

"Mark, Rick, and I can't stay here anymore; I know for sure the Nirka I ran into in the Albedo's mansion saw my eyes, won't be long before Canaan sends soldiers looking for me. The people will just think the forge got out of control and burnt the shop down." Rebecca walked over to the pile of wooden boxes filled with packing hay up against the stone wall of the shop while Rick went inside and came out with a messenger bag over his shoulder.

"Where will you three go?" I asked looking at the brothers and back to her.

"I'm not really sure...do you have any ideas?" she replied looking at me expectantly as the fire burning in her hand and the red glow of the forge quickly became our only light as night began to fall.

"Well, my family's home is in the Mill, next to the forest, I can always ask them if you guys can stay there for a while, if nothing else you can stay in the woods." I offered reluctantly as I returned my new sword to its sheath and slid it into my belt. " This is gonna be awkward…" I muttered under my breath and turned around, walking through the open door in the back fence and up the alley back to the street.

I made my way out front of the shop followed by the Kats with my head hung low, as we waited for Rebecca to catch up. The three of us turned and watched from the other side of the street as flames burned from the inside of the shop and crept around the stone engulfing every burnable substance. At this point a crowd had begun to form from the surrounding shops to watch the shop succumb to the fire, Rick threw on a light jacket he had bunched up in his bag and pulled his hood up to mask his face. The patrol arrived quickly and got their pressure hose hooked up to the outdoor hub that was connected to the city's pump system. They began their work to drown the fire in a deluge of water, and while I watched with the crowd that had begun to form a safe distance from the blaze, I felt a small but unbelievably hot hand gently grip my shoulder.

"Let's go." Rebecca's voice floated by my ears and for a brief instant I got this weird feeling of warmth but without any harshness to it, her hand was still hot from the fire she held earlier

I could still feel it through my jacket even after she removed her hand.

Shrugging off the feeling with the more pressing matter on my mind of how to tell my parents about our new guests, the others and I left the city street and disappeared into the crowd until we could get out of the district. We strolled down the dark streets of the city in the direction of my house, and as the twilight gave way to a starry moonlit night the gas street lamps begun to light one by one illuminating our path. The four of us walked in silence though, Rebecca was already getting fidgety. I had never really spent any time with her since she usually wasn't there when I would hang out with Rick at the shop, but she always seemed like…like she was constantly trying to distract herself. One thing about her that was hard to miss, she was actually really pretty, though she usually kept her hair pulled back in a tight ponytail. When I pulled her and Rick out of the canal she wouldn't even let me near her, maybe that was because she couldn't use her fire that now I see she is quite fond of, she just disappeared.

When Rick came to I just showed him to the Trade District, but he said he could take it from there. I could tell Rebecca was following us the entire time but I didn't say anything, I figured why rock the boat? I wondered who she really was though, the Rya that can make their own fire are supposed to be one of Ryagan's closely guarded secrets, I've only ever heard rumors of them and now there was living proof walking next to me. I didn't think they even let her kind outside of the country.

"See something you like?" Rebecca was looking over at me with one eyebrow cocked, apparently I had been staring.

"I uh…I've just never met a Rya that could create fire like that." I recovered truthfully; she just laughed and kept on walking.

We got to the Mill archway just in time to meet the evening guards. The two large Ater were just barely shorter than Mark, and it was clear they knew Kats when they saw them.

"It is past curfew. Where are you going with these…gentlemen?" the one on the left demanded an answer from me with a booming voice that echoed through the relatively empty street, practically ignoring Rebecca entirely.

Not willing to deal with anymore annoyances this evening, between getting attacked by a giant Kat and heading home to ask my folks if three foreigners can stay the night, I reached up and pulled the collar of my shirt down to reveal the brand that was evidence my station. The brand of the Kyn is simple enough, a full moon with a sword stabbed into its crest, what makes the brand impossible to imitate is the title, unique to each bearer, etched into the base of the moon. Every member of the Kyn is branded with the same seal so that they will always be known, the permanent brand also serves as a reminder that no member may ever leave the Kynodontes Tou Vorro. The guards eyes both widened and then narrowed tight with disgust as they lifted from the mark back up to my face.

"Let us pass." I ordered calmly as I stared back, matching their disgusted expression with a look of cold wrath.

The four of us passed by the guards and through the archway without another word. I navigated the dark roads of the district for our group until we reached the dirt road that led up to my house, I could see the lights inside from here, which meant Mum and Dad were still awake… We continued down the dirt road until just a few steps shy of the front porch of the house where I turned around to face the group.

"Guys, my family is old fashioned, so just try not to stand out too much and we'll be fine, and Rebecca, please don't light up." With those obligatory words of warning I spun back around with a light click in my heels and marched up the steps of the porch and opened the door to the log house that my father had designed himself.

The heavy wooden door creaked on its hinges as it swung open slowly, and we all filed inside the dimly lit house. Inside the house was spotless as usual, ever since mother was able to leave her job and stay at home all she does is read and clean. The front door led straight into the common living room where there was a fireplace, a couch, and a couple of reclining chairs. The only other piece of furniture was a large-back leather chair that was reserved for my father as the man of the house and it sat squarely in front of the fire. This chair was where he would take his coffee in the morning while reading a newspaper, and where he would relax in the evening with a cigar before bed. The aroma of a freshly burnt cigar hung in the air as we entered the room letting me know that he had recently taken his evening indulgence, which meant he and mother were probably getting ready for bed.

"Wait here, I just have to go tell them you're here, and then I'll show you where you'll be sleeping."

I ducked out of the room without waiting to hear a word from the others and headed upstairs to my parent's bedroom, though I was stopped in the hall halfway to their room. My mother was already in her dressing gown and on her way downstairs to put out the sconces and candles that kept the house lit, I guess she thought I wasn't coming home tonight.

"You made it home tonight after all. Your father said you had left after work today to go see your friend in the Trade District again. Why didn't you stay out there tonight?" She asked looking concerned, even now after I fought in the war she still gets worried when I'm not home.

"Actually… something happened. Rick's forge overheated and caught fire to his shop. Rick, his brother, and their friend made it out alright but now they need a place to stay. I thought they could chill here for a couple days until they can find another place to live, if would that be okay?" She and I exchanged a glance, both knowing how my father feels about guests especially since it's not just one person, but three.

"Let me talk to your father, are they here now?"

"They're in the living room, I told them to wait there until we got an answer." She looked at me one more time with a hint of disbelief in her eyes, the kind a mother has when she knows you're not telling the whole truth. She didn't say anything else though, instead Mum just turned and went back down the hall to the room where my father waited.

I returned to the living room where the others were, Mark had taken up a spot standing by the book shelf, glancing at its contents every few seconds, and Rebecca was leaning back in one of the recliners.

"Where is Rick…?" the question rolled slowly from my lips as I scanned the room for him. Rebecca just pointed lazily at the leather chair in front of the fireplace.

"You folks have a nice place here." a familiar voice came from behind the back of my father's leather chair. Rick stood up and leaned on the chair with one arm. "So what's the verdict?"

Before I had the chance to respond my mother came softly down the stairs and stopped at their base. She looked from one face to the next of the inhabitants of her living room, now dressed in casual pants and a t-shirt, before her eyes came back to me.

"Your father said they could stay tonight but he needs to meet them before he agrees to let them stay any longer." She walked over to Mark first and shook his hand, then Rick and Rebecca, and then introduced herself to them. "Hey, I'm Dorian's mom, Leah. It's nice to meet you all. The guest room is down here, and you must be Rebecca, you can stay in Dorian's room upstairs." Then turning to the three of us men with eyes that had a tinge of warning in them, she said "You guys will be sleeping downstairs."

Without saying anything more Mum disappeared back upstairs, she must have been pretty exhausted by the way she sounded. Rebecca turned and looked at me with a devilish grin as soon as Mum was out of sight. She had been assigned my room to sleep in tonight, and when it came to a mischievous girl like her, that couldn't be good for me.

"Don't mess with anything alright? She is just wants to keep the boys and girls on different floors because she's old-fashioned that way." Rebecca's grin stayed plastered to her face as I showed Mark and Rick the spare room.

I quickly set up a cot to serve as a second bed in the spare room downstairs and left Rick and Mark to retire for the evening. Rebecca and I walked upstairs to my room which I unlocked and she went bounding in ahead of me and dove onto my bed. I went to work putting away all the papers on my desk wary of whether she would set fire to them accidentally, or worse... read them.

"We're getting up early in the morning so you can meet my Dad and we can get started on figuring out where to go from here." I stated flatly.

"Our first date and I'm already staying at your place and meeting your parents, everything is happening so fast..." She embellished the tone in her words just to mock me as I headed for the door. "Seriously though, thanks Dorian, and goodnight."

Somewhat surprised at her change in demeanor as I was about to close the door I looked back inside, "Goodnight Rebecca...". After closing the door I went back downstairs to the second, smaller living room where more bookshelves lined the walls and stretched out on the couch that would be my bed for the night.

"Why did my house have to become the frickin hotel...?"

Chapter 10: Mark's Regret

I can't believe this, somehow I've been roped into working with the man I came here to kill, and now I'm staying in his guest room. I laid down on the cot in the spare room that my brother and I shared, waiting to fall asleep. I tried countless times, and each attempt only seemed to frustrate me even more than the last. Though I must've dozed off at some point because when I rolled over facing away from the wall I noticed Rick's bed was vacant. A thin beam of white light poured through the door that Rick had left behind partially open, probably in an effort to re-enter the room without the noise of opening the door. I got up, took Nyma's knife from its place by my pillow, and decided to investigate why my brother would want to sneak out in the middle of the night.

As I slipped through the dark house with only the moonlight spilling through the windows to illuminate my path when I heard voices coming from the back door. Following the sound of the voices I found myself at the window by the backdoor peering out into the darkness. A few yards out stood the familiar silhouette of my brother and just past him, another person was standing there facing him. It was a young man, with dark skin and short dark hair, wearing a collared shirt and pants with no shoes on, and with an oddly shaped sword-in-sheath in his left hand. Dorian faced Rick without a word, a dark wrath present on his face as he stared at Rick.

"You owe me some answers Dorian. What Rebecca said earlier, that you were an assassin, and you had master Nyma's knife. Did you kill him?" Rick tightened his grip on his staff though he hadn't yet released its length.

"Yes, I killed him."

"Why…?" There was little malice in my brother's words, more like genuine curiosity.

Dorian hesitated for a moment, his fist clenched but he made no attempt to reach for his weapon. I couldn't stand it anymore I threw open the door that had kept me hidden from sight until now. Dorian's eyes narrowed in anger as I stepped out into the cool night air.

"Tell him, tell him what happened that night." I demanded, but instead of rising to my angry order Dorian's voice became stone cold.

"You're pathetic. You're so blinded by anger at losing your master that you have forgotten, it was just war. People die in war. I killed Andre Nyma because he was an exceptional general and a real threat to our efforts. I followed my orders. You aren't really angry at me, you're angry at yourself for failing to do your duty and protect him." His smug look like he knew everything, made my blood boil.

"So it was just the war, nothing personal... Did he at least have the chance to defend himself?" Rick interrupted calmly.

"Yes, I made it all the way into his room without being noticed but in the last instant he caught me, there was a struggle, and I killed him in combat." Dorian replied. I could tell by the sincerity in his voice that he was telling the truth.

"See Mark, just let it go for now. It's late we should get some sleep, I just wanted to hear from Dorian what had happened, and now we know. Like it or not right now we have more important things to deal with, if you want to go back home then go, I'm staying until we figure out this mess with the Nirka." After his ending statement, Rick turned and went back passed me and headed for the door. Dorian started for the door as well but stopped in front of me, looking me dead in the eye.

"I am not sorry for following my orders, but I am sorry that you lost your master to that pointless war, that I do understand." He gave me an unexpected salute and went back inside.

What game was he playing…? Dorian then poked his head back out of the door when I turned back to go inside myself. The indignant expression he had moments earlier had completely vanished. "Oh and we'll have to get up early for my parents, they'll expect us to go to church with them in the morning."

Dorian jerked his head back inside leaving me outside alone. I hadn't noticed I guess because of the tense situation, but somehow the warm night air had turned into icy daggers in my lungs and when I breathed a deep sigh before going back inside a thick cloud of vapor dispersed in the air. Church...? I trudged back to my room to try and get some sleep without thinking about anything. I didn't want to think about what tomorrow was going to be like if I really had to sit in some foreign church that was sure to be heretical, surrounded by people who would have me arrested if they knew I was a soldier from south of the border. Rick was already passed out by the time I had returned, and as I focused on the thin stream of moonlight coming in through the window by my head I finally fell asleep as well.

The next morning I awoke to a bustling household, I smelled fresh ham and eggs frying in the kitchen and the aroma of coffee spread through the entire house. For a second I thought I was back home, that when I left my room I'd be greeted by my mother's smile as she cooked breakfast for everyone. Unfortunately that wasn't the case, which kicked the day off in disappointment. After I left the room with Rick still fast asleep, I entered the kitchen where Dorian's mother stood over the stove tending the breakfast. I heard footsteps above me and the unmistakable sound of rummaging, no doubt Rebecca digging around in Dorian's room. I also heard voices coming from the living room we had waited in the night before. Dorian's and another man were arguing, and since there was no one else in the house I figured the other man was Dorian's father.

"You must be Mark, I'm sorry I wasn't able to give you a proper welcome last night, Andy and I like to go to bed early these days. Did you sleep well?" Mrs. Vesco asked cheerfully as she looked over her shoulder with a smile but without turning away from the food, doing a good impression of my mother.

"Yes, thank you. I'm sorry for the imposition, like Dorian must've told you, the shop where my brother and I were staying burnt down. He was kind enough to offer us a place to stay for the night." I said trying to keep up a polite manner; after all she seemed nice enough.

"Well that's Dorian, he's always been that kind of person, before the war he went to the Consilium University, spent more time helping other people with their work than he did on his own." Mrs. Vesco explained while she piled on slices of ham to a serving plate and put more in the frying pan.

"I thought only the Candor were admitted to the university?" I asked for the sake of conversation, if nothing else.

"My husband is from the Ater breed, I am Candor however, though it was still a bit of a struggle for Dorian to be admitted because he is a half-breed, but he proved himself more than…capable…" I could hear the strain in her words as they trailed off. I guess having a son with such potential turn into a killer had taken its toll on her.

"So…, breakfast looks good…"I said trying to change the subject, just then, the sound of pounding feet came from up the stairs. Rebecca followed her nose straight from the bottom of the stairs to the kitchen.

"That smells amazing Mrs. V!" she yelled, running up to the counter where the food sat on the ceramic serving plates. "Do you need any help?" Rebecca asked with her eyes locked on the ham.

"Ha-ha, if you want, you can set the table. The dishes are in that cabinet over there." Following Mrs. Vesco's instructions, Rebecca pulled out a stack of plates from the cabinet and flatware from the drawer and arranged them on the table while I stood back and opted to stay silent for the rest of the morning.

Once the table was set Mrs. Vesco called her husband and Dorian in from the living room and just as we all sat down, Rick showed up suddenly in the open door of our room looking half awake, somehow he always knew when a meal would be ready. We all took our places at the table, Mr. Vesco sat at the head of the table, he wasn't as tall as the Ater I saw in the war but his tanned skin, dark hair, and muscular build, were all typical of his breed. Rick and I sat next to each other, and the girls sat across from us with Dorian at the opposite end of the table from his father. Mr. Vesco looked from Rick to me with suspicious eyes before addressing his son.

"So these are your friends." He said, matter-of-factly, and then he looked over at my brother and I. "Will you be going to church with us this morning?" Rick knew I wasn't much for masking my dislike for other religions. We were raised in a colony of believers in Jagés and taught other faiths were nothing but lies to control the masses.

"Yes, we're looking forward to it actually, Mark and I have never been to any religious other gatherings besides our worship back home since we came here, and we are interested in your faith." Rick answered Mr. Vesco's question honestly, at least from his point of view. My brother is the sort that enjoys learning about other cultures.

The rest of breakfast passed with small talk, mainly between Mrs. Vesco and Rebecca, though Rick and Mr.Vesco's did talk a little about where we came from and what we will do now, only Dorian and I remained silent throughout the meal. As each individual finished eating and excused themselves from the table eventually, I was left alone. I waited for a few moments in the empty kitchen before getting up to go get ready for church. It wasn't long before the others gathered in the living room, the Vescos having changed into their dress clothes with Rebecca wearing one of Mrs. Vesco's modest black dresses. Dorian and his father both wore dark pinstriped suits with Dorian in black while his father wore blue, though Dorian had a matching hat of the same material. Mrs. Vesco had on a modest blue dress and stood by her husband. I joined them along with Rick, he and I wore casual yet church-appropriate clothes we had borrowed from Dorian. We waited for Rick to finish getting ready then we all headed out the front door to the horse drawn carriage that waited for us in front of the porch. Dorian must have pulled it around after breakfast.

Mr. Vesco climbed up and took the reins while Dorian held the door for the rest of us to enter the carriage before climbing up to ride next to his father. At the snap of the reins the carriage sped off down the dirt road of the Industrial District. The ride was short though, before long we had come to a stop right in front of an old wooden building that looked like it had been a barn at one point in its history. I made sure to exit the carriage first so that this time I could hold the door for the others, and I never really liked other people waiting on me.

Dorian's parents seemed like good honest people, though his father was definitely still suspicious of Rick and me. He kept looking back at us with this squint like we were hard to see or something. For the sake of keeping the status quo till we got out of this situation, I needed some way to make a good impression and I was never as good a talker as my brother so I just decided to be silent, polite, and well mannered. I stood with the door open as the ladies disembarked first, followed by my brother while Dorian and Mr. Vesco climbed down from the driver's bench.

The six of us headed towards the church and the large gathering of Lykos in their Sunday finest that were socializing in front. Mr. and Mrs. Vesco left us to go talk with their acquaintances before the service, while Dorian led the rest of us inside. Immediately after we sat down in one of the long benches close to the back of the large open 'auditorium' of the barn, the rest of the people outside began to pour in. They all took their seats quietly, though one Ater and his wife gave us a bit of a dirty look when they passed. Dorian leaned over from his seat at the far end of our group and explained what happened with the Ater and his wife.

"Sorry, some people sit in the same place every week and get a little offended if someone takes 'their' spot." he said with a look embarrassment.

Everyone slowly found their seats and settled down, with the exception of a few fidgeting children and a baby that I could already tell were going get on my nerves. As the noise from the crowd began to subside, a heavyset Canden-Lykos with slicked grey hair, and a suit that matched, took the pulpit. The pulpit had some sort of rune inscribed into its face which looked familiar, almost like the symbol that pops up in the writings of Jagés. Anyway, the hefty Lykos man cleared his voice and began to address the congregation.

"Good morning folks, I'm glad y'all could come out this morning! Looks like we have a full house! Do we have any visitors this morning?" His booming voice carried through the entire building as my brother, Rebecca, and I realized at the same time, that he was looking straight at us when he asked about visitors.

"Let's all shake hands and welcome any newcomers while my lovely wife plays us a song."

A Canden woman, not nearly as heavy as her husband, but still a bigger woman and around the same age, walked up to the piano on stage. She took a seat at the bench, and began playing a beautiful flowing melody. Everyone who had just sat down, stood back up and began socializing again. I couldn't help but wonder if was a worship service or just an excuse for people to have a get-together? The three of us saw a few people begin making their way back to us, we exchanged uneasy glances at first, but my eternally charismatic brother took charge and stood up shaking everyone's hand that passed with a smile. Rebecca soon joined him in greeting everyone as they welcomed us to the service, she's so cheerful and outgoing it's annoying…

As I watched the rest of the crowd, I became more and more agitated. It seemed like these people cared more about socializing than they did about their faith, in the colony the only words spoken during a worship service were the priest's, everyone else remained respectfully silent. Even though Rick grinds my nerves most of the time, at least he kept these oddly warm people from invading my space.

Soon the melody died down and the pastor's wife left the piano bench for a seat behind her husband, who once again took his place at the pulpit and began his sermon with a prayer,

"Father, father, forgive your children their transgressions and guide us ever forward in your will and grace that we may serve thee…"

"All our days…" Rick and I finished in hushed voices under our breath as we looked at each other simultaneously with astonishment.

The Pastor's prayer was the same one my brother and I were taught since childhood, the words we prayed to Jagés every night at our bedside as kids. Dorian leaned over and signaled us that we were being rude by pointing back up to the pastor whom had already begun preaching.

"Alistair who guides and protects us, teaching us to live rightly by his words and to always remain vigilant for the great day of regeneration…"

Chapter 11: Rick's Faith

This was so incredibly different than the way my brother and I were raised to worship, yet the prayer, and even their day of regeneration were the same as in Jagés' teachings. In the colony, people came to the temple to worship in rags to symbolize their humility, but here everyone wore their finest clothing. The men were scattered about in suits of grey and brown, wearing collared shirts and ties, some of the ties had the oddest designs stitched into them. Then there were the women, in modest dresses with ribbons tying the collars of their ankle length dresses to their necks and they all shared the same uptight hairstyle that made them all look so cold and callused. I was a little unnerved by both the similarities and differences in the way that our cultures viewed religion.

The four of us sat and listened to the preacher's words as he ranted on for at least an hour about the evils of every little thought anyone may have, without offering any real solution except to just 'stop it'. The wind was picking up outside, howling fiercely and I noticed through the windows, that the sky had begun to grow dark. I heard a strange sound almost like hushed laughter and looked down to see Rebecca quivering slightly. At first I thought she was afraid of something, but the fire in her eyes and the eerie grin she wore, said otherwise. She didn't even seem to be paying attention to the sermon, and while the preacher went on, she was staring straight at a tall man sitting close to the front of the church. The man was wearing an overly expensive black suit with golden accents that set him apart from the middle-class church attendants that sat around him, as if that wasn't enough, he had a top hat in his lap.

"Something wrong?" I whispered quietly to her as she continued to stare.

"That's him, he's the one I ran into when I was in Canaan's mansion yesterday." She barely breathed the words out. I looked at him then back to her.

"You mean…"

"The Nirka." she confirmed.

I sat back in my seat and tried not to look over at our adversary that sat on the other side of the room. I thought for a moment that maybe he didn't know about us, he could just be here by coincidence, but then he looked over his shoulder past me to Rebecca and gave a sly smirk. At least he wouldn't try anything in a room full of Lykos. I looked across the makeshift auditorium but I couldn't see any other Nirka, coming alone didn't make any sense though. I decided that I would wait and see how this would play out.

At the end of the preacher's sermon his wife stood up and returned to the piano, this time her song was much lower, almost somber. People from all over the room gathered at the altar in front of the pulpit and fell to their knees in prayer. The man with the top hat even got up and sauntered on over to the far side of the altar and knelt as well. Then Rebecca stood up and began walking in the same direction. I held my breath in silent preparation, just in case she tried something stupid. Rebecca knelt down next to the man with the top hat, they were hard to see from where I was standing but from what I could tell they never said a word to each other. I wanted to follow her over there but there was no point in adding another new face to the one the man with the top hat already knew was involved.

The song slowly died off and people began getting up and leaving, Rebecca's companion stood up first and I saw them exchange a look as she cocked her head up at him from her knelt position. The man left her side and strolled out of the building placing his top hat on his head as he passed through the side door, but before he stepped out he turned and tipped his hat to the three of us left standing at our bench in the back, looks like we had already been pegged as Rebecca's accomplices. She returned to us without saying a word, only an apprehensive expression. Dorian's parents crossed back by our little group while we all stood in awkward silence, to remind us about the family dinner they had planned for after church today.

"Guys, we need to talk." The three of us turned away from the direction the elder Vescos had left in to see Rebecca standing behind us holding up an envelope.

The three of us gathered around Rebecca outside the church after telling Dorian's parents that we would walk back to the house. She opened the envelope and pulled out a letter, when she unfolded it the writing was in an old Kat language my brother and I knew well. Rebecca handed me the letter and I read out loud.

"Good afternoon, Ms. Rya and friends.

I serve as a manservant in the Albedo's estate, and as you undoubtedly have already noticed, I am from the Nirka tribe of Kats. I have come here today to offer you a chance to learn what you were unable to at the Albedo's mansion last night. The Albedo is no longer following the plan my master has given him. But unfortunately, my brothers are still loyal to him rather than our master who led us to Canaan in the first place. In my current position I am unable to do much, but you and your three friends have already shown an interest in the same goal that I hope to achieve though our motivations differ. I already knew that you had been poking into Canaan's affairs and when I saw you inside the mansion, I thought you might have the gall to unravel his treachery. To that end, I'm sure you've heard of the fabled 'Undercity', the eighth district of Crown Lykou. If you go there you will find a man by the name of Cayden Vel, he will have the information you need. Pretty helpful wouldn't you say? After all, I am one hell of a servant, no matter who I'm serving.

I hope to see you again soon,

Lucas Deimo

P.S. Try and play nice with Cayden, he can be a bit of a handful."

Nobody said anything for a moment, though to me our direction seemed pretty clear. "Rebecca, do you know of a way into the Undercity?" I asked snapping her out of contemplation.

"I've heard of it, the only way I know in is still closed off from before, but should we really trust this guy?" I could tell by her tone, she knew more than she let on, something about the way she acted when I said the word 'Undercity' reminded me of how she was after we nearly got killed trying to get into Crown Lykou.

"I say let's go for it. It's a solid lead and if this turns out to be a trap, which is what it sounds like, then we should just spring the trap and let the pieces fall where they may. At least we'll know more than what we do now, since all we have is guess work. We should also hold onto this letter, it will be useful in proving our case to the council when we are ready to show them evidence of Canaan's treason." Dorian was the last person I'd expect to want to jump back into another conflict like this, but he had a point. Mark just nodded to his words but didn't say anything.

"I guess I can find us a way in, but isn't your family expecting us back at the house, Doriaaan?" She looked back at Dorian with devious grin that I could tell was fake this time, I guess she knew he was trying to avoid the family dinner they had mentioned earlier and also wanted to deflect some of the attention she was getting from us because of the letter.

"Do we really have to go…?" Dorian muttered as we started walking back.

"Let's just lay low for right now. We'll deal with the Undercity later." I suggested as I started following Dorian with the other two close behind.

What really bothered me was that last note at the end of the letter. We are being sent after this Cayden, and what did that guy mean 'he can be a bit of a handful'? I guess right now our biggest hurdle is getting into the Undercity. The letter said it's a whole other district underneath Crown Lykou. That must be that place that Rebecca and I came up through to get into the city. If that's true, we can't go back through the canals like we did before. I wonder how Rebecca plans to get us in, and why she didn't say anything about us already having been there. Maybe she ran into that Cayden guy the last time we were down there. For now I'll follow her lead and keep my mouth shut until I learn more.

"Alright guys, it won't just be my parents this time. My brother, his wife, and their son will be there. Sorry about all this, my family likes to get together once a week after church, but if we can get through this without any problems then they shouldn't care about letting ya'll stay for a few more days." Dorian explained as we approached his house. Off to the side of the house we saw his parent's carriage accompanied by another, newer carriage that was parked next to it with the horses already eating from the trough.

"No worries bro, we'll be on our best behavior!" I reassured, giving Dorian a good smack square on his back.

"If you say so..." He sighed opening the door for us.

When we entered the house, the strong smell of grilled meat and steamed vegetables filled the air. It smelled so good my mouth began to water as I automatically found my way to the kitchen. The table we had eaten at this morning had been extended, and at one of the seats sat a Lykos woman I had never seen before. The woman's hair was a darker shade of gold, which didn't match any Lykos breed I was familiar with, but then I remembered Dorian had different hair as well since he was a half breed. The woman had a young child sitting next to her with her same hair color, he couldn't have been more than three or four years old, she was tending him while he ate a minced burger.

"Well hey, I guess you're one of Dorian's friends. I'm Marie, Hod's wife." Marie wore the same broad smile that Mrs. Vesco always had. I wasn't sure if they were faking kindness or if these people were really this nice to total strangers.

"Hey Rick, Mr. Vesco and Hod are on the back porch over there grilling the steaks if you want to join the guys." Mrs. Vesco said as she set the table large enough for the nine of us.

I simply nodded to her and smiled to Marie before started for the door, but Dorian's father and brother came through first carrying two large platters stacked high with freshly grilled steaks. Apparently I had been staring because I looked up from the center of the table where they placed the platters to see Mr. Vesco and his son looking straight at me. Hod was every bit his father's son, they looked almost identical minus the age gap and Mr. Vesco's lack of hair on the top of his head. If I hadn't already met Mrs. Vesco, I wouldn't have had any idea Hod was a half-breed like Dorian, he looked just like a pure blood Ater only shorter, which I heard sometimes happens with their breed.

"How's it goin?" Dorian's brother extended his hand and shook mine firmly

Just then Dorian, Mark, and Rebecca, all emerged from the other side of the house after changing back into their casual clothes and took their places at the table. Once again the ladies sat on one side of the table while the men took the other side with Dorian and his father at either end. We passed the food around the table as everyone took a portion with little conversation, then Hod looked over at Dorian.

"So how do you like working with Dad?" he asked with a slight chuckle. Dorian just shot him a dark glance and finished making his plate.

"What do you do?" I asked Hod in an attempt to shift the attention away from Dorian, who was obviously uncomfortable.

"Oh, I run my own company, basically we crunch numbers for the businesses here in the Industrial District. It's not a bad job, Marie and I run the company together. Mom and Dorian actually used to work with us before we bought it out. Of course that was before mom retired and Dorian ran off to war." He said with the faintest sneer.

"That's cool, before moving here I worked with my family too, heading up a traveling ministry from Katzen into Ryagan. I was very interested in the church service this morning. Your prophet Alistair has many of the same teachings as Saint Jagés that we worship back home." My reply got wide eyed looks from every Lykos at the table, excluding Dorian with whom I had already discussed my beliefs. Mr. Vesco stifled a grunt of displeasure sounding not unlike my brother when he is angry but wants to refrain from making a scene.

"Who is Jagés?" Marie asked curiously as everyone else went to eating nervously and quite fast.

"Jagés was a saint that whose soul ascended to heaven after his body became one with the earth itself. Some of our people have the innate ability to understand the earth and it's components on an instinctual level, this is said to be a watered down skill that Jagés once possessed. History says he had the ability to reshape the earth according to his will, making mountains shift and even moving entire land masses. Not so different from what the preacher said about Alistair's influence on the ocean, it's all very intriguing.

By the time I had finished explaining, people were already excusing themselves from the table. Marie stayed back to be polite but I could tell even she was put off by the presence of another faith at the table. Dorian left his plate at the sink and went straight outside without saying a word, he must not have wanted me to go on talking about having a different belief than his family, but what's done is done I guess.

Rebecca gave me a glare that let me know my assumption was correct, and then proceeded behind Hod and his family along with Mr. and Mrs. Vesco out of the front door. I followed along behind and once their carriage left the property she turned and glared at me again, waiting for Dorian's parents to leave us alone on the porch.

"Why did you have to go running your mouth?! We have nowhere else to go, all you had to do is sit there and be polite through one dinner!" She whisper-yelled to keep from drawing any attention from Dorian's parents inside.

"Number one, I was just making conversation. Number two, as conservative as these people are, maybe you shouldn't have come to Sunday dinner in a skirt that's more than a little too short!" I began to yell lashing out at the first thing I could think of to shift some of the blame. Because of the look on Rebecca's face, I realized I had been getting louder and louder. I took a deep breath and started again. "None of this matters at the moment. We have a more important issue to deal with right now. Isn't the guy mentioned in that letter the same guy that chased us into that underground canal on the way into the city?" I asked, cutting straight to the point that I knew she had been trying to avoid.

"Yes, Cayden Vel is the one that runs the Undercity, an underground community of thieves, murderers, and criminals, beneath Crown Lykou. He welcomes this city's outcasts, of any kind, and because of that I thought they would help you and I. But, when I went down there to scout a way for us to enter the main city I met Cayden, and learned how they operate. Things are different down there, they have their own laws, the most important being power. They follow Cayden because he is the strongest, and if we want anything from him then we'll have to fight him. Listen Rick, I already fought him and lost, I can't fight him again by their law. Cayden has some sort of weird skill with his whip, it moves on its own…and no I'm not crazy." She lifted her shirt to expose her left flank above her hip to show a large slashed scar that looked like the flesh had been ripped open. Her eyes burned in dark anger at her own failure as she explained pulling her shirt back down.

"So that's why that pack of Lykos chased us through that underground passage to the canals. You challenged him for our right to stay down there and lost…, and now we're going back.

Rebecca, what will they do to you if we go back down there? I asked, realizing just what kind of danger she would be putting herself in.

"I can't fight, so one of you will have to, normally it's just a test of strength but because of what happened before Cayden will have to lose for us to get the information we're after. Tonight I'll go find us a way in, I have a few contacts in the Pit that can help us. I need to blow off some steam anyway, I'll be back." Rebecca walked off towards the woods on the side of the house and disappeared into the trees .

Her frustration was understandable, ever since I saw her take down that Nirka back home on the colony, and in every fight on the way here she barely broke a sweat, so it's hard for me to imagine her losing to anyone so utterly. I couldn't help but get a little excited however, looking ahead, with Dorian and Mark's experience in the war, they shouldn't fight Cayden. We will need them at full strength, in case we have to fight our way back out of the Undercity, which leaves me to face Cayden.

The thought made me anxious and a bit restless as the air turned cold whipping across the front of the house. If he is tough enough to beat Rebecca then I might finally have the chance to really let loose, I can't kill him though, not if we want the answers we're going down there after… I turned around and went back inside as the afternoon air turned even colder with the high level of moisture in the air making each breath feel like ice in my lungs.

When I closed the door behind me the heat from the fireplace radiated against my skin, as I looked around to find the common-room deserted. Mrs. Vesco could be heard in the kitchen still, washing dishes while her husband sat at his desk in the living room off the side of the kitchen, sifting through papers as I walked by.

I went to my temporary room closing the door behind me and lighting the lamp hanging from the ceiling. I went under the pillow and pulled out my extendable staff, staring at it as the lamp light reflected off of its polished surface, and for some reason I noticed it felt lighter than before, I looked at it for a good minute before I realized… I was shaking. I wasn't scared or nervous at all I just couldn't stop thinking about the chance to test my skills that was fast approaching.

Chapter 12: Rebecca Has a Meeting

"Stupid, stupid, stupid, Rick! Why couldn't you just shut up and let me deal with this?!" I whispered my little rant to myself since I was still close enough to the Vesco's house to be heard.

The scene from a few months ago kept playing out in my head. I could barely see in the dimly lit red-rock cave standing in the ring facing a colossal Kokin with a whip in hand that had to be at least three feet longer than my entire body. To this day I don't know how Cayden fought the way he did. That whip of his moved like it was alive and was so tough that my knives couldn't cut it, and was so fast I didn't have time to use any fire. Then he broke my knives and all I could do was run. As soon as my feet left the battle circle it seemed like everyone in the city was after my head. Now I'm leading three more people down there and running the risk that they won't just kill us all on the spot.

I ran through the forest near the Vesco's house, birds scattered in every direction as I barreled through the pre-cut path. Running has always been a good stress reliever when my anger begins to overwhelm me, but the further I got the more I got the sense I wasn't alone. I stopped in the middle of the path when I heard a loud crash deeper in off of the trail. It sounded like some sort of large branch fell from one of the gigantic oaks that crowded the forest. Since I was looking for a distraction anyway, I decided to check it out. I dashed into the forest with only the meager light that broke through the canopy of leaves to keep me from running smack into a tree.

The closer I got to where the sound came from, the more chaos I could hear. As I drew near, another sound accompanied each dying branch, the sound of a person bellowing a destructive roar before each strike. The sound was fierce, like a wild animal. When I finally reached the clearing where the noises were coming from, I found freshly cut tree branches littering the ground and Dorian standing at the far end. The tanned skin of his bare chest glistened in the low light of the forest as he stood there, sword in hand and a little out of breath, when he turned to look at me.

"Hey Rebecca…sorry was I making too much noise?" he asked meekly, not even sounding close to the wild beast I had heard on the way here.

"N…no, I was just out for a walk after dinner. What are you doing out here?" Like it wasn't evident that he was training…

"Just blowing off some steam, my family has never really forgiven me for joining the Kyn." He shrugged and turned back for the fallen log his shirt hung on next to his sword sheath and slid his sword inside like he was getting ready to leave.

"Blowing off steam, huh? Sounds fun." I smiled, and let my hands drift down to the long knives strapped to my thighs.

"What are you doing…?" he asked, turning around with his shirt in hand, but I wasn't in the mood for any more talk.

I sprinted toward the unprepared swordsman as fast as I could, drawing my weapons ready to strike, I could already feel the heat rising off of the metal. The closer to him I got the more I could see the wheels in his head process the situation, the grin spreading across his face made me even more anxious to see what he could do. I struck, stabbing at his neck but all my knife pierced was air, he dodged right and spun as he drew his sword in one motion, striking from the sheath. I parried the stroke of his sword with the blade in my right hand but was caught off guard by the blast of cold air that came off of his sword. Dorian seemed as surprised as I was as we both leapt backwards and took our stances ready to fight. Steam rose off of the knife I blocked with as mist fell from his raised sword.

Dorian shot toward me at incredible speed, flipping the sword sheath in his hand over. He swung with both sword and sheath simultaneously from opposite directions, I tried striking straight down the middle but I was too slow to do anything but block. We stood at a stalemate, our weapons grinding together. The harder I pushed against him, the hotter my blades grew until they were glowing red, but the harder he pushed back more and more icy mist fell from his sword and sheath. Our weapons began to spark green as they shifted in force and then suddenly, like magnets they repelled, knocking us both in opposite directions.

Neither of us had seemed to notice the thunder clouds gathering until roaring thunder shook the ground and cold rain started to fall. I looked down at my blades, the raindrops evaporated as they hit the surface of the red hot metal that was rapidly cooling down. I returned the knives to the sheaths strapped onto my thighs as Dorian returned his sword to its sheath. We looked at each other in confused silence for a moment.

Rain trickled down his face as Dorian's expression returned to its usual calm state, he looked almost sad as he stood in front of me. Just then I heard footsteps tromping through the forest coming for us. Dorian belted his sword in sheath and returned to the log where he dropped his black t-shirt and slid it on over his head before the others joined us. Rick and Mark came running into the clearing with concerned looks on their faces and their weapons in hand.

"Guys what's going on back here? We could hear fighting all the way from the house!" Rick yelled as he came into sight.

"Nothing is wrong. We just wanted to have a little fun." I said shooting Rick a wink. "Now I better get going on that entrance into the Undercity, don't wait up." I flashed one last smile before running off back toward the main road by the Vesco's house.

The rain didn't last long, by the time I reached the main road it had already stopped. I knew the only way I'd find out how to get into a den of thieves was by asking a thief, so I went to the best place topside where plenty could be found. The sun was falling on the horizon, setting the sky ablaze with orange light as I reached The Pit. The preparations for the nightly parties were well underway, Kokin ran back and forth with large casks of brewed alcohol and bags filled with other vices. Unlike most of my visits to this district, I wasn't looking for a party this time, I needed someone with connections. The only ones that would know how to get into the Undercity are real criminals not the riff-raff close to the gate. I walked down the dirt roads of the slums past all the rickety houses and scrambling people, headed for the one place I could find someone that could tell me what I wanted to know, Casino Lane.

The bright fluorescent lights shining from the southern end of the Pit led me all the way to Casino Lane, a long strip of gambling halls and night clubs. The wide open road ran along the inside of Crown Lykou's outer wall and was home to the headquarters for a number of criminal organizations based in the city. Gambler's Row was the only paved road I had seen in the entire district, as I walked down the cobblestone path I scanned every building for the obvious signs of illicit behavior. What made my search both difficult and easy was that every establishment had evidence of foul deeds, so I decided to go to the place that looked the most fun.

"Go big or go home." I muttered with a smirk as I approached the largest casino on the strip, knowing who ran this particular racket, I couldn't help but be somewhat impressed.

The large neon letters of shaped glass tubes filled with phosphorous material read 'The Kennel', flashing lights and smoke poured out of the large open entrance, which was guarded by two Ater who looked like they had both just gotten out of prison. The line to get in was at least thirty strong and was filled with the more affluent breeds in fine personally tailored suits or designer evening gowns, I looked down at my sleeveless top and denim pants with the long knives strapped to my thighs and felt more than a bit underdressed. I looked down the street for any place that I might be able to buy some clothes and not far from The Kennel was across the street from a local boutique, they were sure to have some clothes that would help me fit in with this crowd. In the window an army of mannequins stood half in ritzy cocktail dresses and the other in classic men's tuxedos. I figured this was as good a place any.

When I entered the small boutique I saw even more mannequins lining the walls, each one in the most elegant apparel I've seen since leaving the empire, though the designs were kind of peculiar. There were clothes for everything from the most formal of events to exercise outfits (those were tucked away in the back like someone was ashamed of them). I waded through the sea of clothes making my way to the section with dresses in my size when I was nearly accosted by a flamboyantly dressed Candor man with an unnaturally wide smile. Well at least I think he was a Candor, his hair had the telltale bleached white color but at a second glance it also had a noticeable pink luster that only highlighted his effeminate demeanor. The pink haired boutique wardrobe consultant wore a croc-skin blazer with bright red slacks and a flashy buttoned down shirt that had a golden sheen to it which made me doubt whether I should take his advice on fashion, like I had a choice since this place was filled with nothing but foreign designs.

"Good evening Miss, how may I help you? I see you're looking at the gowns, looking for something to impress a special someone or for a night out on the town? Come with me I know just the thing!" he wrapped his arm around my shoulder and almost forcibly drug me into the heart of the store to the fitting platform. He led me up to I pedestal that had three mirrors in front of it and left me there, disappearing into the mass of dress-clad mannequins. Seconds later he reappeared with several dresses draped over his arm, the first he produced was a deep blue floor length dress.

"What do you think? Tasteful yet modest, enough to leave your special someone wanting more." He said with a wink holding up the dress.

"Eh not really my type, I don't really like blue all that much…" I answered reluctantly. He seemed so enthusiastic and I didn't really want to disappoint him. Then he came uncomfortably close looking me straight in the eye.

"Oh I am so sorry! I had no idea, you're a Rya, you're going to need some warmer colors!" With that he dashed back into the clothes without even suggesting any of the other dresses he had brought the first time. I could only hear him in the sea of clothes sifting through rack after rack of hanging dresses.

In the blink of an eye he returned holding the perfect dress, exactly what I had in mind, I was in love as soon as I laid eyes on it. I snatched the dress from him and held it up against my body staring at myself in the mirrors, it looked almost like black croc skin but higher quality than what my consultant was wearing, and when the light caught it at a certain angle it shined a deep crimson. It was the perfect length, stopping just above my knees, not too low cut and sleeveless, with a four inch slit from the hem making it just risqué enough to attract a particular someone's attention. I looked over at my oddly dressed and newest friend,

"Can I?" I asked, and he gave a knowing smile, big and wide as he pointed to a changing room door without a word. I ran over to the door and locked it behind me, quickly undressing and slipping into the form fitting dress, it even fit perfectly. I stuck my head out of the dressing room and looked around, I had not been seen in a dress in a good while and I wanted to keep it that way.

My new friend sat in a chair next to the pedestal with the mirrors; he was fiddling with something that looked like a pair foot-and-a-half long polished black metal bars that were kinda thick and connected at one end by a small hinge. When he noticed me he stood up with the same big smile he seemed to have permanently plastered to his face holding the metal bars in one hand and a pair of polished red shoes in the other.

"What's that?" I asked a bit confused. He held out the bars to me as his grin got even wider.

"You seem like the kind of girl that likes to keep her weapons on her all the time, which is smart if you'll be alone on these streets, so I found a way for you to take them with you. May I?" he held out his hand for the long knives still sheathed on top of my folded clothes in my arms. I was a bit wary but if he tried anything suspicious I always had my fire to fall back on if I needed to defend myself. He removed the knives from their sheaths and slid both weapons into the hollowed out bars at the end with the hinge, since there weren't any hand-guards on my blades they slid all the way inside past the handles. Once they were inside he pulled two metal caps out of the breast pocket of his croc skin jacket and secured them onto the open ends of each bar. I looked at him suspiciously since he had yet to explain what he was doing, immediately I thought the best thing to do if he tried anything was threatening to burn down his store.

"Here now you can carry this with you anywhere you go and no one will ask any questions. Go on, open it up." He said with a grin that was quickly beginning to annoy me. I took the tool from him and inspected it quietly. "Just hold that end and flick your wrist." He urged. I did as he instructed and the hinge opened up the opposite end spreading a large cut of cloth between both bars forming the shape of a rather large fan, the type I had seen noblewomen carry back home, though the ones they had were much smaller. The cloth was made of silk and had a large red dragon breathing fire stitched into its surface.

"Wow, thanks a lot! You know I never got your name." I said with a smile feeling pretty good about myself in the fine dress with a silk fan that hid my weapons making this look both beautiful and deadly.

"No ensemble is complete without the right pair of shoes, here sit down." He directed me to the seat he had used while working on the fan, and I did as he asked. "My name is Paul Schneider, a pleasure to meet you Miss…"

"Kasimi, Rebecca Kasimi, and the pleasure is all mine." I said as he fastened the four inch heeled shoes to my feet.

"Well Miss Kasimi, this dress highlights your exquisite beauty in the most elegant fashion, shall I wrap it up for you, or would you like to wear it out?" Paul asked as he finished with the clasps on my shoes before standing up. I reached into the pocket of my folded pants and pulled out my money clip, not even Rick knows about my personal stash. I liberated most of this money while developing the criminal connections I was about to make use of tonight.

"I'll be wearing it out, thank you again for all of your help sir, here." I handed Paul a few bills and got up to leave.

"Miss…" He called after me, but I raised my hand to silence him and turned around to smile at him.

"Worth every penny." I smiled again as he looked back down at double the cost of the dress from what I had seen on the tag while in the dressing room.

When I walked out of the boutique I turned around and looked at the bright Neon sign on top of the building I had just left, to my surprise it read *Schneider's*. I smiled to myself and then looked down at the casino "Here we go" I muttered as I walked up to a crate sitting in a nearby alley and stashed my clothes for later.

Now that I had the perfect costume, I was ready for the main event. I stood in the back of the long line to get into The Kennel for all of thirty seconds before I had enough of waiting. I marched past everyone in line and walked up to the bouncers. The two Ater in tight t-shirts and pants stood with menacing glares as I approached, both were all scarred up and the parts of them that weren't scarred were covered by tattoos. I looked up at them without a trace of apprehension.

"Don Pericci is expecting me."

The two guards looked at each other then back at me suspiciously, they might've had no reason to believe me but on the chance that I was telling the truth, no one working for one of the shady businesses out here would keep their boss waiting. After all, crime bosses out here are so fickle they'd kill over something so petty. The two guards stepped aside revealing the ten foot tall double doors that were wide open. I gave them a wink and went into the dark smoky club.

The minute I stepped inside I was surrounded by colored smoke and the sound of the violent music Lykos seemed to love. The dance-floor was filled with people and breeds of all ages and origin, except Kokin, women trying to lose themselves in the music and men taking advantage of the opportunity to convince them to make a decision they would regret later. The smell of liquor and tobacco smoke hung heavy in the air as I entered. Past the dance floor was the main casino, as I walked across the dance floor towards the casino, the sounds of various slot machines ringing grew louder and louder, accompanied by the voices of dealers calling out cards and patrons either celebrating or cursing the outcomes of their various games. As soon as I set foot on the casino floor, two more Ater approached me, clearly blocking my path. These two were completely different from the ones outside, both in matching black suits and ties wearing tight black leather gloves.

"I figured it wouldn't be long before someone showed up." I said with a smile as one Ater motioned for me to follow him and the other took his place behind me.

I knew all I had to do was mention Pericci's name and word would get back to him quickly, now his goons will take me straight to him. I clenched Paul's ornamental fan tightly, knowing this little reunion could either go really well or horribly wrong, it felt good to be armed. The suited Lykos led me to the back of the casino floor and the one in the lead pulled out a key from the inside pocket of his jacket and unlocked a large oak door in the back wall with a monstrous wolf emblazoned in silver above the door looking down on all that entered.

The room we entered was almost completely covered in black velvet, from the floors to the walls, even the ceiling, and at the back, a large desk sat with a portrait behind it displaying the face of the man who sat at there. A Candor-breed Lykos with snowy white hair, a pure breed, he wore a white suit with black pinstripes, and was calmly watching the door as we passed into his office. Pericci stood up and left his leather arm chair behind his desk, as he approached his expression turned dark. My escorts took their spots standing on either side of me as he came closer.

"You have a lot of nerve coming here, sweetheart…, after what you did to me and the gang." He leaned down, his fierce gaze cutting right through me, causing my hand to slip unconsciously down to the end of my fan.

"Hey you guys knew the risks, it's not my fault you…" Before I could spit the words out a broad smile broke out on Pericci's face.

"Haha I can't believe it! I haven't seen you in months! How have you been?" He practically yelled.

"Umm...." I started, trying to make sense of what just happened. When he saw my confusion he straightened his suit jacket and stood back up straight. He took my hand and kissed it humbly then looked up to my escorts.

"Leave us alone, we have some catching up to do." They quickly obeyed his orders and a moment later I was left alone in the room with my... 'old friend'.

"So... looks like you've done pretty well for yourself since I've been gone." I said as I walked past him looking around the room and then up at the large portrait at the back of the room.

"Yeah after we pulled that last job in Everest, the gang and I pulled together our money and opened this place. But you know Rebecca, you didn't have to leave." I could feel his eyes on me while he spoke, it made me shudder internally but he was always weak to me so this choice of dress gave me a bit of an edge.

"You and I both knew that we were only working together out of necessity, I did my job and then left, end of story." I said plainly, turning around to face him.

"Then why did you come back now?" He asked as his eyes narrowed and the look of cold business dwarfed his smile.

"A job, I need information, is this enough?" I flashed my money clip.

"What sort of information are you looking to buy?

"I need to get into the Undercity, there's a man I need to speak to down there, that's all you need to know." I answered clenching my fan again.

"The Undercity huh?" Pericci said as he walked by me up to his desk, he leaned over it and pulled open one of the drawers and took something out. "This is a map to an entrance, don't worry about the money just deliver this letter and we'll call it even." He quickly scrawled something on a piece of paper, and slipped it into another envelope, and handed it to me along with the sealed envelope containing the map. "Don't worry, the one you're delivering the message to will find you."

"Just like that?" I asked, Pericci only replied with a sly smile.

Chapter 13: Dorian's Backup Plan

After Rebecca ran off from our sparring match in the woods the Burke brothers and I decided to head back to the house, I sat in front of the fireplace warming myself against the freezing temperatures that had seeped in after I cooled off from training. I stared into the dancing flames trying to figure out what my next move should be, with Rebecca off chasing down a way for us to get down the Undercity I felt a bit useless. Mark was sitting across the room thumbing through one of the books on the shelf and Rick went back to their room probably sleeping. Scenarios kept running through my head, maybe Rebecca is working with the Nirka, I had no real reason to believe her loyalty after all, she could be informing them as we speak, but what would the point in that be?

Rebecca brought Rick here and that drew Mark, she roped me into this too, if she was planning something the only thing I could think of was insurance. If Canaan was working on the inside of Parliament to orchestrate this whole thing then he may need a scapegoat... or three... to take the fall if his coup fails. Rebecca could be working with him and if she is, two Kats and a member of the Kyn would be perfect to pin the blame on if something goes wrong. Fox knows the situation, but he can't risk his position by siding with us. I need some insurance of my own in case this gets ugly.

I stood and headed for the door, knowing exactly what I had to do as much as it would pain me to do so. I left the Mill on my way down the main road of the city for the Garrison. Each step I took across the pavement around the broad circular road caused my anxiety to build, but about halfway there I got that feeling… the one you get when you're being followed. The street was empty this time of the evening since it was the last day of the weekend most of the people in the city were home early to rest up for the work week…so why was I hearing footsteps? I turned around and there stood Mark, I thought as much.

"Why are you following me?" I asked already half expecting his suspicion from the dark look on his face.

"You tell me. I find you fighting Rebecca in the woods after that strange man delivers us a letter sending us into some sort of trap no doubt. and then you just up and leave the house headed straight for the city's military installation." Mark's logic was sound however misguided.

"Do you trust Rebecca?" I asked calmly

"A hell of a lot more than I trust you." He shot back tersely

"Touché but really, you don't know her and neither do I. Now apparently Rick has lived with her and your family for some time after your father found her during his travels in Ryagan. But do you know anything about her before that? Rick doesn't, and its possible with all the information she keeps from us that she was a plant, to lure people back here from Katzen that could take the fall in case this little operation of Canaan's fails. Rick told me that what brought them here was a Nirka that attacked your family's compound, what if that was staged? Rebecca spoon feeds us just enough information to keep us going and now we're about to head into some underground den surrounded by the enemy if she really is with us then we have to, but I for one don't want to put all my trust in one very suspicious Rya." Mark stood quietly listening to me, no doubt studying me for any sign of dishonesty, though I had nothing to gain by lying to him at this point.

"So what's your plan? Go to the military and ask for an escort?" his calm tone could have passed for an approval of my assessment, if I didn't know better.

"No, I have a connection with one of the Garrison officers, I didn't want to have to use it but under the circumstances right now it's our best bet. I'm going to discreetly inform the military of our actions, they won't take us seriously but at least this way I can ensure that we have an official report of what we're doing if Rebecca turns on us." Mark donned a puzzled expression as his offensive stance relaxed a little after hearing my plan.

"It couldn't hurt, but is your contact going to take kindly to two illegal Kats in the city?" His point was valid but moot, I had already accounted for that possibility.

"Normally yes, but I am still with the Kyn, all I have to do is claim both of you. I'm allowed to cover anyone beneficial to my mission, which is classified. The military cannot interfere with me nor make any inquiries about any of my missions. While we are there I will request clearance documents for you, your brother, and Rebecca." I explained.

"Why Rebecca, won't documentation make it easier for her to move about the city?"

"It will, but it will also make it easier for us to track her movements. Any time her name is checked we'll be able to see exactly where she's been." At hearing this Mark smirked.

"That's playing dirty." He almost laughed as he and I started back for the Garrison.

"Backup plans are how I've survived so many solo missions, and if she's really being honest with us then she doesn't have to know. All the same, I don't think we should tell Rick about this, he trusts her and he might tell her what we have planned." I returned Mark's smirk looking up at him out of the corner of my eye as he walked next to me.

"Agreed." Mark's tone returned to its normal, flat inflection.

It was ironic that the first time Mark ever showed me any amount of trust or approval was because I was doing something out of distrust for someone else. This did confirm my thought that

Mark himself didn't have anything up his sleeve, in spite of his offensive manner he was a very honest person, maybe too honest and that's why he's so offensive. This realization certainly made dealing with him that much easier.

As we approached the gates to the Garrison the guard took one look at me then at Mark then back to me."You're here to see him? He's in his office, I'm sure you remember where it is." The guard stepped aside and I nodded to him as my foreign companion and I passed.

Mark gave me a curious look, no doubt wondering why I didn't have to show my brand or even say a word in order to be allowed inside "Must be some connection you have in there if the soldiers know you just by your face." Mark's words carried that same suspicion as before, and I thought he was finally warming up to me.

"You could say that, you'll see when we get inside." I mumbled

We marched through the central courtyard, though neither Mark nor I were soldiers anymore, the atmosphere of the base brought out the military training we both had pounded into in. There were two squads on either side of the courtyard performing maneuvers; I could hear the drill sergeants bellowing commands at the top of their lungs at the green recruits and the recruits complying with every insult and order. I looked up at Mark and he was wearing a half-smile, I could tell he was remembering the days when he went through the same training it was hell but something every soldier looks back on fondly.

We reached the large wooden doors quickly compared to the university this building was archaic, grey stone and wood were all that were used since it was the oldest building in the city. The Garrison outdates even the Royal Quarter originally the city was built around this base. The guards on either side of the large double doors pushed them in opening the way for us, the groaning wood of the old doors as we passed through were evidence of their age. The inside hall was lit by the eerie glow of the long thin bulbs developed at the university, between that and the metallic air ducts with the low hum of the rotating fans circulating air through the base made the whole place seem somewhat foreign.

The entire city had begun to undergo these modern changes as new ideas from the students of the Consilium became a reality. Long tables stretching half the length of the hall sat back near the entrance but the far half remained clear for indoor assemblies of the men. As we passed I received the customary indignant stares of the soldiers scattered about, however today they seemed particularly hostile. I realized they were looking past me to my companion, I had forgotten that the war, especially for these men, had not been too long ago and they still held strong animosity for Mark's tribe since they made up the bulk of the Kat's forces. I sped up our pace to make this visit as short as possible, passing through the back door of the main hall into a small corridor that led past several rooms till I reached a thin wooden door at the far end. I stopped and turned to Mark.

"When we go in here let me do the talking, it'll go quicker and I'd rather not draw this out." My demand was in a half-hearted whisper as we stood before the door and Mark's curious look turned to a slight grin as his eyes rose from me to the brass nameplate bolted to the door bearing the name 'Captain Wayne Vesco 101st division'. Mark just nodded and with that I knocked on the door.

"Come in…" the labored voice on the other side of the door groaned.

I swung the door open wide and with all the dignity I could muster I sauntered on in and stood before the desk of 'Captain Vesco'. The first expression to cross Wayne's face was of wide eyed surprise, but that quickly faded to the arrogant grin he carried when he was looking right through me, this time he was looking right through me to Mark. Wayne stood and walked around his desk and past me to offer his hand to Mark shaking firmly.

"My name is Wayne, I'm glad to see Dori in the company of a soldier. Thank you for looking after him." Wayne's sincere tone showed evidence that to him I was still a child.

"Dori….? I'm Mark Burke " Mark was confused for a moment but also very stoic as he shook the captain's hand. Never has anyone that I've seen, not in my family or even his own brother approached him so carelessly. The kinship between soldiers, even from opposite sides of a conflict, seemed to create a very strong respect towards one another. Unlike the other soldiers on the base Wayne held no grudge against the Kats for what happened in the war and I guess he could tell Mark was a soldier even without being told.

"Ha, well I guess no one calls him Dori anymore, I hope my brother hasn't caused you too much trouble." My brother stepped around the side of his desk and leaned on it looking at us. "So what are you doing here Dori?"

I answered without hesitation, having rehearsed this conversation many times in my head on the way here from the house. "I've been investigating, the particulars aren't important right now, but we have reason to believe that the Albedo may be conspiring against Canile and working with the Nirka tribe from Katzen." Wayne's eyes widened in surprise but quickly narrowed to a slit at me as I cut straight to the point. My brother then glanced up from me to Mark, and he nodded gravely in affirmation. I guess my word wasn't enough for my brother to believe the story. "I just want to inform you in case we find any hard evidence so the military can be prepared to move on Canaan. I have no intention of confronting Canaan directly. This operation is simply for proof of conspiracy."

"Let me stop you right there, is this a Kyn operation?" My brother made his own cut straight to the heart, as he did with any serious matter. His whole demeanor shifted, in this moment I wasn't looking at my brother but instead a loyal captain of the lykos military.

"You know I can't answer that. Just know that if you hear any reports of Nirka in the city the first place you should look is the Albedo's estate in Everest." I stated plainly. "Also, would you mind signing three documents of asylum for Mark here, his brother Rick, and a Rya named Rebecca Kasimi?" I asked with slight apprehension.

"Asylum? Are they not legal immigrants?"

"No, but they are a part of my mission. I just want to avoid them having any trouble in the city since I can't always escort them around." I explained, straightening up and giving him a nod out of respect before turning around to leave when I heard my brother say to Mark.

"I know it's a lot to ask but would you look after my brother for me?" I almost busted out laughing right there. If he only knew, the man he was asking to take care of me plans on killing me after we sort this mess out. Mark's reply was unintelligible as far as I could tell being halfway out as I was, leaving the door open for him. I knew he had rejoined me when I heard the door close.

"What'd he say to you?" I asked rhetorically, curious too because Mark had lingered a little longer than it would have taken for a single reply. The tall Vikan simply gave his usual grunt and kept walking.

It wasn't long before we found ourselves passing through the outer gates of the Garrison. The pair of us walked through the night air as the gas lampposts flickered to life lighting up the dark streets of the city. Silence settled between us for half the walk before to my surprise Mark spoke up first,

"So your brother is a captain, why didn't you join the military?" He asked curiously.

"My brother wouldn't allow it, he made officer pretty early and when the war broke out and I tried to join up he denied me." I answered honestly, and a bit of that old frustration slipped in to my answer.

Mark opened his mouth to speak but just then we heard someone yelling from over the wall as we passed Everest and the odd scraping of stone. Immediately we realized someone was coming over the wall, Mark drew his knife as my hand dropped to the sword on my hip when we saw Rick jump down from the top of the ten foot stone wall separating Everest from the main road. I took my hand off the sword and heard Mark return his weapon to its sheath while we both stared at Rick as he approached us.

"Hey guys, what're you doing out here?" he asked as though nothing were out of the ordinary.

"Um, what was that just now?" I asked both deflecting his question and a bit suspicious as to why Rick would be hopping walls in the middle of the night.

"I was just visiting a friend...then her father decided to come in without knocking... haha." He answered joining us on our walk, Mark and I sighed in unison and continued on down the road.

Rick continued talking about the tryst he had just escaped from and others like they were the most epic stories we could ever hear. I think Mark and I both knew him well enough to just let him talk, every once in a while I'd chime in with a 'Wow,... what'd you do then?' or a 'least you made it out of that one' Just near the end of one of his stories the three of us heard footsteps coming from behind but before we could even turn to look a familiar voice rang out through the night.

"Heeeyy! You guys where have you been!?" Rebecca almost sung the words as she called out to us. Rebecca came running and stopped right in the middle of our group though she locked eyes with me right away. "When I got back to the house I looked for you guys because... I have news! ...But first, I'm hungry."

"We have food at the house…" I answered slowly as she studied my face closely, I was almost convinced she could read my mind and saw what I had just done out of mistrust for her.

"Yeah… but I don't feel like cooking anything." Rebecca looked across the three of us with a devious grin…"I have an idea, why don't we have a race back to the house, it's not far and whoever gets there last has to cook for the rest of us." At first I thought she was just messing with us and even if she was serious I knew there was no way the brothers would agree to a race…it seems I was wrong.

Mark's stern expression shifted into a grin as he and Rebecca shared a glance and Rick smiled as well. "This will be fun, I'm in." Rick's agreement was followed by an affirmed nod from Mark and then the three of them turned to me.

"Alright, alright, you're on. Don't forget, it's my city." I smiled at her and turned to look down the empty road as the others lined up next to me and Rebecca began to count off.

"Ready…One…Two…Three…GO!!!"

Chapter 14: Mark Begins to Understand

The four of us took off at top speed down the empty city street passing the gates of Everest and staying neck and neck all the way around the street until we got past the Consilium grounds. The air grew cold and icy in my lungs though I could feel a distinct heat radiating from Rebecca as she pulled ahead on my left. As soon as we reached the section of the street that ran alongside the Pit Rebecca began to peel off close to the wall that separated us. The Pit was the last district before the Industrial District, or the Mill as I've heard it called, where Dorian's house was, and sure enough as soon as she reached the entrance Rebecca slipped off into the Pit with me close behind her.

Following Rebecca through the winding paths and back alleys reminded me of navigating the deep jungles during the survival training all Vikan soldiers undergo. She leapt over carts and dove around the random people in the alleys with ease all the while I kept close at her heels until we got to the solid stone wall dividing the Pit from the Mill. Rebecca stopped in her tracks and turned around staring straight at me as I approached,

"Take off your belt." She demanded.

"Excuse me?" I asked barely winded as I came to stand in front of her.

"You want to beat your brother and Dorian? Give me your belt and then give me a boost over the wall, I'll pull you up from the top of the wall." I looked the Rya girl from the ground up and she knew what I was thinking. "Just trust me, c'mon!"

I decided it was best not to argue with her plan, I stripped my belt off and pulled the knife-sheath from it, stuffing it into the waistband of my pants and handed Rebecca the belt. I stood with my back to the wall and cupped my hands low. She took a running start and jumped up landing her right foot into my hands as I heaved her up onto the wall. Rebecca landed gracefully on barely a foot thick of stone as she let one end of the belt hang down for me to grasp. No sooner had I taken hold of my thick leather belt then I looked up to see her hop over the side. As light as she was there's no way she could pull me up but I was able to use the tension on the belt to climb, lowering her at the same time.

I reached the top of the wall and jumped over landing next to Rebecca, she gave me a wink as I slid the knife-sheath back onto the belt and secured it to my waist. I surveyed our surroundings for a moment and realized we were just outside of the wooded area that was next to Dorian's house. Rebecca and I quickly took off through the woods, able to see the outside firelight from the lantern hanging at the door in moments. When we reached the house I looked around and saw no sign of my brother or Dorian, that's when I got an idea.

"Wait here for a second…"

I quietly slipped inside the house and retrieved one of Mrs. Vesco's long wooden spoons from the kitchen, when I reemerged Rebecca gave me a curious look, "Just for a little fun." I shot her the same devious grin I saw her wear countless times and she responded in kind.

A few minutes passed and before long I could see Dorian and Rick running, still neck and neck down the path to the house. I grinned again, this time because I knew that Rick was just playing with him. Even among Kats, who were known for our swiftness, my brother was faster than any in our tribe. The pair was only about thirty yards out when Rick started pulling away from his Lykos pursuer; only slightly at first but the gap between the two was growing at a rapid pace. The smile on my brother's face was evident and almost amusing as the distance between he and Dorian became too great for his competitor to make up. Rick reached us just in time to turn around and wave at Dorian, as he approached I produced the wooden spoon with a grin and when he stopped facing us I tossed it to him.

"It's kind of chilly out tonight; I'd like something hot for dinner." With that smug statement I turned around and went inside.

After our little race I decided to go back to the room Rick and I shared and rest while Dorian got to work on dinner, though Rebecca took pity on him and started in helping him cook. Rick left, probably to go see another girl in the city, according to his stories earlier, he had many. I wasn't surprised; he always had at least one or two girls on the hook, even back home.

I laid on my cot staring at the ceiling thinking about everything, my mind was racing. It wasn't long ago I left home for the military, Rick and I fought that night. Rick said I was abandoning the family and our work, spreading the word of Jagés as it were. I knew better though, I wasn't like him, I couldn't feel the earth and I couldn't speak to people the way he and our father could. I decided to pack up and leave home, following my own way. I also knew part of it was jealousy. Rick had always wanted to join the military and go off to exotic places and lead a military life defending our people, but he was born different…special, and because of that he was denied many freedoms. In the end though he got his wish, he landed smack in the middle of our former enemy's capitol city and here I am, stuck here with him.

I still couldn't believe it… somehow I ended up working with the man that killed Andre…along with my brother and some strange foreign girl my father brought back from Ryagan, and for what? Helping the Lykos? They used the Nirka tribe as an excuse to pass judgment on all of us, to invade our lands and kill our people! I understood, I didn't need to take Rebecca's word for it, I saw that Nirka at the Vesco's church earlier. I knew that I couldn't risk letting the Nirka run free here, all the Lykos need is another excuse to go to war.

What really bugged me as I turned to watch the starlight pour in through the window of my dark room was, I was beginning to understand Dorian and Andre's last words kept echoing in my head…"It's just war"… Dorian was only following orders, like I was, and he had no support, no brothers in arms and even his family didn't approve of him. Dorian's own brother denied him when he tried to join the regular military so he did what he had to do, maybe that's why he and my brother get along so well. Then there's Rebecca… a savvy young woman that seems like she pulls valid information from thin air. Dorian was right to suspect her, but I can't help but trust her. She is can be pretty shady but if everything she's said is true then the four of us may have bitten off more than we can chew. Rebecca can be so childish at times, but that fight between her and Dorian earlier showed more than anything else, she is anything but a child.

That fight was another of recent events that haunted me; Dorian's sword almost seemed to radiate an icy chill, I even saw frost fall from its edge when he pulled away from her. Rebecca's own weapons seem to heat up during any fight she finds herself in, when she held them to my brother's throat and again when she fought Dorian. That fight in particular caused them to glow a dim red as though they had just been pulled from a forge, I wonder if Rick made her knives like he made Dorian's sword.

I pulled out Andre's knife and stared up at its glistening edge as traces of light bounced off of its surface. I was reminded of when Rick and I were children. Nyma was a captain back then, young and strong. He was part of the detachment that was assigned to our colony during one of the many skirmishes between the tribes. Captain Andre Nyma spent a lot of time with my brother and I, teaching us survival skills, tactics, and self-defense. Back then Rick was apprenticed to one of the craftsmen in our settlement and when it came time for Nyma and his men to leave us, Rick stayed up for three days straight working at the forge to make this knife, he even asked me to help him so he could finish it in time. When it came time for me to join the Vikan were the only tribe with an organized military and Andre welcomed me with open arms. I was surprised to see he still carried the knife Rick made for him, and now it was all I had left of him.

I continued to stare at the ceiling, holding Andre's knife, which seemed heavier now than something of its size should be and conflicting thoughts of my current predicament turning in my head, distracting me from the oddity. I could hear Rebecca in the kitchen laughing with (or at) Dorian, as the smell of hearty potato soup began to fill my room. I guess Dorian was warming up to her after all, though when it comes to someone like him, I doubt he would trust her yet. I sat up but stayed in my room thinking for a good twenty more minutes or so before I heard a knock.

My brother didn't open the door, instead he just spoke through it, "Hey, Dorian and Rebecca are about done with the soup, just thought I'd let you know."

I wasted no time in getting up and heading out into the hall leading to the kitchen after all I was getting really hungry. I found Rebecca ordering Dorian around as she stirred the soup, she had him preparing tea, setting the table, and cleaning up the mess they had made in an apparently short-lived food fight that I must not have heard while lost in my own thoughts. Now I knew why Rick had decided not to stick around for the meal preparations, he must have learned early on how bossy Rebecca could be and conveniently didn't tell Dorian or myself. It was more than likely he left it out for his own amusement, which I had to admit, it was pretty funny watching an infamous assassin get ordered around the kitchen. Rick was sitting back at one of the places already set at the dining table enjoying the show. I joined him and sat on his right and as we watched the comical display, I realized why Dorian was doing everything he was told so obediently. While Rebecca stirred the pot with one hand, the other had a firm grasp on Dorian's sword.

"How did she…?" I began, before Rick cut me off.

"Dorian wasn't paying attention and she snatched it, sheath and all right off his belt as he entered the kitchen. That's why I left, didn't want to get caught in the middle of a fight between those two, so I decided to visit a nice farm girl I had seen earlier that only lives a few houses down on this road. By the time I got back I guess she had convinced him that the only way he was getting that sword back was to do as she says, so I thought I'd just sit back and watch the 'Wolf' get ordered around... haha." Dorian shot a look of contempt at Rick as he no doubt overheard him talking to me.

Not long after I sat down, Dorian and Rebecca placed four large bowls of soup and a glass of iced tea at each of the four seats around the rectangular table. Only after everything was set did Rebecca extend Dorian's sword-in-sheath to him, he snatched it from her hand and sat down leaning it against his chair without a word. Rebecca gracefully sat in her chair next to Dorian with her devilish smirk was aimed at him before she began to take part in the meal. We all started in on the dish and it was surprisingly delicious, I didn't expect Rebecca to be such a good cook, the creamy texture and tender slices of potato with a hint of melted cheese blended perfectly. While the four of us ate I knew it wouldn't be long before Rick or Rebecca started a conversation so I just sat back in wait.

Today was a long day and we were all very tired, after ten minutes of silence I thought perhaps I had been wrong and that we would have a peaceful quiet dinner before going to bed...Then Rebecca leaned forward just as we all finished our bowls around the same time.

"Down to business, or had you forgotten I had news?" we all shook our heads 'no' in turn. Rebecca let out a short sigh and pulled out two small envelopes and one large folded paper from her back pocket, though one envelope was a little bigger than the other. The larger one was obviously the envelope she received from that Nirka butler with the top hat at church, Lucas Deimo I believe was his name, the other one looked plain and unassuming.

"This is all the documented evidence we have right now, Deimo's letter, and the Nirka's orders from when they attacked the colony. I still haven't had much luck fully translating the orders, neither has Rick, but right now I think we should put all our focus on dealing with Cayden and the Undercity. Rebecca slid the smaller of the two out into the center of the table.

"I haven't opened this yet, it's supposed to be a map to an alternate entrance to the Undercity instead of the one Rick and I used before. I know everything up till now you've had to take on my word. Rick saw the Nirka attack back in Katzen, and all of you saw Lucas Deimo, the Nirka butler for Canaan, but beyond that none of you have any reason to believe what I've been telling you this whole time." Rebecca's voice was serious and I saw the point she was trying to make. "I left this sealed so that we all could look at them together for the first time, that way you won't have a reason to suspect me if this turns out to be a trap, I'll know only as much as the rest of you about how we're getting down there. First we have to go over this one more time." Rebecca pulled out Lucas Deimo's letter from its envelope. "Whoever Deimo's master is may be an issue, but right now the task at hand is dealing with his 'brothers' and Canaan. Cayden Vel, Rick you said you'd challenge him when we got down there, but if you lose then we're all done, they'll kill us. Are you sure you can win?" As Rebecca asked, she looked at Rick and he met her gaze with a look that could kill. He took her question as a deep insult, like any of us would. "Fine, but remember you'll have all our lives on the line."

"I understand, so let's see where we're headed." Rick grabbed the sealed envelope from the center of the table and tore it open with one of his claw-like nails and pulled out the folded piece of paper and tossed it on the table, there was no drawn map or lengthy instructions, only one line and it read,

"Beneath Erus' most trusted guard."

The four of us sat back in our chairs, not sure what to make of the cryptic message. A few minutes passed with us all staring at the table deep in thought. Dorian raised his head to speak and we all turned attentively,

"Well the Eruses are the royal Canden family that united Canile before establishing the Council of Parliament, their descendants still live in the castle in the Royal Quarter at the center of the city next to the Hall of Parliament. Maybe one of the royal guards knows the way into the Undercity…" Dorian's thought trailed off as he must have realized the problem with his theory.

"Then why would it say 'beneath' the guard? It must mean something else, unless the guard stands on some sort of hidden door." Rick's logic was sound as he voiced his take on the riddle and Dorian seemed to agree, but I wasn't so sure and by the look on her face, I could tell Rebecca wasn't convinced either.

"I don't know, but right now that seems like our best bet. I feel like tomorrow the four of us should try to find a way to sneak into the Royal Quarter, and then we can check the guard postings from a distance to see if any of them are standing near anything that could be used as a hidden door." She said as she sat back in her chair.

It was a sound plan for the moment and we were all very tired. After putting together our plan we all returned to our rooms for the evening, though as I was falling asleep I noticed Rick, still sitting up staring at his weapon.

Chapter 15: Rick's Chance to Fight

After dinner and planning the four of us decided to get some much needed rest since it was around one in the morning before we all got settled, however I didn't get to sleep till three. Throughout most of my time here I couldn't help but feel like I was just along for the ride, but today was the day that I proved to myself that I could do more than work a forge back at the colony. Today the others were counting on me to win against Cayden.

Just as I closed my eyes they snapped open again, it was morning and through my window I could see hints of light creeping their way across the sky creating a faint hazy glow through the heavy clouds. I had only been asleep for four hours but I felt like I hadn't slept at all. Mark was already dressed and heading out the door when I got up and slipped on my hooded shirt. I shook off the thoughts from the night before and slid my collapsed staff into my belt at the small of my back and headed out after Mark into the living room. I found everyone standing waiting for me,

"Let's do this." I sighed, still a little groggy.

Rebecca and I headed out the front door, followed by Mark and Dorian, and off we went down the street toward the main road. Rebecca was quiet, solemn even. I had never seen her act this way. Usually she'd be loud and obnoxious, talking about anything under the sun except what we were doing. I expected her to be cracking jokes at Dorian for last night, losing the race and being at her beckoned call all night making dinner, but instead she stared intently forward and walked slightly ahead of me. I guessed she had an idea of where to enter, after all the main road encircled the Royal Quarter and I doubt Dorian's status as one of the Kyn would get us in, so I just followed her as we turned onto the main road headed west for the entrance to the Pit.

I heard Dorian say from behind us, "The entrance to the Royal Quarter is the other way…"

Rebecca turned around with an almost angry look aimed straight at Dorian. "Did you think they'd let us just walk right in through the front door…? I have a plan, so just c'mon."

Our group walked in silence for about twenty minutes till we reached the entrance to the Pit. Once there, Rebecca led us through the unguarded gate and up to one of the shacks just inside the district. There was an old man waiting out front, Rebecca approached him and forced a smile. He looked the three of us up and down and then back to her before nodding and allowing us inside. We all quietly followed Rebecca into the rundown shack and back to an old storeroom filled with ladders, tools, and bricks of all shapes and sizes stacked to one side, before she turned around to face us.

"I left again last night, came out here to figure something out, I came across the old man that lives here, he works with his sons in the early mornings doing spot checks and maintenance on the inner walls. He has agreed to help us get into the Royal Quarter, in here are all the tools we need and there are overalls in the drawers over there for us to wear over our clothes. We'll pack our weapons in the tool bag and use a ladder to climb up and over the wall, and we'll use another ladder on the inside so we can get out the same way. Our cover story will simply be that we were slacking this morning and haven't yet finished checking the walls." Rebecca explained flatly.

Rebecca went straight to work, pulling out four pairs of overalls in the appropriate sizes (or close enough anyway). Mark's was a little too small, so the pant legs barely stopped above his ankles and the arms stopped above his wrist. I would have laughed if not for the grave air Rebecca was giving off. I quickly jumped into my overalls, which were a little snug but looked fine. Each of us placed our weapons in the duffle the old man and his sons used to carry their tools, thinking ahead Dorian placed a large cloth over them and piled a few of the tools from the room on top, I assumed just in case a soldier doubted us and asked to look inside. Dorian and Rebecca finished zipping up their overalls and we each wore a cap with the bill pulled low enough to cover our eyes but not low enough to look suspicious. Dorian grabbed one folding ladder, and Mark grabbed the other, and together we all marched back out. The older man waved at Rebecca as we passed and she returned his wave before heading out into the street with us.

Rebecca walked straight out from the entrance to the Pit to the inner wall surrounding the Royal Quarter and motioned for Dorian to put up his ladder. I saw what she was doing, since there are never any guards posted at the Pit entrance it was less likely we would face any questions if we set up here. Dorian unfolded his ladder and leaned it at a stable angle against the wall and stepped away to make room for Mark, who slipped his arm through the bars of his ladder up to his shoulder and climbed up to the top of the wall. We all stood in silence watching him as he unfolded his ladder and lowered it down the opposite side of the wall and quickly made his way down.

"Ladies first." I said to Rebecca with a smile, trying to soften the tension a little.

Rebecca walked by me without a word and climbed up, I followed and Dorian brought up the rear carrying the duffle with our weapons. Once we all made it down I looked around to see what part of the Royal Quarter we had ended up in, it was a small paved courtyard that looked to be centered directly behind the castle. The sun was just getting high enough to cast a dim grey light through the clouds, which gave the rear courtyard an eerie aura as we collected ourselves. What caught all of our attention immediately was the large stone statue of some sort of ancient knight that stood right in the middle of the courtyard. Rebecca just nodded to us and we all started in towards the castle, but when we passed the statue something hit me.

" 'Erus' most trusted guard'…" I mumbled the words scrawled on the slip of paper from the night before.

I broke away from the others and walked up to the base of the statue, slowly looking it up and down. It was just so odd that instead of facing the castle, the statue was facing the wall we climbed down.

"Rick! Get back over here, we can't get separated!" Rebecca hissed from behind me, trying very hard to keep her voice low.

"Just one second…'Beneath Erus' most trusted guard'. What if it's not talking about an actual guard, think about it. Mark, as a soldier, who would you have to trust most in a battle?" I asked without looking back to see his expression.

Mark hesitated to answer at first but in low tone he said, "I guess, the soldier watching my back."

"Exactly, and this courtyard is right behind the castle, what if the 'Erus' in the letter was 'Castle Erus', not the family?" I crouched low at the base of the statue and there it was, behind the statue there were two grooves in the stone right in line with the corners. "There are tracks here, Mark, help me with this."

I moved around front of the statue and Mark joined me, helping me push while Rebecca and Dorian kept a lookout. Surprisingly the statue slid back quite easily revealing a dark, narrow stairway leading deep underground. Rebecca came around and studied the passageway with an astonished look on her face.

"Well that was easier than I thought." She remarked.

Dorian slapped my back in congratulations before following Rebecca down the stairs. When we all had entered the stairway Rebecca plucked an old dusty torch from the wall and raised the fire in her palm to it. The torchlight revealed a handle underneath the lip of the statue which Mark quickly pulled, covering the entrance and leaving us with only the torch to light our way. Dorian dropped the bag full of our weapons while we all stripped out of our disguises and piled them next to the bag at the top of the stairs before strapping on our weapons. The four of us were now ready and we began our descent into the depths below Crown Lykou. We travelled down for about thirty minutes but it felt like hours and the further we went down the more damp and crowded the path seemed. Rebecca seemed to get more and more agitated the further we went down, it could have been because she felt boxed in with no easy way to slip away and escape, though it was probably that she hated losing that fight with Cayden before, and it frustrated her to face him again. It wasn't long before I had enough.

"Look, Rebecca we can't afford any stupid mistakes down here and the way you're acting you're going to say the wrong thing and get us all in trouble. So what? You lost, that doesn't give you the right to act like a child about it, get over it or stay up here and wait for us." Rebecca seemed taken aback, like no one had ever stood up to her in that way, for someone with no home or family she seemed pretty spoiled.

I walked past her without giving her so much as a look, Mark and Dorian seemed to agree with my point as they followed me with grim expressions on their faces. The three of us kept going down for about five more minutes when we finally stopped at the bottom of the staircase. I heard the oddest sound off the stone floor, it sounded like… footsteps. I turned around and looked past my brother and Dorian scanning for the source of the sound and hoping it was only Rebecca, Sure enough, the young Rya girl was almost prancing down the stairs.

"You really think I was going to sit this out? You should know me better by now Rick… Plus you three wouldn't make it out of here alive without me, even if you won the right to enter the Undercity from Cayden." She had a ring in her voice that sounded like a song as she skipped on by, "Finally, we're at the bottom! Now where…" Her words cut off as she saw what we had moments earlier, the ceiling in the passage gradually got higher and wider until it could accommodate doors that were ten feet high and a good six feet across.

"Well… looks like we're here, go on 'fearless leader', I believe it's your move." Dorian said nudging me forward from behind.

I placed both hands on both doors and pushed in spreading my arms as I did, (when passing through double doors it looks more epic this way) and stepped out as the light engulfed me, dim but blinding for me having just come through a pitch black tunnel with only one torchlight with which to see. It took a second for my eyes to adjust and then I realized…this was sunlight. As our eyes recovered we stood in awe of the sight before us, the cavern was so large, it was about the size of three districts from the city above. The ceiling was at least a hundred feet above us and I could see the light was coming from large mirrors reflecting it through holes that must have led up to the surface. We stood on a large, round, arena style platform that had a staircase leading down from it into the city below. I walked to the nearest edge and looked down and at the bottom of the long staircase was what looked like a small city, shops and people walking up and down the roads, children playing in the street.

The whole Undercity was surrounded by water cutting out a large circle around it which was probably how Rebecca and I got in last time. I could see where the water flowed in through holes at the bottom and then back out. Rebecca left me in one of those tunnels when she faced Cayden so long ago, and now it was my turn. I snapped back to the moment at hand when I saw a group of Lykos running up the stairs from the city to meet us. I slowly walked back towards Rebecca and the others, steeling myself for what came next.

The pack that came up the stairs all carried the rifles that we had seen in the hands of the Lykos soldiers around the city, and were led by a large Kokin Lykos. His skin was strangely tanned, odd for his breed and he wore a low cut v-neck shirt that allowed me to see a large scar on his chest. I could see he had a large leather pouch hanging off his hip that sloshed with each step he took and out of the top poked the handle to a whip, this must be Cayden. My only question at the moment was, why he would keep his whip in a water-filled pouch?

Cayden's familiar face and green eyes seemed to burn as they settled on our little group, especially as he looked to my left where Rebecca stood defiantly. When I saw his eyes trained on her I stepped forward to ensure the attention of the pack, and Cayden in particular, would be directed at me.

"Are you Cayden Vel? I hear the only way to get into this place is to fight you. My friend here fought and lost against you the last time she was here. I am also fighting for her to be pardoned." My voice carried throughout the cavern as I stood, shoulders squared, asserting my claim.

"I don't know how you found the way down here, but Rebecca already lost her chance to enter the city. You can fight for yourself and the other two there, but coming back here means her life is forfeit. Give me one reason not to have these men execute her right here and now." Cayden's bellowing voice could probably have been heard all the way down in the streets bellow as it resonated off of the walls.

"Here's a reason, if you have her killed then I will kill you in our fight, and that is a promise. Another reason, if you need another, is that if you let this thing go with her, then I will fight unarmed in our match." I kept a stern, cold tone of voice as I made my arrogant threat.

"Haha, you know, I like you. Sounds good to me, if you fight me bare handed then I will let all four of you in. Just out of curiosity, why are you all down here?" I had been waiting for Cayden to ask this question ever since I saw him come up the stairs.

"Well, all of us want to speak with you, they have their reasons but as for me, I want to talk to you about your brother." My words cut straight to his heart and everyone saw it, I had poked the bear.

"Tell me your name Kat." Cayden grunted.

"Richard Burke."

"Alright, let's get on with it then, Mr. Burke." Cayden's right hand hovered above his whip while the other dropped to the machete hanging on his other hip. "My men will keep an eye on your friends since we know the girl has a tendency to run away when things get bad." At their commander's words each of the ten

Lykos that followed Cayden up leveled their aim directly at the others behind me.

"This time she won't need to run, but enough talk. I want to get this over with." I stated firmly as I let my closed staff slip from my hand and fall to the stone platform.

"Let's." Cayden replied fiercely, drawing his machete and quickly pulling the coiled whip from its pouch.

I had to end this quick, I had no intention of getting torn apart by Cayden's whip. I took the opportunity of him having the last word to strike, launching forward to close the distance as fast as I could, at close range that machete would be difficult to handle, but easier than the whip if I had stayed back. With a flick of his wrist the water-soaked whip struck, he intended to lay open my right shoulder but with a quick leap forward and left I avoided the whip and charged in for Cayden himself.

'This was too easy, there's no way Rebecca was too slow for…' Before I could finish my thought the whip was wrapped around my throat and I was choking as I sailed through the air, slamming face down into the stone. The whip had unwrapped itself from my throat as I was flying so when I tried to stand I felt the first lash rip into my back as the whip simultaneously cracked the air. I had no idea what happened, I thought I had avoided it, how could he have caught me when I was so close? A second lash tore into me and I smelled the red mist of blood as it hit. I kicked my feet under me and sprung to the side and quickly jumped back to avoid the impressive range of Cayden's weapon.

I saw it, as I raised my eyes back to my opponent, Cayden's whip layed out on the ground as he stared at me with murderous intent. The strange thing was, Cayden's arm wasn't moving in the slightest and yet the whip was writhing... just barely, but enough to catch my attention. It looked like the whip was alive, but I knew better, like mine and Rebecca's, the Lykos also have bloodline traits that sometimes manifest themselves. Some Lykos were said to be able to influence the flow of water to some degree. Cayden must have the Lykos' trait and he's controlling the whip fibers with the water it's soaked in like a muscle. If I couldn't avoid the whip then I just had to get it away from him.

Cayden came running this time, closing the distance so he could put me in range of his weapon, but this time I was ready for him. I saw the flick of his wrist and just as he sent the deadly tendril for my neck I raised my arm in the last instant to catch the whip. I pushed the pain from the sting of his weapon to the back of my mind and torqued my arm to coil the length of Cayden's weapon around my forearm. When I pulled the whip tight it groaned under the tension and by the contorted look on Cayden's face, he knew what was coming next. I jerked my arm hard, snatching the whip out of his grip and threw it to the ground behind me. Now that he had lost the advantage of range I could end this.

I kicked off the ground at full sprint as he readied the blade in his other hand to defend against my assault. Finally it was my turn to go on the offensive and he was going to pay for making me bleed.

Chapter 16: Rebecca's Frustration

I had forgotten what it was like to see Rick fight, aside from the skirmishes with raiders and such on our way to the city I realized that I had never really seen him fight seriously. His unarmed technique was perfectly in line with the rigid style of military martial arts that the Vikans teach, I expected to see his brother fight that way, but not him. I honestly didn't think he had a chance against Cayden or that whip of his, not until this moment. The whip wrapped tightly around his arm before he ripped it out from Cayden's grasp and the determined look in his eyes made me doubt my first assessment of the situation.

That look in his eyes was the same one he wore in the tunnel when he confronted me on the way down here, I had only seen it before when he was out training and thought no one could see him. Rick liked to put on an arrogant front, like he was god's gift to the world (or at least to women), but deep down he had something to prove, not to anyone else but himself. Now his eyes were alight with that same passion, and a faint smile crossed his lips as he shot forward towards his opponent.

Cayden reacted quickly to the head on charge, raising his blade to come down on Rick from above, as tall as the Kokin was for his breed, he was still only equal to Rick in height. When Cayden swung his machete Rick instinctively caught his wrist and threw a punch straight for Cayden's face, Cayden saw it coming and caught Rick by the forearm. There they stood locked, leaning into one another, though equal in height, Cayden had the advantage in muscle. I could see Rick's knees begin to buckle under the weight of his opponent, that's when he saw his chance. Rick stretched one leg out behind him and leaned back, letting go of Cayden's wrist he raised his other leg and thrust his foot squarely into his enemy's stomach. The kick sent Cayden tumbling over the stone floor gasping for the air that had been forcibly ejected from his body. Rick locked his eyes on the machete as it skidded away from Cayden, at the same time Cayden raised his eyes from the ground to see where it had gone. They both turned from the weapon to look at each other and in that moment it became a race.

Cayden scrambled to his feet as Rick took off towards the blade. It was a close race…but not close enough for Cayden. Rick scooped up the blade and brought the tip of its edge to bear on Cayden, barely an inch from his throat. It was over… and just as I was about to let out a sigh of relief I heard the clicking of ten rifles as Cayden's men chambered their rounds and aimed their weapons at Rick. My hands dropped to the knives at my thighs and out of the corner of my eye I saw Dorian and Mark going for their weapons as well…

"Stop." Cayden ordered with one hand outstretched toward his men. "The Kat won, let them pass." Cayden relaxed and stood up, still laboring for breath. "There's a doctor that will patch you up in town, I'll send word." Cayden turned to look at one of his men over his shoulder and gave a slight nod. The one he nodded to shouldered his rifle and ran off down the stairs.

Rick nodded respectfully at Cayden and turned his weapon over, extending it back to its owner, handle first. Cayden took it without a word and Rick backed away, heading for the rest of us standing there waiting for him. Rick's staff lay on the ground between us and him, Dorian walked out past Mark and I and stopped in front of the staff. Dorian slipped his foot under the staff and kicked it straight up in front of his face and caught it, offering it to Rick as he approached. When Rick stretched out his hand and grasped his weapon Dorian smiled,

"Good work."

"Ha, yeah I thought I might lose for a second there, he was pretty tough." Rick replied with a half cocked smirk.

"Hey! You said you were all here to see me about something; come to the Crossroads Pub, it's right off of the center square in town." Cayden's words carried from behind Rick as he stood in front of us. "I'll be there in an hour or so, come find me after you finish up with the Doc." With that Cayden took the whip from one of his men that had apparently retrieved it for him as he spoke. Once he was finished Cayden coiled his whip with a grunt and headed off down the stairs into the town below.

Rick was trying to hide it, but I could tell he was in a lot of pain from his wounds. Mark tried to help him by offering his shoulder but Rick refused and kept walking as we made our way into the city. The Undercity was as I remembered it, yeah there were some hardened criminals here, but a lot of the people were actually soldiers from the war with Katzen and their families. The soldiers didn't exactly receive a hero's welcome upon returning and most of them were discharged as soon as they got back in0to the country. It wasn't a surprise, the bulk of these men that were sent across the border were recruited solely for that purpose.

It wasn't right though, they served their country and instead of getting congratulated the government gave them the proverbial boot. All of the former soldiers down here ended up turning to crime simply to survive. I didn't blame them, if the government wouldn't give them what they were owed then in a way they were justified in taking it. They came down here, started a new life, and many of them also had families. The ones that couldn't or didn't want to become criminals set up businesses and created an economic base for the Undercity. The four of us walked through the Undercity streets and passed shops of all kinds, there was even a toy store with children out front staring through the glass at the handmade toys in the window. I stole glances at the others who were astonished to see that this place wasn't some pit of dark underworld people, but a bastion for the outcasts from the city above. Honestly I was surprised Dorian didn't end up here after the war, I had guessed it was because he had a family with a firm foothold in Crown Lykou's society. When it came down to it, in the end these people took the short end of the stick they were given, persevered and are now finally experiencing prosperity for themselves.

It wasn't long before we saw a sign hanging over the street with the Physician's Cross on it that marked the door to the Doctor's clinic. When we approached my hand swung over the pocket of my shorts and brushed Pericci's letter, the one I was supposed to deliver in return for the information on how to get down here.

"Alright, so… you guys can take it from here right? I'm gonna go look around for a bit, I'll see you guys at the Crossroads Pub." I tried to sound as upbeat as possible to hide my true motive, the last thing those three needed was to find out I had been holding out on them.

I took off down the street, not waiting for a response from the guys and wanting to get this over quickly. Before long I found myself at the stairs leading down to a tunnel with barely any water flowing out. This was the tunnel Rick and I used to get down here before, where I made him wait while I had my fight with Cayden. I shuddered for a moment as the feeling of despair I had in that fight washed over me once again, my muscles all tensed at once as I sensed the another presence coming closer, the slight sound of footsteps coming to a stop behind me.

"Well well, look who's here all alone." I spun around and there stood Cayden with an evil smile on his face. "Your friend is quite a fighter, wasn't he the one you drug out of here when you ran after our fight?" I only nodded in response. "Maybe you should have let him fight last time, things might have turned out differently." Cayden mocked.

I quickly regained my composure and met his mocking smile with one of my own. "At least I had some entertainment this time, watching you get beat was pretty funny. The look on your face when Rick kicked you across the floor almost made me fall down too…laughing." Cayden let that comment roll off of him without much of a reaction, which I expected. Though the next thing he said I definitely didn't see coming.

"One thing I'm curious about though, that entrance you four used, the one that leads up to the castle, it hasn't been used since the first of us came down here. An old friend and I discovered it the day we were assembled in the Royal Quarter for our 'honorable discharge', how did you find out about it?' The suspicious ring in his voice made it certain in my mind that he already knew the answer to his question. "I guess we have a friend in common, did Pericci give you anything for me?"

Just that quickly, Cayden had figured out everything about how we got down here. Pericci never told me that he had served in the war but I guess we all have our secrets... I pulled the envelope from my pocket and handed it to Cayden, who had closed the distance between us while he had been talking. "He didn't tell me

who to deliver it to, just that the person it was for would find me."
I explained.

"And he was right, by the way I like the new knives, it was
a shame what happened to the last pair." Cayden added smugly
while he opened the envelope and quickly read its contents.
"Everything's going as planned then." Cayden lifted his eyes from
the letter with a satisfied smile. "I'll see you at the pub." Cayden
chided as he turned, trotting off down the street.

I walked along the ridge and up the slope to the next tunnel
where the water flowed more vigorously into the moat that
surrounded the underground city. The sandy red stone down here
reminded me of home, I never thought I'd miss it but now it
seemed so much further away than before. I was lost in thought for
a moment looking down the short ledge into a small section where
the water collected from both tunnels into a small whirlpool before
flowing back out when I heard the low crunch of dirt behind me…
I turned around and Rick was standing less than a foot away about
to push me!

I grabbed both of his wrists to stop him but he was already
committed, and we both went over the ledge into the water. The
roiling water flowing of the whirlpool disoriented me for a moment
and it was so dark, all I could hear was the sound of rushing water
and my own body struggling against the current. I tried to calm
down as fast as I could and quickly swam for the surface. When I
exploded out of the water I looked up and saw Dorian and Mark

running up to the ledge. I looked around and Rick was nowhere to be found, I turned my eyes back down into the dark water but my sight couldn't penetrate its depth in the low light. I dove back down and the further I went the more faded the sound of churning water became. Even though I couldn't see anything this deep, I could hear Rick fighting the water. The lashes from Cayden's whip must've been deeper than I thought if he wasn't strong enough to fight the current.

I swam for Rick as fast as I could and reached out for him, I grabbed his forearm and he jerked for a second, it was the same arm he caught the whip with less than an hour ago. When he figured out it was me he calmed down and together we started to swim back up. Rick helped as best he could but with the current getting stronger the further we went the more of his weight I felt as I pulled him towards the surface. Finally we broke out of the water, both gasping for air, by now Dorian and Mark had jumped in and helped Rick and I to the shallow end of the water at the bottom of the slope. I was a bit dizzy but more angry than anything else, and Rick was just a little waterlogged but otherwise he seemed alright and I wasn't going to waste a moment before tearing into him.

"What's your problem!?" I yelled, a little louder than I intended by the look of Mark and Dorian as they backed away.

As soon as Rick finished coughing the water from his lungs he looked up at me from his seat on the ground at the water's edge. "I was just messing around, I didn't think you were going to freak out and pull us both into the water. I just wanted to scare you a little, that's all."

"I'm out of here. I'll see you guys at the Crossroads Pub, where you should have been waiting for me to begin with." With that I angrily sloshed off towards the city again, this time in search of a clothing store and if I was lucky I might find a place to take a shower.

I wandered through the relatively empty streets for around twenty minutes before seeing anyone. I guess that's because they're all above ground during the day, running whatever robberies or crime they're involved in. The one person I did run into caused me to freeze in my tracks, she was a slender girl with pale skin and the telltale red hair of the Kokin, my friend that as far as I knew was still working as a maid at the Albedo's estate, Margot.

As soon as she laid eyes on me she froze in her tracks. We both stood there about thirty feet apart on the side of the empty street, neither of us said anything for a moment until I decided to break the silence.

"Hey Margot! What are you doing down here?!" I ran up to her whipping water with every stride.

"I...uh...well... My boyfriend knew how Mr. Canaan is a little paranoid and told him that I let you cover for me that night in exchange for a reward. I ended up homeless and some guys in the

Pit told me about this place, I had nothing left to lose so…here I am, haha. What about you, why are you so wet…?" Listening to her explanation I felt so bad for getting her into this situation, but at least she was doing better now it seemed.

"I took a little swim earlier… and… forgot to bring a change of clothes." I sighed, looking down at the soaked mess that was my outfit.

"You can borrow some of my clothes if you want to come back to my place?" Margot offered with a smile.

"Sure! I guess I have a habit of borrowing your clothes." I smiled back

"I'm glad this time I don't work for some creepy paranoid elitist, If I got kicked out of the Undercity, well then…I'd really have no place to go haha." I could hear slight regret in her voice as she tried to make light of her situation. I had to make this up to her somehow.

We made our way back down the street into the heart of the underground community and came to a stop in front of an establishment with a very familiar name.

"The Crossroads Pub, huh? What are we doing here?" I asked Margot.

"I work here, and I rent the loft apartment upstairs. I was really lucky to get this place, it's even tied in to the pub's boiler and pump system so I have hot running water!" Margot sounded so excited and I admit I was pretty excited too, I hadn't had a real shower much less a hot one since Rick and I left the colony.

"What are we waiting for then?!" I exclaimed, eager to get out of my drenched clothes and into Margot's shower, but when I started for the door I noticed Dorian and the Burke brothers trudging up the street.

"Hey…" I shot a contemptible glance at Rick before letting my eyes cross Dorian and Mark.

"Did you all go swimming?" Margot asked, looking from them to me.

"Something like that." I let my reply stop short with a tone that made it clear I was not happy with at least one if not all of them.

"Well… I have some spare clothes for Rebecca but I don't have any men's clothes, there's a store across the street if you guys want something dry to change into." Margot adopted my tone, which made me feel a little better having someone on my side, not that I needed anyone, but it was still nice to have another girl around.

Without saying anything else, the trio turned and headed across the street for the clothing store that Margot had pointed out. Margot and I went inside the pub which was littered with six or seven older Kokin and Ater men, it couldn't have been past eleven in the morning, (it was kind of hard to tell what time it was down here without the sun) yet the smell of alcohol was thick in the air. The bartender smiled at Margot and winked at me from behind his large cherry-wood bar as we passed by, headed for the back door and the stairs. At the top of the narrow flight of stairs was a thick wooden door with three massive locks on it, I watched as Margot pulled out a key ring with three keys on it big enough to match the locks.

"I've never had any problems with anyone downstairs, but you know a girl living alone can't be too careful." she explained as she worked on unlatching the locks.

Margot undid the final lock and held the door open for me, as I passed into her apartment I couldn't help but notice how nicely she had furnished her modestly sized living space. The common area had an easy chair and large rug with a low table in the center and two couches on opposite sides. There was a short hallway leading back with a door at the end. I followed Margot down the hall and into her bedroom which had a large wardrobe just across from a single metal framed bed with a small nightstand on the left.

"The bathroom is right through there." Margot motioned to a door on the far side of the room. "There are clean towels on the rack, go ahead and get cleaned up while I find you something to wear."

I nodded and went to the bathroom, shutting the door behind me and began to undress. It felt so good to finally get out of those wet clothes. I unbelted my knife-sheaths and thigh straps and laid them on the sink, then I tossed my still dripping outfit into the empty basket in the corner of the small bathroom and walked over to the shower. I pulled the curtain aside and before I reached for the fixture to turn the water on, I heard Margot humming a soft melody through the door while she sifted through the clothes in her wardrobe. I smiled to myself at her sweet innocence and turned the shower on, cranking the hot water up so hot it would scald most people, but as a Rya I liked it hot. I stepped into the burning water and let it run over me for a minute, I could feel the heat relaxing me, washing away all the dirt and bringing every nerve in my skin to life. I didn't want it to end but I didn't want to impose any more than I already was, in case she wanted a hot shower as well. I hurried and cleaned myself, turned the water off, and reached for a towel on the rack.

As soon as I cut the water off I heard a knock at the door. "I have your clothes whenever you're ready." Margot called through the door.

"Just bring them in if you don't mind, the curtain is closed." I answered still working vigorously to dry myself.

I felt the rush of cool air as the door creaked open and Margot stepped in, "I have a question, when did you meet Cayden?" I asked as she laid the clothes on the edge of the sink.

"Well...Mr. Vel found me in the Pit, I told him what had happened with Mr. Canaan and he offered to set me up down here. Why do you ask?" I could hear the slightest bit of suspicion in Margot's voice as she spoke, so I decided not to pry any further.

"No reason, I was just curious. Thank you again for letting me use your shower by the way." I deflected

"No problem at all, haha. So... who were those guys we ran into outside?" Margot asked as she finished with my clothes and turned for the door.

"Friends of mine...I guess." I answered. Margot's curiosity was understandable, but I was still not happy with Rick or the others for letting him push me into the water even as a joke.

"Those two tall guys were Kats and the other guy was a half-breed, you have some strange friends Rebecca." She commented, now doing nothing more than making conversation, or so I thought.

"Yeah, the one with the tattoos is Rick and the other is his brother Mark, the half-breed works in the Mill, his name is Dorian." I explained.

"Oh... You wouldn't happen to know if Dorian is...involved with anyone; would you?" Her question surprised me for a second but she must have noticed my hesitation because she quickly retracted, "Oh I'm sorry, were you interested in him?"

My surprise quickly turned into annoyance. "Haha, go for it if you want, but I definitely never would. Would you mind stepping out for a moment so I can get dressed?"

"Oh yes! I'm sorry." Margot whipped out of the bathroom closing the door behind her and freeing me to step out from behind the curtain to inspect the outfit she picked out for me.

Margot had a real talent for understanding other's taste in clothing, or at least mine. The outfit was a pair of knee-high black leather boots, dark red slim-fit pants, and a black sleeveless shirt with the collar cut into a V and buttoned high enough to remain modest. I slipped into my new clothes relatively quick and then went to drying off my weapons. I drew my knives one at a time and dried the beads of water from their polished surface with my towel. After I finished with the knives I picked up the sheaths and straps and clicked my fingers to lightly ignite a small intense fire in my palm and held it just close enough to let the heat do its work. Before long the whole rig had steam rolling off of it but was dry enough to wear. I slipped the belt on with the sheaths and secured them to my thighs with the straps and then quickly shoved the knives back in their sheaths. It felt good to be dry and clean again.

"I'm finished!" I called out to Margot as I stepped out of the bathroom to find her sitting on the bed. "I wonder if the boys are done getting their change of clothes, we're supposed to meet Cayden downstairs pretty soon."

Margot's eyes went wide in surprise, "You're going to meet Cayden…?"

Chapter 17: Dorian's Threat

"You really shouldn't have pushed Rebecca, you know she has a real temper and now she's probably mad at all of us." I scolded Rick as he, Mark, and I crossed the street to the clothing store.

"I was just playing around! I didn't mean to push her in…or for her to freak out and pull me in with her. How was I supposed to know?" Rick protested. I knew where he was coming from, and why he went a little too far playing around, Rebecca saw how deep those gashes from Cayden's whip had gone into his back and she may have blamed herself since he had to fight bare-handed because of her. Rick was just trying to lighten things up so she knew there were no hard feelings, but now things were probably worse off this way.

I let Rick's question go unanswered as we strolled on up to the swinging doors of the store and let ourselves in, if what the mannequins wore in the window outside was any indication, then the clothes here were nicer than one might find even in the city above. However, as we stepped inside we found no racks of clothes nor piles of assorted folded garments on large tables, there was simply a few dressed mannequins lining the walls like the ones in the window and a desk with an old man sitting behind it.

"Excuse me, we were looking to buy some clothes, just something dry to wear." I stated to the proprietor displaying our soaked situation. The old man who was sitting alone behind his desk reading a newspaper that was clearly out of date looked up at the three of us with a blank look in his eyes... until he realized we were leaving a puddle of water where we stood in the middle of his shop.

"What do you think you're doing!? You kids are going to clean this mess up, you know!" he yelled, though rather than feeling guilty, the three of us exchanged a glance of disbelief at being called 'kids' at our age.

"I'm really sorry sir, we fell into the water at the edge of town and a girl across the street said we should come here if we needed to buy clothes, and don't worry we have plenty of money." Rick explained. I was relieved that Rick took the lead of this encounter from me, he was a much better talker and frankly, I thought for a moment the old man was about to roll up that newspaper and take a swing at me.

Rick pulled out a hard plastic case from the messenger bag over his shoulder and popped open the airtight container, in it he sifted through a small pile of papers, his ID, business license, and some product orders from the shop, underneath were neatly ordered stacks of small bars of precious metals stamped with the seal of the Lykos Parliament. Crown Lykou had begun using paper currency as part of its modernization, allowing for the government to keep track of exactly how much money was flowing in their economy with numbered codes on each bill. Before this modern economic practice, these bars were the main form of currency and now they were valued much higher than paper money for their rarity. The old man's eyes lit up at the sight of Rick's rare currency and he dashed over to us with a small thin tape measure, then Mark spoke for the first time since we got down here.

"...We don't really have time for anything to be custom made..."

"No no, I wouldn't guess you gentlemen would, you have important business to attend to I'm sure, I am only taking down measurements to find something in each of your sizes. You see, when people do make custom orders and they either do not come back or cannot afford the work they commissioned I simply hold onto them just in case anyone of similar size comes looking to buy. I'll be done in just a moment, one quick question though, what type of clothes were you three looking for exactly?" the old man asked while he went about taking each of our measurements. We were all so taken aback by his complete turnaround in personality that we almost didn't register that he had asked a question.

"Nothing fine, something functional that looks halfway decent will do." Rick answered politely.

"Coming right up sirs!" and with that the old man dashed back through a small door behind his desk with the speed of a Lykos in his prime. Almost as soon as he had left, the old man burst through the small door pushing a multilayered cart, each layer was a shelf with three outfits to a shelf. "Alright gentlemen, each shelf has three options for each of you. You sir, the Lykos, your three are on the bottom and the next shelf is yours sir, the tallest Kat, and finally the top shelf has your three options good sir" The old man explained, though he barely ever broke eye contact with Rick and proceeded to shake his hand before stepping away. "Oh and where are my manners, my name is Oliver Withers but you can just call me Mr. Oliver as most of the folk around here do."

It didn't take long for the three of us to decide on our new attire, mainly because we wanted this shopping trip to be as short as possible, after coming all this way we didn't want to be late for our meeting. We took turns changing in the small bathroom off to the side that doubled as a dressing room. Rick went in first, coming out only a few minutes later in a pair of blue denim jeans with a white shirt and a dyed green, thick leather vest that had thin metal plates bolted into it which covered his vitals. Rick was very satisfied with the setup Mr. Oliver had picked out for him; he stood in the mirror and straightened the military style leather vest just so he could admire the fit. Next up was Mark; the outfit of choice was a dark grey hooded shirt and a pair of simple black pants, now it was my turn. I chose a black shirt and a darker blue thin hooded jacket with the sleeves rolled up and some black military pants. Outside I could see the streets beginning to fill with people as the time passed. Mark and I waited for Rick to finish paying Mr. Oliver which apparently came with a long conversation about the difficulties of running a business here as opposed to running one topside.

Once they finished we said our goodbyes and went outside, as soon as the three of us made it out of the shop I laid eyes on a familiar face. Walking down the middle of the street and obviously heading for the Crossroads Pub was a tall Kokin man with a whip and a machete hanging off of opposite hips. Cayden looked our way when he heard Mark close the door to Mr. Oliver's shop and I guess the others noticed him too because from behind me I heard both of the brother's stances widen defensively. I didn't take my eyes away from Cayden and at first he did not move from his spot just before the entrance to the pub, but then his expression of surprise softened a little and he sauntered across the street to meet us.

"Well, look at you guys, now that you're all cleaned up are you ready to go inside and talk?" he asked casually while we glared. "Aw come on, don't give me that. It was an honest fight. It's how we deal with outsiders here, and thanks to the Kat there, all four of you can come and go as you please, so long as you don't cause trouble. I don't hold a grudge against any of you, so why are you all acting like that?"

I couldn't argue with Cayden's logic or even his methods, there was just something about him, something he had done not long after I saw him for the first time on the terrace above the city that made my blood boil, though I couldn't put my finger on it.

The irony was that Cayden's mannerisms and the tone in his voice when he spoke so closely resembled Rick. Of course I held no particular animosity against Rick, we had been friends a good while now, but with Cayden even looking past the fight earlier I just couldn't bring myself to accept him. I was actually surprised that Rick didn't have anything to say at the moment, though I was just ready to get to doing what we came here to do. "Let's go inside then, Rebecca and some girl went in before us so they're probably waiting." My low grievous tone was not lost on Cayden, or the others.

Without another word or acknowledgement to Cayden, I walked past him and through the door into the pub. The place reminded me of an old style tavern, a hanging candle chandelier made of wood with iron fittings. The bar itself was a polished dark red wood, and the walls were lined with benched seat booths with assorted round card tables strewn across the floor. When Cayden and the brothers made it inside, both Mark and Rick made a straight shot for the bar. I guess after all that's happened up until now we all could have used a stiff drink. I looked at Cayden who simply shrugged his shoulders and stepped off towards one of the tables in the back corner.

"If you want to get a drink with your boys before we get started I'll just wait back here." Cayden's offer was tempting but there was something I wanted to say to him away from the ears of the others. I followed Cayden to his table and sat down opposite him, there was a moment of silence between us before I began to speak.

"I get what you're all about down here. The city up top is unfair to most and rather than deal with whatever they give you, if anything, you all decided to come down here and make your own rules. You should know however, if you fought in the war with the Kats like most of the people down here, who the Kyn are and what we do." I pulled my shirt to the side so that my brand could be seen. "I don't care how things work down here, I don't even care that much how things work above, but the people I am with are trying to make something good out of a very bad situation. You'll hear about the situation once everyone gets over here, what I am saying is that they are under the protection of the Kyn, and you know unlike the regular military, the Kyn will come down here and burn all of you out…if you give us a reason. Like I said, I don't care what you do down here, I'd even like for us to work together on this problem that we're here to discuss, just don't lay a hand on those two guys or Rebecca and we're square." I warned, though I never liked having conversations like these, I usually preferred to let my swords do the talking.

Cayden sat back in his chair for a moment, the grim expression he wore was akin to how he looked before the fight with Rick this morning, and then he leaned forward to match my intensity as he spoke. "I have come a very long way with these people down here, the ones that were here before me and the ones I brought in, and I am doing the best I can to hold this community together and defend it. You seem to care about your friends a lot, and that's suspicious to me. I wouldn't think anyone who would join the Kyn, let alone survive a war's worth of their missions, would care about anyone so much. Either way, I was only a threat to the four of you all so long as you were not proven; the tattooed one over there took care of that so, I have no hard feelings against any of you. As far as whatever all of you came down here to see me about, I'm not making any promises on helping…" Cayden's words slowly grew more casual as he went on and his explanation, which was enough to placate me for now, though our conversation was cut short by the slam of the door not far behind me at the back of the pub.

The sound from the door drew the attention of half the pub, Myself, Cayden, and the brothers included, only because the other half were more concerned with their drinks or card games. Rebecca glided across the floor without making a sound as her feet carried her over the bar where Mark and Rick sat drinking some amber liquid from small glasses. I couldn't hear her over the noise of the people as the place became more and more crowded, all I know is that whatever she said to the brothers made them give her a serious nod and leave their drinks straightaway to head directly for the table where Cayden and I sat. Rebecca followed closely behind the boys and her devious grin made me a bit uneasy, knowing her capricious nature she's probably looking to pay us back for earlier, like Mark or I had anything to do with it. Anyway, the three of them came over and sat down at one of the larger round tables closest to the booth. Cayden nodded to me and we both stood and sat down at the round table, I did find it odd that Rebecca chose to sit in between Cayden and me, though I chose to ignore it. Once we were all seated she looked over my shoulder to the door she had come in and waved her hand calling someone over. My first thought went to the girl she had come in with earlier who had obviously been responsible for Rebecca's new clothes, which I couldn't deny fit her quite well, especially for being borrowed clothes. Rebecca directed the girl to the seat on the other side of me and when she sat down, introduced her to the rest of us

"Guys, this is Margot, she's going to hang out with us for a few minutes before she has to start her shift."

The brothers and I shared a curious glance since what we were here to discuss couldn't really be said around just anyone, after all if Canaan found out we were looking into his dealings he could have us all arrested for treason. None of us argued the point though; Rebecca usually had a reason for doing what she does so we just let things play out. I decided to be the first to say something to Margot to make her feel welcome.

"Hi, I'm Dorian. So how do you know Rebecca?" I asked, not entirely innocent. Sure, Rebecca made friends quick but I got the feeling they'd known each other for more than just one afternoon.

Margot looked over at Rebecca for confirmation then back to me with more confidence, "Rebecca and I met in the Pit several months ago, she saved me from some guys that tried to mug me…I guess I'm not the strongest girl out there. I was lucky she came along when she did."

"Then how did you end up down here?" I asked, moving along my not-so-subtle interrogation while everyone else began their own conversations.

"Well, I was a maid at the Albedo's Estate and Rebecca offered to cover my shift one night so I could see my boyfriend. Mr. Canaan is kind of paranoid and my boyfriend decided to sell me out for some extra money… So I found myself back where I started, poor and in the Pit until Mr. Vel found me, he invited me down here and got me this job. I work here in the pub and my apartment is upstairs." I could see Rebecca smiling at me over Margot's shoulder and I guessed Margot noticed the look I was giving Rebecca, "I don't blame Rebecca though, she was just being a good friend and letting me have a night off, my ex is just a jerk."

"Well I suppose it all turned out for the best." I responded, stealing another glance over Margot's shoulder, though this time it was Cayden that caught my eye. He was talking to Rebecca now and they seemed to be having a very entertaining conversation, for some reason that made me feel a twinge of anger like before.

"What about you? How did you meet her?" Margot asked, she seemed intent on keeping my attention.

"We met when her and Rick first came to the city, I didn't really spend a whole lot of time with her since she was out doing…whatever she does. You know Rebecca, haha…" I let my sincerest fake laugh trail off. As soon as Margot mentioned she used to work for Canaan I knew offering her details about any of us could be dangerous.

Just when Margot was about to ask her next question, the bartender called out over the noise of the crowd. "Margot! It's getting pretty heavy in here, would you mind starting a little early?"

Margot looked a bit frustrated as her sweet demeanor changed, "Alright I'll be there in a second!!" Then she looked at me apologetically, "I'm really sorry… I have to go, but it was nice meeting you, we should talk again sometime."

I gave her a smile as she got up to leave, "You bet."

When she left the table I looked around at the others sitting there and they were all staring at me with these goofy grins, even Mark was smiling.

"Look at that, Dorian found himself a girlfriend." Rick mocked.

I just ignored him and looked over at Cayden and Rebecca.
"Let's just get to business…"

Chapter 18: Mark's Contemplation

I couldn't believe what I just heard. Rebecca came out of a door in the back of the pub, walked right up to my brother and I and told us that she wanted us to stay here while she and Dorian went back up top to investigate Canaan. She didn't say much as to why, only that she had reason to believe there was more going on down here than we could see that had something to do with Canaan and Cayden. Rebecca asked us to see what we could find down here while she and Dorian continued working in Crown Lykou. There wasn't much we could do to protest with Cayden in the room but nod in agreement and follow Rebecca to the table that Cayden and Dorian had settled at to wait for us. They looked like they had already gotten into a pretty serious conversation from what I could tell from the bar, I'd have to ask him about that later…

Once we sat down Rebecca called her friend we saw on the street from the door she came out of and introduced her as 'Margot'. Dorian and Margot talked for a few minutes while Rick tried to talk to Rebecca though she seemed much more interested in Cayden for some reason. I only thought it was odd seeing as a few hours ago, even before Rick pushed her into the water, Rebecca was giving him that death-glare of hers. I switched back and forth between listening to both conversations, Rebecca was asking Cayden about his trick with the whip and Dorian was basically questioning Margot. My interest was sparked when I heard the name Canaan briefly from the conversation Dorian was having, apparently Margot was his maid at some point, but before anything else came of that conversation the bartender called Margot to work and by the look on Dorian's face we could all tell he was a little disappointed, whether he knew it or not.

Dorian deflected our stares and went straight to it, "Let's just get to business…"

"Fair enough, what brings you all down to my city?" Cayden answered, leaning back in his chair and scanning the four of us.

Rebecca started in on Cayden first, "We're here because a mutual acquaintance directed us to you, we believe there may be something going on between Neil Canaan and the Nirka tribe from Katzen, you remember them. Since the war began with the Lykos soldiers capturing Nirka on this side of the border with classified documents, and since that event occurred only days after Canaan pushed through his petition to station more soldiers along Canile's border, I am suspicious as to whether or not he's been working with the Nirka all along. Rick and I came here to the city after intercepting orders from a Nirka that attacked us back in Katzen, those orders so far as I can tell, were for his unit of fifty to make their way here to the city. We decided to come here and investigate, because I don't think either Canile or Katzen wants another war. You of all people should understand, another war would only create more casualties and lost people that, in the best case will only find themselves down here for protection. Dorian helped us get set up in the city after we arrived, and Mark came later in search of his brother, right now all we care about is getting to the bottom of this." I thought it amusing that Rebecca didn't mention who it was that sent us down here but I decided to let things play out on their own.

"Well that is quite a story, lots of conspiracy and all. That still doesn't answer how you think I can help." Cayden responded without showing much interest.

"Are you involved in Canaan's plan?" Rick asked suspiciously.

Cayden brought his chair back down and leaned on the table, "So what if I am?" Cayden's response was met with astonished looks from our group. "Everything up there is so stagnant, they look down on us from those pedestals of breed, no one chooses what breed they were born into but they can choose what they do with the life that they have. Canaan understands that it doesn't matter if you're Canden or Kokin or anything in between, so long as you work hard and persevere there's nothing that can't be accomplished!"

"So what?! You'll start a rebellion? You'll bring war not just to your people but inside the walls of the city?" Dorian retaliated.

"If that's what it takes. If that's what it takes for them to see that we are not some sort of servant breed, we are just as capable as anyone." Cayden's voice became cold with resolve as he started again. "I don't know what sort of deal Canaan has worked out with the Nirka, though he did mention that he was gathering others to help us, what I do know is that I have a hundred and fifty men here and almost as many rifles, ready to fight for equality. We could take this city right now, kill parliament and the Erus's but that would leave a power vacuum, and by the time anyone could fill it the entire country will have fallen apart. That is why I need Canaan, he can take control of the country by right as the Albedo if all the other elected officials and the royal family are gone. Now you have what you came here for, but since you are working specifically to stop what Canaan and I have cooked up, you all will have to stay here. You could try to escape like last time, but last time we didn't have the rifles. This time hunting you down would be easy." The dark look on Cayden's face was matched only by the one Rebecca wore, then the corners of her mouth turned upwards and I knew now what she was planning all along.

"There's just one problem with all of that, Cayden..." Rebecca's voice almost seemed to dance at the words as they rolled off of her tongue.

"...and what might that be Rebecca...?"

"You are working with Canaan, yes? A man that is about to become a traitor to his own people and specifically his own colleagues. Now you learn that he is dealing outside of the box, you have plenty of men and weapons to take the city from within, so why would he need the Nirka? Would you really put it past him to pull one over on you? From what I heard back in Katzen, the Nirka are discriminated against pretty badly, sound familiar? He could be running the same con on both, you and the Nirka. Then, when he sets both of you loose on the city, you'll kill each other leaving the entire country for him to rule unchecked and without any grand promises to keep. How does that sound?" Rebecca's broad smile left no room for misinterpretation, anyone that knew her could tell she was playing him.

"Do you have any proof that Canaan is planning on betraying me?" Cayden asked, showing some real concern as he became trapped in the picture Rebecca had painted for him.

"Maybe... I do have a connection in the Albedo's estate, if you want to know for sure whether you can trust him or not, then let us go. We'll look into Canaan's involvement with the Nirka and report back to you, he doesn't know about what we've been doing, he won't suspect that we're working with you." Rebecca's proposal wasn't complete just yet; she was drawing him in, waiting for the right moment.

"The problem is, I don't trust you, what if he is legit and you just kill him? Then our only shot at freedom is gone."

Cayden's eyes narrowed as he stared into Rebecca's while Dorian sat in silence and my brother and I waited for her to make us hostages.

"Then keep the Kats." She said plainly, imitating Cayden as she leaned back in her chair.

"What?" Dorian and Cayden asked in unison while Rick and I leaned back, having expected this from the beginning.

Rick decided to finish what Rebecca had started I knew he couldn't sit through this entire conversation silently. "Yeah, keep us here, Dorian and Rebecca can look into the matter with Canaan and if they do anything you don't like then you can just kill us, you can think of us as willing hostages."

I simply nodded in agreement as Dorian took turns looking at both of us and then back to Cayden. I could see the wheels turning in his head as he considered the option. After a few minutes of awkward silence Cayden looked up to Rebecca again.

"So you would just leave them here, and trust that I wouldn't just kill them outright and then tip off Canaan so he could deal with you and your half breed friend?" Cayden had a point and it was funny that he was talking about Dorian like he wasn't even here.

"Come now Cayden, we both know that, for the whole tough guy act , in the end you are a soldier. You aren't like Canaan, you have honor, and if you accept this agreement that you will respect it. Plus, Rick won your duel earlier, if you try to have him executed without cause it will be against the rules that the people here have lived by long before you ever found this place. You will lose their loyalty and they will not follow you in your plan to take the city." The power dynamic had completely shifted, now Rebecca had control of the situation and we all nodded in agreement to her terms as Cayden looked to the rest of us for confirmation.

"It's a deal then, stay here tonight and in the morning you and your friend will leave the same way you came in, and the Kats stay here until you come back." Cayden sat up from the table, pushed his chair back, and headed for the door.

I decided to go for a walk to think about things, I didn't like this situation at all. I got up without a word and made a line for the exit. When I stepped outside of the pub I looked around and could see the lights reflecting inside from the mirrors in the cavern ceiling were beginning to dim, I guess outside the sun was getting low. As I walked down the street there were various men and women rounding up their children for dinnertime, most of them were Kokin but there were a couple random Ater families that I passed. It all seemed so quaint, here they were outcast from their own society and still living and working like nothing had ever happened, or so it seemed. Though I could imagine how they all must hate having to live underground just to be treated equally.

Walking down the street I noticed a pair of men going down the streets lighting the lanterns high on the poles on either side of the road. Unlike the city above the street lamps here were not gas fed, they were the old world kerosene lanterns hanging on wrought iron poles only about nine feet in the air. The yellow glow of the lamps lit the road leading me to the ledge where Rick and Rebecca fell off into the water this afternoon. I stood on the edge looking down at the slowly turning water as it collected in the pool and flowed out, the sound was almost soothing. In the water I saw images from the past few days, but the one that stuck out in my mind was of Rebecca fighting Dorian, there was something about that fight that I just couldn't get out of my head. I pulled out my knife and stared at the hazy reflection looking back at me from the blade's surface. These weapons my brother made… there's more to them, I just couldn't figure out what, though it seems that both Dorian and Rebecca were learning it whether they knew it or not.

"It's really something else isn't it? We did a good job on that knife." The voice coming from behind me was my brother's, I didn't turn around, I just kept my gaze down as he stopped beside me looking down into the water.

"How did you do it? Is this knife…is it like Rebecca's knives and Dorian's sword?" I asked looking up from my weapon to Rick who was smiling.

"…and this?" Rick drew his staff from his belt and with a flick of his wrist it extended to full length. "Yes they are all made from an ore vein I found close to where the colony was founded."

"Interesting…" I muttered turning my eyes back to the water and wondering if there was something special about the metal Rick used to make his weapons but before I could ask him directly a voice calling out from behind caught my ears.

"Hey!! We thought we'd find you two out here!" Rebecca was approaching at a brisk pace with Margot and Dorian in tow. Dorian was carrying some sort of sack over his shoulder that I did not recognize as the group came to join us and we formed a small circle standing at the ledge.

"So guys, sorry for dropping that whole 'hostage' thing on you but it was the only way I could think of to get Cayden to trust us." Rebecca's apology didn't sound very sincere but at least she tried.

"What are you two doing out here?' Dorian asked seemingly out of genuine curiosity.

"I just sort of ended up here I guess, what's in the bag?"

"Eh, Mr. Oliver came to the tavern right after you guys left, he had all of our clothes cleaned and dried. So…here they are, and Rick, he sewed up those tears in the back of your shirt." Dorian explained.

"Guy's, I have a great idea!" Rebecca's elated voice broke through the very monotone, exhausted atmosphere. "Let's do some sparring! No weapons just hand to hand, I think we could all use the chance to blow off some steam. Rick, are you up for it or is your back still in bad shape?" Rebecca's question was met with an insulted look from Rick before he answered.

"I'm still not ready to fight any currents yet, but I could definitely go for a fight."

"Dorian, let's see what you can do." I took the opportunity to claim my opponent early. I had been looking for the chance to fight Dorian since I got here though under the circumstances I couldn't actually hurt him.

Dorian donned a cocky smirk and out the corner of my eye I saw Margot pick up the bag of clothes and back away to a safe distance.

"Alright, c'mon Rick, I guess it's you and me then." Rick and Rebecca walked a little ways off for their fight.

Dorian's entire form seemed to shift as his eyes locked on me. He no longer looked tired, a slight grin crossed his face as his muscles tensed and I could feel my own body flexing, preparing for his attack. We began circling each other slowly without a word between us to signal the start of this duel. In the same instant we both leaned in and lunged forward for the attack.

Chapter 19: Rick Goes on a Date

"Whew… Where did that come from?" I sighed as Rebecca and I laid out on the ground a few feet apart, staring up at the stone canopy of the cavern. Our fight had just ended in a very painful draw and we were both so worn out neither of us wanted to get up.

"You did pretty good, but you fought better against Cayden. Who do you think won between Dorian and your brother?" Rebecca asked, propping herself up on her elbows and looking down at me.

"That's a tough one… wanna go find out?"

"What? Did you two just decide to take a nap?" Rebecca and I jerked our heads in the direction of the voice to see Dorian and Mark slowly walking up. From what I could tell they both took their share of hits. Dorian's voice sounded hoarse and low, he was breathing pretty hard it, Mark must have hit him pretty hard. Mark on the other hand was hunched over rubbing the back of his neck and walking with a slight limp.

"What happened to you guys?" Rebecca asked, hopping up quickly, studying them in the low light.

"It was a good fight." My brother's answer came with the slight twinge of approval that was devoid of his usual gruff attitude when referring to Dorian.

I got up and joined Rebecca in front of the other two, Rebecca already had a big smile on her face and I couldn't help but smile as well. She must have had a particularly infectious smile because even Mark and Dorian were grinning at her. Without a word the four of us left back for the central square. When we passed the ledge where I found Mark earlier, Margot was still waiting there with the bag of clothes.

"Hey, do you mind if I stay with you tonight?" Rebecca's question snapped Margot from the almost creepy, dreamy expression on her face as she stared at Dorian when he approached.

"Uh sure…" She answered a little confused. "I don't have a spare room but you can sleep on the couch or something." Margot's dreamy look reminded me of the girl I went to see the other night that lived down the street from Dorian's house, but she only had it when her eyes crossed him.

"I've had to stay with these guys for so long, it'd be nice to have a girl's night for a change" Rebecca stepped out in front of the group and winked at the three of us guys, Margot joined her and the two of them headed off for the pub.

"So… where are we going to stay guys?" I asked

"There's a hotel up the road." A familiar voice came from behind us, the three of us whipped around on the spot to see Cayden standing there clapping. Then he looked directly at Dorian, "I'm lucky you didn't decide to fight me, that was a good match between you and the Kat, but I wasn't expecting a clean fight from a Kyn." Dorian's eyes turned dark and his fist clenched at Cayden's last statement. "What? I was impressed, all the Kyn I've ever fought beside fought dirty, I was surprised to see you fight without taking any cheap shots. Don't worry, despite their methods, down here the Kyn have a lot of respect for what they've given up. Anyway, about two blocks up there's a hotel where you can bunk down till tomorrow." With that Cayden left off down the road in the opposite direction from us.

By the time we got to the hotel, paid and got to our rooms, I was so beat that as soon as my head hit the pillow I was out. The next morning, at least I think it was morning since it's kind of hard to tell down here, I got up and looked out of my second floor window to see light reflecting from the holes in the cave ceiling and my suspicions were confirmed. When I looked down to the street below I saw Dorian heading out for the central square where the Crossroads Pub was, I guess he was anxious to get out of here. I checked in Mark's room and he was still dead asleep, since neither one of us are leaving it didn't really matter. I headed out to join the others but by the time I got to the pub Dorian was already coming out with Rebecca and Margot, Rebecca's face had an expression I had never seen before, if I didn't know any better I would have thought she was embarrassed. Margot didn't seem too happy either for some reason, though I didn't have long to think about it since Cayden was approaching us, giving me a slight nod as he passed me to stand in front of the others.

"Alright, it's time for you two to head out. Margot, could you stay here with our friend? I'm going to show these two an easier exit to get out of here and I don't want to give the Kat here any ideas about escaping that way." Cayden gestured down the red dirt road, and Dorian with Rebecca close behind, followed him silently as they disappeared off into the city.

"So…. How did the night go with Rebecca? I see she didn't burn the place down, haha." My attempt to break the awkwardness of the situation didn't do much good, Margot just stood there in silence. "Well want to get some breakfast? My treat, since we didn't really have the chance to eat last night I'm kinda starved."

"That sounds fine, come this way." Margot ordered flatly.

I followed Margot down a couple blocks. The streets were pretty busy this time of the morning, I guess from the thieves, because they'd just be getting in from their midnight activities. Margot didn't say a word the whole way to the little diner-style restaurant. We entered and sat down near the back, sounds of random conversations from the semi-filled restaurant and the hissing of frying pans through the open window made it difficult to think until I got used to it. The booth Margot chose was far enough away not to draw attention. I got the sense that she didn't like me very much, she refused to look at me at all and after the waitress came and took our orders I decided I had to know.

"Do you have some sort of problem with me?" I asked setting the drink down that had been brought for me while we waited for our food.

"I just don't like the idea of having to chaperone someone like you, but Cayden is the boss down here so it's not like I could say no." She replied tersely. She was definitely more responsive than Mark, but her attitude sure reminded me of the way he usually acts around Dorian.

"Someone like me, huh?" I replied, not so put off as I was curious. I didn't really care that this girl had a chip on her shoulder, or that it was particularly aimed at me, but at least finding out would pass the time until I found the chance to ditch her.

"Your people are nothing but murderers. I hate all of you, Cayden is working very hard to make sure that we will never have to deal with your kind again." As she began to get more emotional I was becoming less and less interested, until I heard Cayden's name attached.

"Cayden is, is he?"

"Yes. Cayden is going to run every one of you out of our city, and then the country." Margot's voice became even more urgent as she went on.

"Tell me this, why do you hate us so much? I am assuming you mean Kats." I asked, egging her on, trying to get her to slip up so I could learn if she knows any real detail to what Cayden has planned.

"I hate you because you and that war you started took my parents! My father was one of the Candor doctors and my mother worked as one of the nurses in an outpost clinic they built over in your lands. They offered aid to any wounded, no matter which side, and your people killed them." Margot's voice kept getting lower and the anger forced her soft features to appear rigid.

"You know, what happened to your parents was horrible, but I had nothing to do with it. I didn't fight, I was in a colony to the north throughout the war. Another thing, you really think that helping Cayden and the Albedo is really going to make things any better? A lot more people will die if you all go through with this little rebellion, I don't think your parents would have wanted that at all. From what it sounds like, they were more interested in saving lives in order to make things better instead of taking them." At this point I was sitting straight up, shoulders squared, and ready for her, just in case she decided to come at me with her steak-knife.

"What do you know?! If you stayed away from the war entirely then how can you possibly understand?" Her voice was slowly climbing back up and I could feel the silent stares coming in from all around the restaurant.

"I can understand. My brother, and my mother, both served in the war. My mother cooked meals for the soldiers and my brother was a guard to one of our generals. By the way, I knew that general as well and he was the most decent man I ever met, he taught my brother and I about the honor and integrity of a soldier and how to be compassionate even for your enemies. Does that sound like the type of soldier that would allow what happened to your parents?!" At this point it was my turn to be angry, I had enough of her generalization. "You saying that all Kats are the same is the same thing your government does by lumping in everyone in a particular breed saying they aren't able to do anything that the other breeds are capable of doing. Don't generalize and say that just because one group of soldiers did something horrible, means that my whole race is evil! I agree the war was terrible, a lot of bad things happened and for no reason, but that is why my friends are here risking our lives, to prevent more people from getting hurt." As soon as I finished my sentence the waitress returned with our food and we ate in silence, though Margot barely touched her food. I could tell my point struck home and that I wasn't going to learn anything more from her about Cayden, at least for right now.

I paid and then the two of us took to the streets again, I was planning on trying to ditch her at this point so I headed for the Crossroads Pub hoping to find Cayden there so he could take this leash. Normally I would have lost her the old fashioned way but since we were down here as hostages I figured I shouldn't start the manhunt so soon after Dorian and Rebecca left. I had to buy them time to find something on Canaan that might tip the balance in our favor, even if it wasn't enough to get the government on our side, it might be enough to sway Cayden. The Nirka in the city were one thing, but if we had to fight on two fronts then things would be that much worse. We reached the pub quickly but when we went inside the only ones that were there were the thieves that had taken their nightly haul and weren't ready to sleep off the day yet.

"Is there any place we can go just to relax? I'm not feeling too up to being around people right now." I asked. Margot just sighed and gave a deep nod, leading me back to the door leading up to her apartment.

"Don't leave the living room, please." She added as she went back to her bedroom for a moment. I looked around and everything was very neat and put away, no mess or anything. I expected to find a big mess from the girls staying up all night, eating and talking. I know Rebecca, she probably wanted to stay up and grill Margot for information but make it sound like 'girl talk'.

When Margot finally reemerged from the back room she looked less angry and more tired as she plopped down on the comfort chair and leaned back. I sat down on the couch and looked over at her for a second, not seeing any sign that she was going to say anything I started in again, "One thing, you've seen me and my brother a couple times here and never once acted like you hated us, why?" Margot sat up in her chair and looked over at me with that slight dreamy look in her eyes, but it looked more like she was looking through me than at me.

"Because of the Lykos that was with you, he is one of the Kyn right?"she asked slowly.

"Yeah, but how did you know, and why does that matter?" I replied.

"Cayden told me about him after his fight with you. The Kyn are admired down here, because the life they chose is the one that was forced on everyone else down here. The Kyn are viewed as little more than mercenaries by everyone else in the city and not even considered Lykos anymore by some, but they made a choice to sacrifice their place with the rest of the their people so they could do what they believed in, noble or not. That means a lot to people like us, we clung to our lives in the city as long as we could and in the end had no other choice but to come down here so we could still do what we want and be free." As she spoke, Margot's eyes seemed to light up, she almost looked like a little kid talking about their favorite superhero. It was odd how quickly Margot had assimilated to the culture down here seeing as she had only come down here a short while ago, then again, the more I saw of the people here the more I understood why Cayden is so desperate for equality in his people.

"You like him don't you? Dorian I mean, it's okay though, I won't say anything." I said with a slight grin that snapped her back from her daze and caused her cheeks to flush bright red.

"N..No…, it's nothing like that, I just have a lot of respect for his decision, that's all." She stammered, as she fell off guard for a moment, that's when I had the opportunity to convince her that our way was better than what Cayden had planned, and if I could do that then I had a shot at convincing Cayden himself.

"Has Cayden ever told you about his brother?" I asked while she stared at the floor trying to will the redness of her cheeks to go away.

"Umm…he's never mentioned having a brother."

"Yeah he has a brother that studies at the Consilium, they've made some really amazing breakthroughs, and I've even helped with one. His name is Albert, he's fighting for equality too, and he just decided to prove that his breed is capable by working his way up through the system." I explained as Margot slowly looked back over to me, her face wore a quizzical look.

"They actually let a Kokin into the Consilium?"

"Haha, yeah though I heard it took a lot of work, but he did it and that is definitely a step in the right direction." I answered with a half cocked grin and a slight smile began to cross her lips.

The door to her apartment swung open and Cayden stepped over the threshold just in time to hear my last sentence. Margot's expression instantly changed, she didn't really look afraid or angry, just nervous as my brother followed Cayden into her apartment.

Chapter 20: Rebecca's Rescue Operation

"The easiest way out is through here, just take the ladder at the end of the hall and it'll lead you straight back up to the city." Cayden directed as we stood at the far end of the Undercity from where we started at the central square. "Make sure no one sees you come out, we can't afford for anyone to find out about any of these exits, I don't have to remind you about what will happen if anyone does." Cayden gave us both a stern glance before leaving us alone in the dim, torch-lit passageway.

"About this morning… let's just forget it okay?" I looked up at Dorian and gave him the most serious look I could muster. I couldn't believe he would just walk right into a stranger's apartment!

"That's fine with me, never happened." Dorian replied with halfhearted sincerity.

"Alright then let's go, by the way, do you have any idea where we should start once we get back topside?" I asked as we reached the ladder at the end of the hall.

"I've got an idea, but I think I'll tell you once we get out of here." Dorian cocked his head toward the exit of the passage and pressed one finger to his lips. I got the message, someone could be listening, and silently began to climb the ladder, which was shorter than I expected. We reached the top after a few minutes of climbing in silence and, when I pushed on the ceiling, instead of stone, it was a panel of wood. The wooden trap door lifted fairly easily, though I remembered Cayden's warning when I slowly peaked out. It looked like we had come up in some sort of back alley, no one was around though the noise of the street wasn't far off.

"C'mon!" I glanced down at Dorian to make sure he knew we probably only had a moment. I slipped out of our tunnel quickly and quietly, double-checking the area so that it was safe for Dorian to come out.

"Alright , follow me. We're going to have to hurry." Dorian seemed almost desperate as he took off after replacing the trap door. The tunnel had taken us out at the far end of the Merchant District. I followed Dorian as he wound through back alleys and cut-throughs all the way to the main exit of the district.

Dorian quickly pulled me to the side of the main street and looked me square in the eye. "Alright the plan is, Vel. Rick told me before that he went to visit a man at the university, and after that comment Rick made before his fight with Cayden, it wasn't difficult to figure out that Cayden's brother and the Kokin at the Consilium are one and the same. If Albert Vel is Cayden's brother then he will be invaluable at this point as leverage, just in case Mark and Rick can't find a way to stop things from down there." Dorian explained in a hushed voice to keep any of the passersby from hearing.

"Okay… so you want to go to the Consilium and do what exactly? I mean it's not like we can just kidnap him." I asked, while checking over Dorian's shoulder for anyone that might be listening in on the street.

"No, you're going to the university without me, I'm sure you'll think of a way to get Albert to go with you without a fight. I have some other business to attend, I'll meet you at my house, just bring Albert there." I gave a suspicious look at Dorian's reply but he just smiled.

"Whatever you say, I'll head over to get him now." I said, trying to shake this weird feeling I got.

We both took off in opposite directions down the main road, and at first I didn't notice, but the air weighed heavy in my lungs. The sky was grey and I could feel the temperature slowly drop, seemingly with my mood. I was really hoping it wouldn't rain since my fire is pretty much useless in the heavy rain, so this weather always made me a little nervous. That, plus Dorian not telling me the rest of his plan had me a little on edge. I shook my head to rid myself of those thoughts; I just didn't like not being in control of the plan. Orchestrating everything with Cayden was easy, the whole situation was clear, but now I had to rely on Dorian since I was out of moves. Still, going after Cayden's brother is a smart move, had to give him credit for thinking of that at least.

I made it to the Consilium as fast as I could, dashing through the courtyard and making my way back to the dorms. I stopped to ask one of the students if he knew where I could find Albert and threw in a little charm for flair, he told me he had seen Albert in the dining room this morning but he didn't show up for the class they had later. My first thought was that I should just ask which dorm he was staying in and check there, but then it hit me, if Dorian could figure this much out then Canaan probably already knew about the relationship between Cayden and Albert.

I covered my bases and checked the dorm room. Sure enough, Albert's room was ransacked and there was no one to be found. From the signs of struggle it looked like only two or three culprits, if so I still had a chance, I had to get to Everest. Whoever took him couldn't have made it far since it was still relatively early in the day, so I ran as fast as my legs would carry me straight to the wall that separated the university from Everest. The wall was tall but there were a group of boys standing around pretty close, I skidded up next to them quick as I could.

"Could you guys help me out, I forgot something at my house over there and it would be much faster if you could give me a boost over the wall." I pointed over the wall towards Everest and gave them my sweetest smile and a wink. They almost tripped over themselves getting in position to lift me up. They got me just high enough so I could get a hand on the crest of the wall and pull myself over. I gave a yell of thanks as I dropped over the side, Lykos boys were so easy.

As soon as I landed I sped off at top speed again, the streets here were empty since all the important people living here were already off to their prestigious jobs. It wasn't long before I heard struggling coming from one of the paths behind one of the large mansions on the way towards Canaan's estate. I sped up and got there in time to see three Nirka forcibly dragging a gagged and flailing Kokin down the path. I was hoping he was not unconscious because there was no way I'd be able to carry him anywhere without getting caught.

No time for words, I rushed in, the distracted Nirka were unaware of me until I was right on top of them. The first let go of Albert and turned to draw his weapon, when I saw the rifle slide over his shoulder I knew I was in trouble but luckily I had already closed the distance. I impaled his gun arm with one of my knives and spun around, slamming the hilt of the other into the back of his neck, his body went limp as he fell. The other two had already dropped their hostage and were going for their rifles but again, there wasn't enough distance between us to make their weapons effective, it was my advantage and they knew it. I slipped right in between them and swung my arms wide, switching my grip on the knives in the same motion as the knives' edge penetrated the two attackers. They fell instantly clutching the wounds in their backs.

Without wasting any time I cut the bonds on Albert, sheathed my knives, and took his hand, jerking him to his feet.

"We have to get out of here!" I hissed and we both ran for it.

The two of us ran out into street that went right down the middle of Everest, I could feel the cold air burning in my lungs but I didn't care. The rush of the fight was still fresh and the adrenaline that flooded me what exhilarating. I looked over my shoulder and was a little surprised that Albert was doing a fair job of keeping up, though the fear on his face was quite plain. By the time we got to the main street we had to stop to catch our breath.

"Who are you?!" he gasped

"I'm a friend of Rick's, come with me, there will be more coming after you."

We took off again on the long run back to the Mill, I was hoping that whatever Dorian said he had to do was finished because if we were being followed this would turn real bad real quick. I looked around, and every person we ran past that was wearing a hat or hood made me anxious. We passed the Consilium gates and kept going around the long road, as we came up on the Garrison I had an idea. Dorian didn't know but his mother told me about his brother that served in the military as a captain here, if I could convince his brother to let us wait in the Garrison for a little bit then we might have a chance to slip any pursuers. I skidded to a stop in front of one of the soldiers guarding the entrance, forgoing any charm I took a more direct approach.

"We need to see Captain Vesco, it's about his family."

The guard's face stone face softened instantly, and he turned to his partner and gave a quick nod before letting us in. The guard escorted us through the large wooden doors of the main building and showed us the back hall leading to the officer's offices. He gave a quick knock and opened the door, letting Albert and I enter first.

Giving a solid salute, the guard spoke in the flat rigid tone of any soldier, "These two said there was a family emergency and they needed to see you, shall I just leave them here?"

The Captain's eyes narrowed as he studied us before looking back up to the guard. "Yes leave them here." The guard left the room, closing the door quietly behind. Albert stood with me back at the far end of the room by the door without saying anything , but Dorian's brother must have noticed the slight bruising and rope burns Albert had from being bound. "You must be Rebecca, my mother has told me a lot about you, and who are you? Captain Vesco asked, aiming his question at Albert, who was looking away.

"I...I'm Albert Vel, I'm a student at the Consilium." Albert's voice shook when he spoke but that was enough for the Captain.

"Okay…and what are you two doing here? Is there really any trouble with my family?" he asked, leaning forward in his chair.

"Well sort of, there's not a whole lot of time to explain but Dorian asked me to check on Albert to make sure he was safe. When I got to the university I couldn't find him and when I looked in his room it was clear he had been taken. By the time I caught up to him, the abductors were in Everest, three Nirka were dragging Albert off. I got him back and was going to take him back to Dorian, but when I thought about it I decided to bring him here instead. You can keep Albert safe better than we could, and that way we could get back to the work we've been doing." My story was completely true for all Vesco would need at the moment, and there wasn't much point in lying now. If I had left the Nirka out he would have just heard it from Albert after I left.

The Captain's voice turned a cocky tone as he spoke, "And by work you mean something to do with whatever you and my brother along with those Kats were doing in the Undercity, am I right?" Vesco must have somehow found out what we were doing, but how? I didn't think with the way was Dorian was with his family that he would just go and tell any of them what we were up to, especially his brother in the military.

"We're done with things down there for right now." I answered plainly, though at hearing my answer I got an angry look from Albert which seemed kind of out of place.

"I see, well about the Nirka you ran into, you said you caught up to them Everest?" Vesco gave a quick look to Albert and I simply nodded to answer the Captain's question. "Interesting…alright, leave Mr. Vel here, I will have him well protected." Dorian's brother stood for the first time since we got there and walked over to stand in front of Albert and me. "As for the Nirka, don't go saying anything to anyone about them, ok? It hasn't been that long since the last war ended and all we need right now is news of hostile Kats in the city kidnapping university students. Also, please tell my brother I'd like to see him as soon as possible." Captain Vesco extended his hand to shake mine before I left. I looked him straight in the eye as we shook hands and when we made eye contact I saw the same look in his eyes that Dorian would get sometimes, a look like he could see right through me, like he knew everything that was going on already.

On my way out I looked over my shoulder and shot the Captain a wink. "Thanks for taking care of Albert for me."

I headed out alone down the hallway, at the end I saw the guard that showed us in from the gate. From behind me I heard the door of the office behind me open and shut quickly, I turned around slowly to Albert coming up with a very angry look on his face.

"You went down to the…!" He started, but then he saw the guard down the hall. "You went down to the Undercity, is this about my brother?" His now hushed voice still carried venom.

"Cayden is involved in something bigger than he knows and we are doing our best to contain it. I came after you because we thought the Nirka might target you in order to make sure that Cayden stays loyal, now that you're safe we have a shot at stopping your brother before he does something stupid." I let my face turn dark to drive home my point. "Just wait here, Rick and his brother are down with him right now trying to find a way to stop him, and while they're doing that I am going to find a way to expose the Nirka. It's all under control." I fell silent and stared straight at him coldly.

"Fine." Albert turned around and went back to the Captain's office still wearing his angry look but I didn't have time to worry about that now. Dorian might not be too happy that I was leaving Albert here instead of bringing him to the Mill, but this was the best move I could think of at the moment. If the Nirka were seen pursuing us then we would have no way of keeping their involvement in recent events a secret, and like the Captain said, if people knew that could spark a new conflict with Katzen. I pushed those thoughts to the back of my mind as I was escorted back to the front gates of the Garrison at the main road. I thanked the guard and took off again headed for the Mill as fast as I could.

As midday crept along the traffic on the street died down, I was relieved that the impending rains had not yet begun to fall. I ran along the stone city street passing several districts and people I had met during my time here, students from the university, randoms from the Pit, and people I had robbed from Everest without them even knowing…. I felt a little bad about the last group but I did what I had to in order to survive here. I finally made it to the Mill after about half an hour of running and ducked in quickly heading for the Vesco's house and the forest next to it. When I made it up to the house I ran around the side and peered into the forest, I saw Dorian walking out with an old Canden following him.

"So you must be Rebecca Kasimi, I have heard a lot about you recently. My name is Alexander Fox, Parliament's Kokin representative, and the head of the Kynodontes Tou Vorro. It's a pleasure to meet you." The old Canden words almost sounded too soft to back up the claim of his offices as he introduced himself.

"Where is Albert? Did the Nirka get to him first?" Dorian asked, instantly reading the situation.

"Well, about that… the Nirka did take him but I found them in Everest and got Albert back." I explained slowly

"Then where is he…?" Dorian's words trailed off and I could see the wheels in his head turn as he tried to think of what could possibly have happened.

"He's in the Garrison. I took him there in case there were more Nirka following us, we were just going to wait there for a little while but then I decided that your brother could keep him safe better than we can. That's right, I know about your brother in the military, and somehow he knew that we had been to the Undercity. Care to explain how he would know that?" I asked angrily.

"I told him. Just in case we ended up needing something more substantial than the four of us with knives and swords. That still fits into the plan though; Wayne can keep Albert out of the conflict, now we just need to get something from Canaan that we can use." Dorian looked away from me up to Fox who was waiting quietly.

"I guess that's where I come in. I have a meeting with Parliament in an hour and I will hold Canaan back for a discussion. In the meantime you two will infiltrate his estate, look for any documentation that ties him to the Nirka or the Undercity elements. Once you have gotten in and out, you will return to the Garrison and I will meet you there. Between what Captain Vesco learns from Albert about his brother, your testimony, and any documents you find in the Albedo's estate, we will have enough evidence to present Parliament and to send the military to arrest Canaan." Fox's tone had instantly changed, it was no longer hard to believe that he was the head of the Kyn, he certainly had the 'order-people-around' part down.

"What about Nirka at the estate? Last time I was there, an entire wing of the mansion looked like it had been setup as a barracks." I asked, shooting a knowing glance at Fox.

"Avoid engagements with the enemy at any cost. We cannot afford for the public to learn about the Nirka, and a fight in the middle of Everest would attract a lot of unwanted attention. Just get in and get out, if you are confronted and have no choice then end it, quickly and quietly. Dorian has been trained in such things so it shouldn't be a problem." The three of us exchanged confirming glances before Dorian and I left Fox there at the edge of the woods.

"Ugh… back to Everest." I sighed after we got out of earshot from Fox.

"We still have about half an hour before we have to leave, is there anything you need to do to prepare before we head out?" Dorian asked looking down at me walking beside him up the dirt road.

"Now that you mention it…I do have an idea." I said with a sly grin.

"Oh yeah?"

"You'll see…just follow me." I chimed, and with that we headed off to the one place I knew we could find a distraction for any Nirka holing up in the Albedo's estate.

After leaving the Mill Dorian gave me a strange look as I took him into the Pit, we walked a little while longer and finally made it to the front of Pericci's casino, The Kennel. "What are we doing here?" Dorian asked as a little frustrated crept into his voice.

"We're here to see an old friend that can help us get what we need from the estate without having to deal with the Nirka." I explained as we walked inside.

During the day the atmosphere inside was entirely different from my last time here. There was barely anyone here except for a few old people pulling levers at the slot machines and less than half as much hired muscle walking around. I showed myself to the back door leading into Pericci's office where there was a single bouncer posted.

"Excuse me, I'm here to see Don Pericci, it's very important that I speak to him. I was sent by Mr. Vel." Dropping Cayden's name was all it took to gain us entry. The tall Ater spun around and quickly used his key to open the door.

"Sir, this girl says Vel sent her to see you." The bouncer stood up straight waiting for a response from his apparently very busy boss.

When Pericci heard the name 'Vel' his head jerked up from the massive amount of paperwork at his desk, immediately and he looked directly at me without paying any attention to Dorian whatsoever. "Leave us alone, now." Pericci demanded. Without a word the bouncer left, closing the door behind him. "What are you here for now Rebecca?" I smiled an evil smile at his question.

"Now what kind of greeting is that? I came all the way down here to do you a favor and you treat me like some sort of nuisance, maybe I should just leave then." I turned back for the door waiting for Pericci to take the bait.

"What kind of favor?" Pericci asked cautiously

"Oh I happen to know that sometime today, the Albedo and his entourage of guards will be gone from his estate for a small window of time. There could however, be a few unsavory elements still lurking around the mansion, but with about twelve men or so you would have little difficulty looting the entire place. You just need to get together a few of these fine men you have wandering around your casino that can deal with those elements…quietly, so that the city guard won't be alerted." I spun my web very carefully to catch Pericci.

"That is quite a favor, and what do you get out of this little deal?" Pericci asked, standing up and walking over towards Dorian and me.

"Oh nothing major…I'll just be going with the men you send, along with my friend here. There is something Canaan has that I want, just some documents, nothing worth any money. It's a win-win, you get a good haul from one of the richest homes in Everest and I get my papers." I laid out the plan with a slight wink to Pericci who turned the option in his mind for a few seconds.

"Alright, it's a deal. You'll get your cover to retrieve your papers, but that's all you are allowed to take, the valuables are mine. Now what time will Canaan be gone?" Pericci asked meeting my wide smile with one of his own at the thought of how much money he was about to make I am sure. A person's greed is always the most reliable way of motivating them in a pinch.

"Well about that..." I began slowly.

Chapter 21: Dorian's Mission

Rebecca and I quickly made our way down the secret passage from Don Pericci's office that he had showed us after striking his deal with Rebecca. Unlike the torch-lined path down to the Undercity, Pericci had his tunnel lit with the expensive glow-tubes from the university. We reached the end of the passage fairly quickly where a short flight of stairs waited for us leading up to a door disguised as the outside entrance to a cellar for one of the more modest homes in Everest. Before ascending the stairs I stopped Rebecca,

"Why are we working with the Don? Fox said this was supposed to be a quiet infiltration, not a raid of the mansion. If Pericci's men get into it with the Nirka and anyone notices then…" I started before Rebecca cut me off.

"Yeah, yeah, I know. It could start the war with Katzen all over again. Geez you Lykos like to repeat yourselves, your brother, Fox, and now you. I get it, but you don't know Pericci or his methods. Pericci learned a long time ago that disguises aren't the best way to rob someone without being recognized, his men use gas to knock out everyone in the area then they can take what they want more efficiently and without being caught." Rebecca explained, somewhat insulted that I would question her.

"Ah, clever, so we just let them gas the place and wait go in after?"

"No, we go in first while Pericci's men get in position and get what we are after, but they won't wait for us to get out before they gas the place. If we take too long we'll have to hold our breath to get out. I hope you can hold your breath for a while." Rebecca cautioned

"Yeah, I'll be fine." I headed up the stairs and pushed open the 'cellar' doors, Rebecca followed me out.

We ran all out for the Albedo's estate, which turned out to be six blocks away. We didn't have time to check the perimeter when we got there, which I didn't like, but there wasn't much I could do about that at the moment. When Rebecca and I stopped in front of the large iron gate, heard her sigh deeply as she looked through the bars at the statues in the courtyard leading up to the house.

"You ready?" I asked, unsure about what was bothering her.

"Tch… yeah. I just feel bad, the last time I was here, Margot let me cover her shift as a maid. I used her to get in and because of that she lost her home up here, it was my fault, but maybe if we do this she can get her life back. You know, when I first came to this city and saw how the Kokin like her were treated, I spent all of my time working with Pericci, stealing money and weapons to help him in what he called a 'revolution of equality'. But… in the end it all fell apart, and I left him to his fate." Rebecca sounded remorseful for the first time since I had known her and it was odd, but nice to know she wasn't just in it for, whatever started her on this path, that she did actually care about the people here.

Together we pushed open the gate and took off through the courtyard passing statue after statue, Canaan even had one of Alistair V the patron saint of the primary faith in Canile. I thought it kind of ironic that someone who was betraying their country and their people would have a statue honoring one who taught us loyalty and unity. We made it to the large ornate doors of the mansion in no time, Rebecca didn't wait to even check the door to see if it was locked. She raised her hands, holding them close together, then with a click of her fingers there was a spark and then brilliant flames erupted in her hands directed at the door, blowing it off its hinges.

"Well that's one way to get in." I muttered as Rebecca ran in ahead of me.

We made it to the center staircase and I looked down at Rebecca swung her head in all directions, looking for the enemy. No one came, outside I heard thunder clap loud, resounding throughout the gigantic house as darkness began to descend inside. Rebecca's eyes focused on the hallway leading back passed the grand staircase and ran down it without saying anything. This whole thing felt wrong to me, I wasn't sure but something just didn't feel right. I entered to dark hallway and found Rebecca, standing at an open door peering into an even darker basement.

"Lady's first." I joked, motioning for Rebecca to go down the stairs. She held up one palm and when she snapped her fingers, a small flame flickered in her palm providing light.

We went down the stairs together, when we opened the door at the end of the stairs light flooded in from the glow-tubes that lit the basement. Inside there were shelves lining the walls with files and books, in the center at the far end there was a desk, Rebecca was way ahead of me and got to the desk first. She tore through the drawers and across the surface of the desk while I looked through the bookcases. A few minutes later as Rebecca poured through the papers on the desk, finally I heard a sound resembling satisfaction come from her side of the room.

"Here's something…" she mumbled as I came over to see what Rebecca was doing.

"Did you find anything that might work?

"Maybe… this drawer has a false bottom, inside was this." Rebecca held up a large envelope and drew one of her knives to slice it open. Rebecca pulled out a thin slip of paper and unfolded it, when her eyes crossed the two pages they widened in surprise like I had never seen on her face before.

"Rebecca, are you okay?" I asked rushing around the side of the desk and looking over her shoulder to read the small paragraph on the first page and on the second page I saw a map of the city with small markings.

"Neil Canaan,

The Nirka tribe has massed one quarter of their entire clan in the forests outside the city. Coordinate with Cayden Vel, to move the tribe through the tunnels and up through the Undercity to strike at the strategic points diagramed in this letter. Sign this letter and take it to the drop point outside of the city when you have made the necessary arrangements.

K.M.   Neil Canaan

Sure enough, there at the bottom of the letter was Canaan's signature along with the initials of the one who wrote it. I didn't know who this 'K.M.' was but we didn't have time to deal with that right now. I snatched the pages and the envelope from Rebecca and slid the papers back inside.

"Rebecca we have to go! Did you forget about the gas, or the Nirka that might be in here?" Rebecca seemed to snap out of her daze at hearing this and we both took off up the stairs and back to the first floor of the estate.

A gray mist seeped throughout the entire house as we ran out past the grand staircase, headed for the front door. Immediately Rebecca and I threw our arms up over our mouths and tried to keep from breathing in the toxic fumes. I looked over at Rebecca and she nodded as we both thought the same thing. We ran at full tilt for the front door so we could get to the open air but once we got there we were met with a sight neither of us had expected. Pericci stood out at the end of the statue courtyard with his entourage of bouncers and next to him stood the distinct form of a Nirka, strapped with tactical knives and a rifle slung over his shoulder. Rebecca and I knew without exchanging any words what had happened, we had been sold out.

The air was beginning to burn in my lungs as I still clung to the last bit of clean air that I had breathed before running into the cloud of gas that seemed to blanket the entire courtyard. The Nirka and Pericci with his men stood over by the gate just outside of the poisonous cloud's reach and I wondered if I could make it there before passing out or getting shot. The thunder was getting closer and closer as my body felt heavier and heavier without the nourishment of being able to breathe.

When Pericci finally noticed us a wide smile crossed his face as he stared passed me to Rebecca. Without waiting to see how Rebecca would react I dashed towards him as fast as I could, I saw the Nirka take aim and Pericci raised his hand to stop him, no doubt he would rather let the gas take me than to let a gunshot draw the city guard. My legs began to feel like lead and the run that had taken only seconds earlier, now felt like hours. Then I felt it, one numb leg tripped over the other and I went down into the low gaseous cloud. I fell right before the statue of Alistair V. I gripped my sword and drew it trying to use it to get to my feet but having no luck. I stared up at the likeness of our saint, the one I had been taught my entire life to put my faith in, and yet now at the very moment I had a chance to actually do something for my people that would be respected, I failed.

Just as my heavy eyes began to close I felt the first drops of water hit the side of my face while I lay flat, faced down, on the ground. The thunder was so close now the fierceness of the light that flashed from the lightning shocked me back before the sound of the thunder reached my ears. The rain fell in heavy blankets down on the entire courtyard washing the gas away. Slowly I climbed to my feet, staring angrily at the group at the far end of the courtyard that was just now realizing they would have to fight. I saw the Nirka give some order to two of Pericci's men and they ran to two of the statues closest to their end of the courtyard and slid them back the same way the statue of the guard that stood over the entrance to the Undercity slid and revealed two hidden trap doors. Pericci's men pulled open the doors and yelled something down in them as I kept running towards them and Rebecca joined me in my sprint to close the distance before the Nirka with the rifle could get a shot off. Less than ten yards away, I heard the click of a rifle chambering a bullet, instinctively I grabbed Rebecca and dodged to the side. We barely avoided the shot that came from another Nirka rifleman that had come up from under the statue on the left side of the path. I let go of a very frustrated Rebecca and we both took cover behind separate statues.

"Well at least the rain is good for something!" Rebecca yelled angrily through the rain as she kept clicking her fingers, doing little more than making a bunch of sparks.

"Looks like we'll have to do this the old fashioned way!" I smiled, holding up my sword and nodding to Rebecca who drew her knives.

I pulled my hood over my head and shot out through the statues using them for cover and confusion as I circled in the first gunman. While they were hunting the courtyard for me, I was hunting for them. At this point it was almost fun finding out which of us was really the predator, and which was really the prey. The first was easy, I came in fast and low from behind the statue in his blind-spot and cut the back of his left knee causing him to stumble on a leg he could no longer use. As he fell backwards I swiftly sliced the base of his neck and let him fall silently to the ground as memories of the war came flooding back, forcing me into cold indifference. I quickly ducked behind one statue and took stock of my surroundings, I saw Rebecca take on two Nirka by herself, and as I surveyed the courtyard I saw only two more Nirka and the two Ater bouncers that came along with Pericci.

I started to feel an icy chill rising off of my sword and when I looked down, I could see that every raindrop that hit the blade froze instantly and slid off its smooth surface. Though at the moment I didn't have time to worry about the strange weapon Rick had made for me, I needed to focus on the task at hand. I shot in for the pair of Nirka that stuck close to each other as they hunted in a downpour, this time I took advantage of their fear and came at them head on from inside the danger zone where their rifles were no longer more effective than my sword. It wasn't until I watched both of them fall to my sword that I noticed what was happening with my weapon. There was no blood from either of them, not on my sword and not on either body. Their blood was frozen solid in their wounds. I looked down at my sword and raised the flat of the blade to my left forearm, gritting my teeth against the pain I knew was coming as a result of this test I pressed the cold metal to my arm. I expected for cold so intense it burned my flesh but instead it just felt like any other steel. My thoughts were ripped away from the oddity of my weapon by the sound of sloshing footsteps coming my way. It was the two bouncers that came with Pericci, both had brass knuckles gripped firmly in each hand as one would expect from hired muscle. I grinned an evil grin knowing that these two posed no real threat, but then Rebecca swooped in a whirlwind of blades and whipping water and they both fell with a loud thud on the stone paved ground.

"It's just you two and us now!" I yelled across the courtyard at Pericci and his Nirka partner.

"Pericci's mine." Rebecca growled under her breath, I barely heard her over the rain and the strange hiss I noticed later was the rain drops evaporating as they hit her knife blades.

I nodded grimly to her and we both took opposite directions to come at the enemy from different sides. When we found them I looked past them to Rebecca, behind her statue and laying in wait. I don't know where this girl learned to fight, but she had skills that were on par with or greater than some of the Kyn, she certainly kept up with me in this fight. I saw Rebecca and she saw me, we timed the pincer strike perfectly, the both of us lunged in the same instant striking down our targets without giving them a chance to retaliate. As our enemies fell before us we looked at each other and paused for a moment. It was the first time since we met that our skills were proven to one another in actual combat, and in her eyes I saw what could pass for respect as we stood in the pouring rain. I responded in kind offering her a respectful nod before smirking and running off out of the estate grounds.

The two of us made our way to the Garrison as quick as we could with the storm mounting and the strength of the wind growing. By the time we reached the Garrison the wind had blown the rain from that section of the city. The guard posted at the gate didn't even bother stopping us, apparently Fox had already informed him we would be coming. When we pushed open the doors to the main hall Fox was standing there with Albert and my brother as I presented him with the letter.

"Here, this is signed by Canaan and initialed by another conspirator and it contains a brief overview of their plan as well as a map." I gasped, not quite used to operating at this place after spending so long back in the city.

"Good work…" Fox said, as he read the rain-soaked letter. "Captain, are your men organized?" My brother turned and gave a salute to Fox as an answer to his question. "Good, Dorian and Rebecca, you will head out with Captain Vesco and his men to meet these hostiles in the woods outside the city walls."

"What about the Kats in the Undercity, or Cayden?" I asked, concerned that maybe Fox wanted us out of the city so he could raid the Undercity without worrying about our interference.

"We will deal with them later, this letter implicates Cayden Vel in the Albedo's plot so he will have to be brought in eventually." Fox turned and gave Albert an empathetic look when he said this.

"What about Canaan, he is in for a little surprise if he went back to his estate after your meeting. Things didn't exactly go as planned but we did keep everything under control for the most part, though you might want to send a cleanup crew down to his courtyard." Rebecca almost sounded like she thought Fox should be proud of her for not escalating the fight beyond the boundaries of the estate when we were supposed to just avoid the fight altogether.

"I don't think he went back to Everest, a man in a top hat came with a carriage to take Canaan out, and they left in the opposite direction of the district." Fox explained

"A top hat, huh?…" I asked rhetorically looking over at Rebecca. We both knew who that was, Lucas Deimo.

Chapter 22: Mark's Hunt

'At least now I can take Rick and get out of here at any time.' I thought to myself as I walked the roads of the Undercity after sneaking out earlier to follow Cayden with Dorian and Rebecca while he showed them a more subtle exit point than the one that the four of us used to get down here. I headed back into the main city in order to keep from drawing attention to the fact that I had been anywhere near Cayden's secret exit from the city. I got back to the square with the Crossroads Pub and decided to look around, we were going to be here a while it seemed and if what Cayden said was true about the number of his men or their weapons then the latter would be the most easy to find and sabotage. I stood at a main crossroad and quickly took stock of each direction. It seemed like the Undercity was separated into three sections, there was the public area where the pubs and shops were, then there was the domestic area where all the housing for the entire city was set up, and the final third looked like a small expanse of mid-sized warehouses. No doubt the warehouses were owned by the thieves of the city and that was where they stored their items until they could fence them. My best bet for finding the rifles Cayden had hidden was in one of those warehouses, so I headed down into the mass of makeshift storage buildings and steel commercial freight containers to hunt for the needle in the proverbial haystack.

I wasn't surprised that I didn't find anything as easy as a nameplate on any of the warehouses or storage containers. Each warehouse had an unlit lantern hanging out by their doors and they were all imprinted with numbers and each had at the very least, three locks on their doors. My next move was definitely clear; I would have to find a way to get the number of Cayden's warehouse from him or someone else that would know. Maybe that girl, Cayden did get her that job and apartment, Margot…she may know something. I headed over to the Crossroads Pub; even if she wasn't there it was the best place to start looking. I didn't really like the idea of having to talk the information out of her, I'm not my brother after all, but I guess for now I would have to do my best. I took a slow pace to get to the pub while I thought about how I'd go about finding out whether she even knew which warehouse the weapons were stored in when I passed Cayden on the street. He looked like he was headed in the opposite direction, directly for the warehouses. Cayden saw me when I passed and turned on the spot coming back to me, which ruined my fleeting thought that I might be able to shadow him all the way to his warehouse.

"You, you're Mark aren't you? Rick's brother, you're a Vikan soldier aren't you?" He asked, still standing a little further than what would be normal for conversation.

"I was, yes, and to answer your next question I did fight in the war." I stated, only letting a little offense slip into my words.

"Actually I was going to ask why you and your brother look so different, it's almost like you're from two different tribes." Cayden took a step closer, looking over me.

"We are half Furo-Sha and half Vikan. My brother takes more after the Furo-Sha and I have the more Vikan traits. Now if we are done with family history, mind telling me what are you going to do with us while we are here?" I asked as I was getting more and more frustrated with Cayden.

"We are going back to find your brother and Margot, she will take care of you two while you're down here. I do not have the time to babysit the two of you, so please come with me." Cayden turned back headed straight for the door of the pub.

I followed silently till we got inside the pub, sighing as the sight of her patrons and staff came into view, all staring with silent disapproval that I had not noticed earlier. I guess that down here the Lykos' bias was no different than the city above, though since I did actually fight against them before it wasn't without cause. We went straight through the back door and up the stairs to Margot's apartment. Cayden went in first with me close behind coming up the cramped staircase. When I walked inside I saw the Kokin girl, Margot sitting across from my brother in her living room and staring at Cayden, looking like she had just been caught kissing a boy by her parents.

"I…I just brought him up here because we had nowhere else to go, that's all." She stammered, getting to her feet.

"That's fine, this is exactly what I wanted you to do, Margot. Thank you, I am sorry to say I will need you to look after these guys during their stay down here. I will talk to your boss downstairs and get it all settled. In the meantime, I need to talk to your friend really quick, do you mind if I take him for a moment?" Cayden's question was met with a half-disgusted look from Margot at hearing him refer to Rick as her 'friend'.

"He's all yours." She replied, turning back to face away, still sitting in her chair.

Rick looked at me then Cayden and got up from the couch, following Cayden out of Margot's apartment, closing the door behind him. I looked down at Margot and she gave an angry glance at me when I sat down in Rick's place on the couch, things had already started on a bad note and I hadn't even gotten the chance to say the first word to her yet. Margot took a book from the stand next to her chair and began thumbing through it, looking for the place where she had left off evidently. I studied the cover of the book and realized it was one I had read before. During my deployments with the Vikan military I had ample time to myself which I generally spent reading books alone in the barracks, but I was surprised that even across borders Margot and I still had the same book in common.

"That's a good series, how far are you?" I asked as she continued to glue her eyes to the text.

"Riza was just possessed by the foreign goddess...she doesn't know how to cope." Margot mumbled.

"Oh then it's just getting good, I'd give you the other books in the series if I had my collection with me, but I am kind of restricted down here." I said to the girl who was barely tolerating my presence. She nearly slammed the book in her lap and looked over at me angrily.

"What exactly are you trying to do? I am not showing you a way out of the city, Cayden asked me to stay with you and your brother till you leave so that is what I am going to do." She snapped, with daggers coming from her eyes as she stared at me.

"Do you do everything Cayden tells you to?" I asked, a bit amused at both her loyalty and that she thought I needed her to help me find a way out of the Undercity.

"Cayden takes care of everyone down here. After the war with your kind a lot of people had nowhere to go, so he brought them down here and gave them a purpose." She growled.

"A purpose, You mean the rebellion?" I asked rhetorically.

"That's right, Cayden is getting ready to lead us back to the surface where we can all have our lives back and so much more."

Now she seemed to be looking past me as I could tell she was envisioning some sort of utopian life that just wasn't possible.

"So much more, huh? You really think that fighting the other breeds and establishing yourselves as dominant will change anything?" My words sparked her attention and she came back from her daydream.

"Yes! The other breeds treat Kokin like trash and Ater like they are simple brutes. We will show them that we are more, and they will know what it feels like to be the 'lower class'!" Margot yelled, looking like she was nearly ready to jump out of her seat.

"That would make you no better than the other breeds, if you really wanted equality you would be working towards changing their view. Instead of trying to force others down you should raise yourselves up." Margot looked appalled at my words. "In Katzen each tribe proved themselves to the others for their talents and took their place in the alliance through hard work, not war." I continued.

"In Katzen I lost my family!! It was your people that killed them!" She screamed back at me.

"I am truly, very sorry for everything that happened in the war, neither side wanted it, it was instigated by a rogue tribe that we have struggled with in our own country for years. When the Lykos retaliated, they retaliated against everyone living in Katzen, not just the tribe that had crossed into their borders, so we defended ourselves." I said calmly, but still firm, not allowing her to sweep me up in her emotional outburst.

"It's still your fault! If your people had kept that tribe in check then that tribe would never have been able to cause any trouble over here!" Tears began to well up in Margot's eyes as she ranted.

"And now your savior is working with the same tribe that caused all of that bloodshed from both of our people, tell me how that will make things any better?" I asked still keeping as calm as I could, and by the way Margot slumped back in her chair and the way her wet eyes went wide as she stared back at me I could tell my point had hit home. "The Albedo that Cayden has allied himself with is using the Nirka, that much at least is clear." I added. The shocked look on Margot's face said it all; she looked down at her hands in her lap as her face twisted into a disgusted expression.

"We are just trying to make things better for everyone down here. They are tired of living without the sun and even though I haven't been down here long, so am I..." Margot's voice trailed off as she struggled to recompose herself.

"Yeah, but maybe there's another way, but we have to stop Cayden from doing something that will destroy what you and everyone else down here really want. Where are the rifles that Cayden has been stockpiling for this rebellion? If we can get them away from him then we can prevent the killing, then Cayden will have to find another way to help the people here without causing any more pain." Margot's eyes studied the floor for a minute then she looked up at me, tears beginning to grow in her glassy eyes.

"Warehouse 352. Please, I don't want any other children to lose their parents like I lost mine…" She sobbed, burying her face in the palms of her hands.

I stood up and walked up next to her facing the door and placed one hand on her shoulder. "You have my word; I will not let anyone else get hurt." With that I walked out and left Margot alone in her apartment, but when I turned to close the door behind me I couldn't help but notice she was no longer crying, she was on her feet and staring steadfastly out of the window across the room.

I had no time to lose, I ran at full speed straight for the sea of warehouses. When I got there I had no idea where to start looking for 352 so I just started checking numbers at random. The setup seemed to be divided up into numbered grids, and I just needed to figure out the pattern. When I entered in the area I was in the 200s section so I didn't think I was far, I was wrong. After running around for thirty minutes I finally found myself in the 300s. When I passed 335 I knew I was getting close, a few minutes later I was standing in front of warehouse 352. The building was pretty big but it looked old and rickety, the wood looked like it was decades old and the sheet metal roof was rusted out but it certainly was big enough to store the number of weapons Cayden had mentioned earlier. The door didn't have any sort of lock that I could see, yet all the same, the door wouldn't budge when I tried to open it. I thought for a moment and realized, the Undercity was still densely populated with thieves, even if they were just trying to provide for their families. Cayden wouldn't use any normal means of locking this door because almost anyone down here would know how to get by everyday locks. Vel would have had to use some sort of special mechanism to keep his armory safe.

Either way, whatever method that was used to lock this door didn't really matter because it would have been contingent on the thief wanting to get in and out of here without anyone knowing their actions to avoid facing judgment. Since I had destruction instead of theft in mind I didn't have to worry about any of that, I just had to bust my way inside. I stepped back and rammed my shoulder into the old wood of the side of the building, in case there were any traps in place for someone trying to break down the door. The old wood was tough but gave way as I crashed through into the dark warehouse. The inside was much like the outside, old and worn down, though I was in the right place. The entire back half was filled with crates baring the insignia of the Lykos military. I walked up to the nearest crate and pulled off the lid. I had to dig through six inches of packing hay but underneath there was a neatly arranged stack of rifles.

"Gotcha…" I mumbled under my breath as I replaced the lid.

Now all I needed was a way to destroy all of these weapons. On the far side of the room there was a large pile of crates that were a different size than the others. When I opened one of the smaller crates I found that they were ammunition crates. The 'bullets' Rebecca told us about earlier, apparently there were two chambers in the back half of each round and the rifle has a pin that punctures both chambers which allows the water in one chamber to mix with the chemical in the other to create steam which expands rapidly and propels the lead bullet. As I studied the munitions I got an idea, quick as I could I grabbed crate after crate of the bullets and set each to face the crates of rifles so that the bullets were aimed at them, then I rushed outside and grabbed six lanterns from the doors of the nearest warehouses and smashed them on top of the crates of bullets. I took two more trips out for lanterns and smashed the rest on the crates of rifles.

Now that there was thin oil covering most of the crates in the warehouse, I pulled out the flint and steel I kept in the small pouch on the small of my back that was packed with assorted tools for wilderness survival and struck the flint over the oil on the rifles. The instant the sparks hit the oil it burst into flame, spreading quickly over the whole pile. I struck the flint once more from behind the ammunition crates, setting them ablaze to melt the chamber-casings for the bullets I didn't waste any time getting out of the warehouse, I ran through the yard and wasn't more than three warehouses away when I heard the bullets begin to go off, it sounded like a flurry of small fireworks as hundreds of bullets fired at the burning rifles.

"Between the fire and the damage from those bullets there's no way they'll be able to salvage any of those weapons" I muttered to no one in particular as I ran off, getting as far away from as I could.

I made it to the Crossroads Pub without running into Cayden or anyone else that questioned why I was running at full speed through the streets of the city. I went inside and ordered a drink, as I tipped the glass back I heard a loud bang as the doors of the pub flew open with Cayden and Rick standing at the threshold.

"What did you do!?" Cayden bellowed, furiously approaching me. The next thing I knew he had grabbed me by the back of my shirt and was dragging me outside.

Chapter 23: Rick's Staff

After we left the pub, Cayden and I walked out away from town to one of the ledges overlooking the waterway that surrounded the city. Cayden led the way and as soon as he looked around and saw no one was in the area, he stopped in front of me and turned around with a grim look on his face.

"Before our fight you mentioned my brother, what did you want to tell me?" Cayden's face looked dark as he stared at me.

"I met your brother at the Consilium when I was looking into how the rifles were developed. He was working on an engine that ran off of the same principle as the chemical mixture for propelling the bullets in the rifles. The day I saw him is the day he proved his theory along with his professor, his name will be on that invention forever, a Kokin name. Cayden, your brother is succeeding at proving that the Kokin are more than just a servant breed, and he is doing it without some big rebellion. You need to stop this whole plan, if you don't then you'll only be proving that the other breeds are right, you have to beat them at their own game like your Albert." Cayden's anger steadily began to grow as he listened, his expression only softened when I mentioned his brother's name.

"What would you have me do? I could turn around and tell every soul down here that their revolution is over before it began, that we will be stuck down here until one Kokin can prove our worth, and then what? I am not my brother, I am not some scientist, I don't have much if I cannot fight." Cayden's low growl crept into his words and his fists clenched.

"Let your brother have this fight, he is already winning it. You could take the people here and leave if you wanted. There's a big country out past these walls, start a town out there in the daylight, farm the land and live free. You don't need this city, but once your brother has gotten enough credit for your breed you could come back then, live free here again. Think about it Cayden, after the war, haven't you had enough of the killing?" I asked, standing my ground.

"I'll tell you what; let's have a rematch right here and right now. No weapons for either of us and if you win I'll consider what you're saying." The joy at having the chance to fight the one who had beaten him before was not lost on Cayden's face as he spoke.

"And if I lose…?" I asked

"If you lose then your group is down one Kat, deal?" Cayden's smile got wider.

"You're just itching to kill aren't you?" I said, dropping my staff to the ground.

"Just you, I don't like losing." Cayden drew his machete and pulled his whip from its water-filled pouch and dropped them both.

"It's a deal then." I could feel a smile of my own spreading across my face.

Just as we took the first step towards each other a series of loud booms came from off in the distance on the opposite side of the city.

"The rifles…"Cayden gasped angrily.

Cayden reached down and grabbed his weapons, returning them to their place on his hips, and I did the same with my staff. Without saying anything more he took off into the city, but he wasn't headed for the direction of the sound, he was headed for the pub. I stayed right on his heels till we got to the main square, he burst into the pub as I was walking up the steps behind him.

"What did you do!?" He yelled and rushed in, grabbing my brother from his seat at the bar and started dragging him outside.

Cayden threw Mark onto the ground and pulled out his whip, slinging it, he sent the tip to my brother and it wrapped tight around his neck.

"I will ask you one more time!! What did you do!?" Cayden bellowed at my brother as he tried to climb to his feet but only succeeded at getting up on one knee.

"I don't know what you mean…" Mark coughed, maybe it was only obvious to me because he is my brother, but he was lying.

When Cayden jerked my brother toward him with the whip and drew his machete, I pulled my staff out and extended it to full length and blocked his swing. Cayden looked up at me with fury in his eyes and aimed his next strike at me, but because of his awkward stance I was able to get a good swing in and knock his machete away. He was shocked for a moment and drew his now free hand back to throw a punch when the low grind of a metal blade halted the three of us in our tracks. In unison, Mark, Cayden, and I turned and looked down the long main road we were on to see a man walking towards us carrying a very large scythe and wearing a very strange hat…

"That man did not blow up your weapons warehouse. It was I who destroyed your weapons Cayden Vel. You're arrangement with the Albedo is now null and void, and we cannot have you causing trouble on your own." The Nirka in the top hat spoke with a ring of authority that sounded a bit off…

Mark took advantage of Cayden's confusion and unraveled the whip from his neck. My brother jumped up and stood between Cayden and the man in the top hat, switching glances from Cayden to the Nirka.

"You're Lucas Deimo, why are you here?" I asked plainly

"Guilty as charged, and I am here to destroy Mr. Vel's ill-gotten weapons and to notify him that his deal with Canaan is off…oh and that I have to kill him now." With that Deimo slowly slid his top hat off his head in a bow, just as he let it fall from his hand to the ground he shot forward at incredible speed, ready to strike through my brother to get to Cayden.

"Here!! Lock your knife into the top!!" I yelled, tossing my staff to my brother.

Mark caught the staff and drew his knife, sliding it into the mechanism at the top with a loud click as it locked into place forming a spear. He grinned as he spun the spear in his hands dropping into a combat stance just in time to deflect the first blow from Deimo's weapon, then the second, and the third. Deimo threw an onslaught of attacks at my brother who stood his ground, going toe to toe with his opponent. It was then that I heard the soft swing of the pub doors just behind me. I turned in enough time to see Margot run out past me into the street.

"Stop!!!" She screamed, running towards Mark and Deimo's fight.

When Deimo saw her he instantly changed tactics, with a wide swing he knocked my brother back a few feet and dashed for the girl. Deimo swung his scythe, hooking her around the neck, being very careful not to slice through her as he pulled his hostage in, holding her by the hair I saw a thin red line of blood streaking down her neck.

"Oops…looks like I nicked her. Be careful, the next one might be a little deeper." Deimo chided.

Cayden, Mark, and I all rushed up, stopping in a line a few yards from Deimo. At some point Cayden must have retrieved the machete that I had knocked out of his hand since he now brandished it.

"Let her go! She has nothing to do with this!" Cayden yelled.

"Let her go? But we were just beginning to get close…" Deimo smiled and gripped her hair tighter causing her to let out a short scream. "Just surrender Cayden, and she goes free."

"Look around you! What do you think these people will do if you kill Cayden or that girl? They'll revolt against the surface and he is the only one strong enough to lead these people, to keep them in check. Without Cayden they just might make a play for the city without the rifles, then you would only be hurting yourself!" I responded ahead of Cayden who had begun to take a step forward.

Deimo thought for a moment and shrugged, "I guess you're right, here ya go." He whipped her by the hair on her head and threw her down between us and himself. "I can't have any trouble in this city while it is still outside of my control after all." The words almost sounded like a song as the evil Nirka spoke them.

I looked over and saw my brother gripping the spear hard and gritting his teeth in seething anger. I realized what he was about to do, only about a second too late. Mark dashed forward with unbelievable speed and a loud roar, brandishing the spear and with a thrust so fast I wouldn't have been able to see the tip if it hadn't connected with its target. Deimo's attempt at dodging succeeded in saving his body form being skewered, but his shirt was another matter. Mark's attack tore the fabric of his enemy's shirt off of his right shoulder. Deimo responded by burying the the blunt side of his scythe blade into my brother's stomach with a full swing which sent him flying all the way back to where Cayden and I were still standing.

When Deimo stood back up a look of dark anger burned over his face for a split second before he adopted the snobbish expression he had been wearing ever since I first saw him. He stood up, erecting his posture properly which gave me a clear look at the rune tattooed on his shoulder that I knew I had seen before, along with the outside edge of another rune that was tattooed on the center of his chest.

"I am letting you go, be happy with this victory. Normally I would have killed you for ruining my shirt but you're lucky, I decided not to wear a nice shirt down to this dirty place." Deimo threw his scythe over his shoulder and started sauntering away, then he looked back over his shoulder at us. "Oh and if you want to meet your friends they'll be heading for the forest just south of the city, something about a gathering of Nirka may have been brought up to them..." With that Deimo dusted off his hat from where it had fallen earlier and placed it back on his head, with an evil smirk he then disappeared around the corner of one of the many buildings on the street.

Cayden ran over to Margot, checking her over to see if she was okay while I still stood there, staring in the same direction that Deimo had left. I looked down to see my brother join Cayden in pulling Margot to her feet and carrying her inside the pub. I hesitated for a moment, considering whether I should join the others or go after our scythe wielding enemy that had almost killed Mark and Margot a minute ago. In the end I let my better sense take over and ran up the stairs into the pub to find Margot slumped in her chair over a table with Mark standing by holding a pitcher of water. Cayden stood tall, staring down at Margot with a guilty look on his face.

"It's okay Cayden… I am alright. I promise." Margot looked up at Cayden wiping the tears from her eyes. Cayden looked into hers and then back up to us with fire in his eyes.

"You two want to go, to that place outside the walls that guy with the scythe mentioned? I am going too; no one else down here is going to get hurt because of me. If Canaan's story is the only one that anyone hears then the military may decide to raid this place and drive the people from the only home they have left. If I can't fight, I'll at least carry the blame for my part in all of this." The conviction in Cayden's voice was rock-solid as he walked away from Margot towards us, I saw the longing in her eyes as she watched, but she remained silent. She knew this was something he had to do.

The three of us walked out of the pub into the street, turning to look at Cayden for directions to the exit I saw Mark walk ahead of us, "This way…" He muttered walking by Cayden and me.

"That's right… How do you know where we are going?" Cayden asked with a hint of suspicion, though it was still clear that his mind was more focused on the task at hand.

"I could have left any time I wanted, a good soldier always plans ahead, you should know." My brother spoke sternly but it almost made me laugh because I could see the faint evidence of a smile on his face.

Cayden gave Mark a quick nod and returned his grin as they understood each other, I just smiled to myself. My brother had never been good at making friends, but if I didn't know any better I'd say during this whole thing that he had made two…people that also happened to be his enemies once. It was a pretty funny thought but I didn't have much time to enjoy it, we found ourselves at the corridor leading to the nearest exit from the city.

"We don't have much time. I think I know where that guy with the scythe was talking about, the last time he and I spoke he arranged for me to move half of the weapons I had stored down here outside the city walls to the south; that is probably where they are headed." Cayden finished his explanation as we reached the end of the corridor and the ladder that was waiting there.

"Let's go then." I said gravely as I began to climb the old metal ladder. "This has to end."

Chapter 24: Rebecca's Idea

"So... You want the two of us to go outside of the city with only a handful of soldiers to back us up, after your conspirator, who has probably now joined his small army, and I'm not supposed to worry?" I said walking down the hall away from the group consisting of Dorian, Alexander Fox, and Dorian's brother, the Captain.

"We can't afford to send anything large scale in the event of this being a trap. A small scouting party to assess the situation versus a large scale operation, the scouting party is the better option because it doesn't leave the city weak in a time where invasion is a very real possibility. You do not have to go Ms. Kasimi but as one of the Kyn, Dorian is required to follow orders. He knows more about this situation than any of the soldiers, so he is our best choice to attach to the scouting party. You have obviously earned the opportunity to go along with Dorian though I am sure he and the rest of us will understand if you would rather decline, since this is a Lykos matter after all." As I listened to Fox's explanation of the situation and why the plan was as it was, I couldn't help but get a little angry at his tone. The way spoke to me like a child reminded me of how my life was growing up in the empire, and anyone that knew me would know that it wasn't a good idea to remind me of my past.

"Mr. Fox, you're right, this is a Lykos matter, one you would not have even seen coming had I not gotten involved. I don't know about you sir, but I see everything I do all the way to the end. I will be going along with Dorian and the other scouts and we will bring back your war criminal, you're welcome by the way." I was impressed that I kept a steady albeit superior tone instead of just lashing out at Fox for his condescension, though I couldn't resist that bit of sarcasm at the end.

It was then that Captain Vesco turned to the small assortment of soldiers inside the main hall and began recruiting for his scouting party while I went to stand beside Dorian. "Soldiers, fall in!!" There were some fifty men in the hall with us at the time and at the Captain's order they all came together in formation, standing at attention. "We are looking for five men to accompany these two outside the city walls to gather intelligence on the enemy's position. You will have to volunteer since the operation is not on any of the books. This mission is potentially very dangerous, the enemy will probably be armed with our rifles and expecting you, use extreme caution. Now who will go?"

Dorian and I stood back and watched as the men looked at us and then at their commanding officer. They must have known what their Captain's younger brother was and with the common view of the Kyn, I wasn't too surprised to see the entire formation think twice about helping. Finally a man stepped out from the back, an Ater-Lykos with a smaller build than most and judging by the stripes on his uniform he was a relatively low rank.

"Sir! I request permission to accompany the pair on their recon mission, Sir!" The Ater held a rigid salute and kept his eyes trained forward.

"You know what this man is, don't you soldier? A Kyn, he holds no place in our nation, he is faceless. Why are you volunteering to help someone like him?" Captain Vesco spoke so coldly regarding his own brother that it was hard to believe they would be related.

"Sir! I am not volunteering to help the Kyn, I am volunteering because you would not have asked any of us to volunteer if this mission wasn't for the good of our city or the country. I am your man Captain, Sir!" The resolve in the booming voice of the Ater caused stirrings among the other soldiers and only seconds later four more stepped out and formed up in front of Dorian's brother along with the first to volunteer.

"Alright then, we will commence operations immediately I will stay behind to rally our forces here inside the city to prepare for the worst case. Good luck gentlemen."

Dorian and I walked over to the men, and he made stern eye contact with each one of the five, then he came to a stop in front of the group while his brother dismissed the larger formation.

"Thank you all for agreeing to help us, I will go out ahead of the group to check out the situation, the rest of you stay back and if things go bad I may need you to cover our retreat." The five soldiers all nodded in agreement to the plan. Dorian even looked over at me as if to ask for my approval, which was easy to understand considering he had never had to work in a group like this before.

"Let's move out!" I yelled as the seven of us burst through the doors of the main hall out into the rainy courtyard of the Garrison.

We made our way to the southern gates of the city, rain pouring down over us as we finally reached the twelve foot tall monstrosities the Lykos used as gate-doors. Having the other soldiers with us really helped with the whole checkpoint thing, the gate-guards saw us coming and got right to work pushing the large wooden doors open. The doors were opened just enough for the seven of us to pass through by the time we got there, without stopping at all we exited the city, headed for the southern woods.

I looked up at the sky and saw that there was no sign of the rain quitting anytime soon. At that moment I was very glad that if we ran into trouble, it would be under the cover of trees. Everything was still wet but at least I would be able to make fire if I had to, not like the fight in Canaan's courtyard just a little while ago. It was a good challenge, and those rifles sure made it interesting enough, though seeing how Dorian fights reminded me what he really was under it all. He may be nice enough once you get to know him, he is even a lot of fun to tease, but underneath he is still the same person that gave up his future so he could fight and the stories of what the Kyn did in the war were grotesque. But he couldn't be as bad as the stories say, there are a good number of people in the Kyn, he probably had nothing to do with a lot of the horrible things that happened, but that if he did? I must have been staring at Dorian pretty hard as we reached the woods because before going inside he stopped and looked at me.

"What? Is something wrong?"He asked a little agitated.

"No... I was just thinking. Dorian, would you hurt anyone that had nothing to do with this fight if it would make it easier for you to win?" I asked, hoping to be reassured.

"I don't like hurting anyone Rebecca, and if someone does get hurt by me or someone else then I have failed to 'win' the fight. Yeah..., I was an assassin for all intents and purposes. Everything leading up to the target was pure bliss, planning the strike, getting in passed any security, and finally besting the enemy, but I hated the killing. I only fought to protect people, and I am still fighting to protect people, whether they realize it or not."As Dorian finished he looked at me curiously, and I didn't realize for a minute that he was looking at me because apparently I had been blushing listening to his noble intentions.

"What are you looking at?!" I snapped as our scouts that where checking the forest edge for the enemy returned.

"No sign of the enemy yet? That's good, we'll do everything just as planned, follow me."

I flanked Dorian's right as we entered the woods with the other soldiers close at our heels, we ran for a good ten minutes before we noticed anything, it was Dorian that heard it first and gave us the signal to stop. He put his hand to his ear and listened while the rest of us mimicked. At first all I heard was the rainfall on the arbor canopy overhead but the more I strained, I could hear the sound of grinding metal and cannon-fire, though it sounded like an awfully small cannon.

"The rifles..." I whispered

Dorian nodded in agreement and took off forward again with the rest of us only a little behind. The sounds of battle grew closer and closer till I could hear the roar of Kats over the gunfire but not one sound resembling a Lykos. At one point when we were only a hundred yards or so out, Dorian stopped and left our five scouts there with orders that if they did not see him in fifteen minutes to head back to the Garrison and report what they heard. He tried to leave me there but he should have known better than that from the start.

Now just the two of us we got far enough in to see the firelight of torches, we stopped just shy of the light so as not to be seen. We hid behind separate trees and watched the scene that played out in the forest clearing only a few feet away. It was a massacre, there were dozens of Nirka dead or wounded, lying motionless on the ground but all around the bodies were other Nirka dressed differently, wearing these dark black leather uniforms with a white, winged snake painted on their backs. The Nirka that were still standing were all armed with the Lykos military issue rifles while their victims seemed to only have only a few of the firearms. I glanced at Dorian for a moment to see his reaction to what had happened, and his face surprised me, he wasn't angry or upset…his eyes were ice-cold as he watched the aftermath of the battle.

When I turned my eyes back to the clearing I noticed that the Nirka side that had won this internal struggle was not even gathering the bodies, they simply took whatever weapons their victims and allies had and went on. I looked even further back and I could see a group of torches coming from the far end of the clearing. A group of Nirka was approaching, marching in unison ahead of a large horse-drawn carriage. The carriage was black with the same white snake painted on it and the driver's seat had a large black canvas covering that extended out far enough to protect the driver from the rain, the cover also kept the driver hidden in shadow. The carriage came to a halt just inside the clearing. I could see that whatever was inside didn't want to be there by the way the whole carriage seemed to pitch back and forth. It wasn't long before the mystery of the driver was revealed as a tall Nirka man came down the steps of the driver's perch wearing a top hat and a heavy black overcoat. Lucas Deimo pulled a scythe down from the darkness of his perch and walked over to the door of the carriage. He reached in and grabbed someone and pulled them, gagged and bound out to the ground. Even as far away as I was, I knew who the prisoner was, it was Rick. Having Rick meant that he probably had Mark as well, sure enough Deimo pulled a second man out of the carriage and threw him down next to his brother, but what I didn't expect was the third or the fourth that found their place on the ground next to the Kats.

Cayden Vel and Neil Canaan were down on the soggy ground next to Mark and Rick, surrounded by the black leather clad Nirka and Lucas Deimo standing over the four of them with a wicked scythe slung over his shoulder. Their captor paced back and forth in front of them for a few minutes before he said, quite loudly, "I sure hope your friends come, I will give them ten minutes to show up. If no one comes then I will have to execute all four of you, I am sorry we just can't handle the dead weight, if you'll pardon the pun…haha" Deimo laughed as he looked down at the four of his hostages, helpless on the ground in front of him.

Dorian and I exchanged looks, and I knew exactly what he was thinking because the thought had also crossed my mind as well. It wouldn't be so bad if we let him kill all four of them, one was a traitor to his country, the other was a revolutionary that was ready to let half the city die to accomplish his goal, and as for the brothers, Mark is still waiting for this to be over so he could kill Dorian, and Rick would end up like this eventually because he blindly follows adventure without ever considering the consequences. The four of them had a couple of the Nirka looters standing by to kick them in the ribs if they tried to move around too much, I didn't know what to do but I wasn't about to sit here and watch this. However it was Dorian who stood up first, I watched as it looked like he was about to turn and leave them all to their fate, then he looked down at me and motioned for me to come closer. I quickly slipped over to his tree and he leaned in, whispering his plan to me. Dorian came up with a good plan considering that the only Nirka left out there were the looters and Deimo, only about twelve in number, though it was still pretty risky. I gave a confirming nod and that's when Dorian drew his sword and stepped out of the shadow of the tree and into the clearing.

"Deimo! Let them go, now!" Dorian demanded, his performance needed some work, a bit on the cheesy side, good thing I like cheesy.

"Ahh so the half-breed has come, and a bit late it seems, no matter, so what can I do for you today?" Deimo asked, as though he had not heard Dorian's demand at all.

"You can start by telling me what happened here from the beginning!" Dorian shouted.

"From the beginning you say? Well I suppose since you've made it this far there's no harm in telling you now. The Nirka tribe has been looking to expand of late, and the Union of Tribes in Katzen doesn't exactly look on us fondly, so we decided that we would take the whole of Canile. The plan really was genius, we had just planned to take over the government then we could do whatever we wanted. We approached the very ambitious Albedo here with the proposition that if he did as we said that he would be the head of this country's government so long as he would provide any request we made of him. Of course as it is with all ambitious men, Canaan got greedy…he turned some of our brothers against us and planned to make up the difference in support that he would lose from us by taking advantage of Cayden here. We worked hard with Canaan to try and get him to see reason, but he refused so we were forced to put our foot down, as for your friends here, I found them trying to sneak out of the Undercity to find you." Deimo smiled ear to ear as he finished talking to Dorian, all the while I took my time, slowly creeping around the edge of the clearing, just out of sight.

"Sounds like you did us a bit of a favor in the end, eliminating the rogue Nirka, and even capturing Canaan. Why don't you just hand these four over to me and you can leave? We'll just say that the Nirka handled their problem and made it possible for us to handle our own." Dorian looked down at the disgraced Albedo while he made a proposition that Deimo would never accept.

"I am sorry but I do not think I can agree to such an arrangement, these men will be an example to the other members of the tribe of what happens when you turn traitor, I'm sure you can understand." Lucas Deimo seemed off…there was something very dark about him all of a sudden that was different from the last time I had seen him at the church.

I wondered if Dorian had felt the same thing that I had coming from the Nirka that had been watching us and everything else from the beginning, at least if we were supposed to believe what he said. Once I was in position I looked directly at Dorian, and even though he couldn't return my signal without giving us away, what he did next was a very clear 'go-ahead' for the plan.

"Alright, if that is the way it is then how about a challenge? You against me, if you win you get my life as well as those four, but if I win the five of us go free, deal?" I could see that Dorian's second proposition was a bit more enticing for Deimo by the wide smile that split his face, though he lost none of the darkness I had felt from him earlier. Now was the time to strike… quietly.

The rain was still going but it had slacked off very slowly, just enough that now it was barely penetrating the canopy of trees. With the weather slowing down, I felt a little better about Dorian's plan, since it was contingent on my ability to make fire. Dorian's job was to distract Deimo, give him something to focus on while I moved around the perimeter unseen. The other Nirka had stayed off behind their leader to keep an eye on the four hostages, so long as we were outnumbered there was no way we could make a move for them, but if I could pick them off from the forests, then Dorian had a shot at beating Deimo and freeing the hostages. There were four Nirka that seemed intent on staying near their charges, one for each person, aside from them were seven others that walked in random directions off behind Deimo. They must not have been willing to interrupt his conversation but still wanted to check around the clearing. Dorian had succeeded in keeping the attention of Lucas Deimo, now taking care of these seven was up to me.

I located my first target, one that had strayed a little farther than the others. I crept in close, snapping my fingers to start a little spark, just enough to get his attention. He slowly approached the edge of the clearing, I waited with one knife drawn and crouched low in the shadow of one of the trees. When he came near, barely two feet away, I dove from the opposite side of the tree from him and struck silently from behind. I pierced his lung from between his third and forth ribs to keep him from making any sound. After I dropped him, I pulled the body back into the woods so that his comrades wouldn't notice that they were down one man. The next was a bit easier because he did come looking for his 'lost' friend, I took care of him quickly enough since he left the safety of the clearing.

"And then there were five…" I mumbled as I watched my targets roam about the back side of the clearing.

I couldn't figure it out, there were just too many, and not enough time. It had already been a good twenty seconds since Dorian made his offer to Lucas and we both already knew how he would answer, he would just take all of his men and kill Dorian outright. I looked around for any option that might help tip the scales and that was when my effort was rewarded when my eyes fell on the four hostages and I saw them still struggling on the ground. Then I looked back to the carriage that they had come out of and saw up by the driver's seat, secured to one of the torch fixtures, was Rick's staff with that knife that Mark took from Dorian locked into it, there was also Cayden's whip and machete hanging from the composite spear. I knew now what I had to do.

Chapter 25: Dorian's Challenge

Lucas Deimo and I held a fierce gaze as the evil look on his face seemed to spread to his entire form. No longer did he hold himself high with squared shoulders and a raised chin, his form was nearly demonic. The finely dressed Nirka stood hunched over with his broad shoulders flared and his free hand half open exposing his claws while the other gripped tight the scythe over his shoulder which made him seem even more the devil. He looked almost... hungry, and I thought for a moment that he was going to accept my challenge for a one on one duel, until he looked back at his men and then to me again.

"Why should I fight you here when I could just have these fine gentlemen overwhelm you? I came with eleven men to take what they could from the Nirka our main force had slaughtered, and to see if I could get you to come out of hiding. I am a little disappointed that your little friend, the Rya girl didn't come with you. No matter, I will go back to the city and find her once I am done with you." Deimo ripped the top hat off of his head as a low animalistic growl began to build up from inside of him, but just when he was about to give the order to attack I saw Rebecca dash out from the woods going straight for the four hostages laying prone.

"Looking for me!?" she yelled as she bypassed their guards and went straight for their charges, using a controlled burst of fire to burn their restraints. Rebecca skidded to a stop at the carriage as bullets flew by her, she grabbed the bundle of weapons hanging just on the side of the driver's perch and threw them to Rick, Mark, and Cayden while they took advantage of her diversion to use their new found freedom and make short work of their guards. Canaan was also freed but he stayed down on the ground, watching as the others took to the fight.

Deimo and I watched as Cayden with his whip, Mark with the spear, and Rick using Cayden's machete, with Rebecca who joined their formation, fought against the remaining Nirka while they struggled to keep up with their rifles at short range. Their only defense was to use the fixed blades on the barrels to futilely swing at their opponents since aiming was near impossible at the speed the others were moving to combat them.

"Looks like you should have brought more reinforcements. Now, why don't you just surrender and make this easy for all of us." I said mimicking the usual arrogant tone Deimo had been using up until his vile transformation began.

"You think you've won? I could never fall to mutt like you!!" Deimo bellowed as he crouched down and kicked off the ground running towards me.

Deimo barreled in so fast I barely had time to react, it was a good thing I already had my sword in hand or his first strike could have ended it. All I could do was block, but the raw power of his attack still knocked me down. I jumped back up and fell into a ready stance, already I could feel the temperature drop as mist began to fall from my blade. The sheer amount of water in the air made the bizarre effect of the weapon Rick made for me even more obvious than usual. Even Deimo in his apparent madness gave pause for a moment and stared at the weapon in my hand before charging in towards me again. He used the opposite end from the blade to knock my block away and brought around the hooked blade in a horizontal slash that was sure to bisect me.

In the last instant, rage flashed through my mind unlike any I had felt in a very long time. It was this all consuming rage that made me feel numb, like nothing else mattered except for what I hated most at that very moment, and in that split second there was nothing and no one I hated more than Lucas Deimo. I swung my curved sword back around as hard as I could, rather than blocking the insane Nirka's attack, I met it with equal force. The next few seconds seemed like forever as our blades met, there was no grinding of metal or shower of sparks, they stuck together for like half a second as though they were magnetized and then I heard a sound similar to glass breaking. Both mine and my enemy's eyes were drawn down to where our weapons had met. My sword had small bits of ice still clinging to it from the apparent dense coating of ice that had enveloped it before our weapons met, while the scythe's blade was crumbling in shards, falling to the ground. Cutting through the ice must have absorbed most of the impact from Deimo's strike and the cold made my blade dense enough to break the scythe blade. I recovered from the shock first of what had happened first and struck for Deimo's neck to no avail, as he leapt backwards and glared at me with dark fury.

"Give up. There is no way for you to get out of this, no way for you to call the rest of your tribe back. I do not want to have to kill you, but that will not stop me if you keep fighting, look around, it's over." His eyes followed mine over to Rebecca and the others who were coming towards us leaving Deimo's defeated men in their wake. I would have laughed at Mark who was literally dragging Canaan along if not for the seriousness of the situation.

"Stop!!" all of our heads jerked back to the forest in the direction of the city to see my brother, and the soldiers we had left behind, along with a full military detachment charging through the underbrush towards us. "Lucas Deimo, Neil Canaan, and Cayden Vel, surrender yourselves into our custody immediately!" Wayne ordered as his soldiers brought their rifles to bear on Deimo and the others, still a good fifty feet away from any of us.

"I am sorry but this has gone on long enough…" a slow, nearly sensual voice came from one of the trees. Everyone in the clearing turned their heads in time to see a woman with a flaming arrow nocked and aimedin my direction, though I wasn't sure if she was aiming for me or Deimo.

"Kay!!!" Rebecca roared, right before the woman loosed her arrow.

The arrow struck the fifty foot gap between where my fight with Deimo was, and where Wayne and his soldiers were stopped with a fiery explosion. I was blown several yards away, everything was burning but I could still make out some sounds, like feet rushing across the ground and I heard the voice of the woman with the bow and arrow scolding someone that I assumed to be Deimo.

"This is what happens when you get carried away Lu, try to control yourself from now on..." Her voice sounded almost lazy and not really authoritative, but before long nothing mattered as everything went black...

I woke up gasping for air, my lungs still burning from all the smoke I had inhaled in the explosion. I sat up in bed, and noticed first that there were bandages wrapped tightly around my left arm, I lifted it to check the movement. There was a little pain but not enough to bother me. Looking around I saw that I was in a white room with only the single bed that I was laid up in, and one couch. I was actually a little surprised, my mother was sleeping on one end of the couch and Rebecca was asleep on the other, Rick and Mark were also in the tiny room hunched over on the floor against the wall and fast asleep. I rubbed the back of my head and wondered how long I had been out when Rebecca started shifting and her eyes opened lazily. When she saw me her eyes snapped wide open and she nearly jumped out of her seat.

"You're awake!" Rebecca's exclamation started a chain reaction as everyone in the room started coming out of their stasis.

"Ha, yeah… How long was I out?" I groaned as the soreness in my muscles started to set in faster than I would have liked. Before Rebecca could answer me, my mother ran up and gave me such a tight hug I thought my muscles were going to bust.

"Dorian, you're okay! You were out for three days, the doctor said that it was a pretty close call but none of your friends will tell me what happened." My mother's voice was weak with worry as she released her embrace.

"I'm fine Mum. I just got in over my head with some punks…" She knew I was lying and looking past her I could see the grim approval on the faces of Rebecca, Mark, and Rick.

"Well I guess I will just have to take your word for it, you had your father and I very worried, he is in the other room with your brother."

"Wayne? Is he okay?" I asked remembering that he was as close to the blast as I was when it hit.

"He is fine, Wayne woke up yesterday." My mother assured as she started for the door. "I'll go tell your father that you are alright." When Mum left the room I looked over at my three friends that were standing there in silence, Mark had a particularly serious look on his face.

"So you decided not to kill me in my sleep, huh?" I asked jokingly, trying to lighten the mood.

"Well you know, killing a defenseless enemy really isn't my style." He said as his face softened a bit.

"So what happened with Cayden and Canaan?" I asked as the memories of how I got here started coming back to me.

"They were both sentenced to life in the prison colony on Fessel in the southeastern sea. Parliament asked us to take a report of everything that happened along with our own testimony to the Samanéra in Katzen for a presentation at a tribunal to decide what to do with the Nirka back home. We leave tomorrow by boat, I'm glad you woke up in time for us to see you before we had to leave." Rick's explanation of the situation was much as I expected, though I couldn't help but feel a little sad at hearing that he and the others were leaving.

"Rebecca, you're going too?" I asked to confirm my suspicion.

"Yeah… The Furo-Sha colony took me in and made me a member of their tribe, so I have to go give my testimony as well.

I looked over at my sword that was leaning on the side of the bed and thought about how life would be like without these people I had spent so much time with in these past few months. My attention was drawn to the door of the room as it slid open and the doctor along with my father came in. While the doctor started talking to me about my injuries and testing me to make sure everything was as it should be, Mark, Rick, and Rebecca quietly exited the room.

After the doctor left I decided to lay back and try to get some rest, though I was woken up by a homely looking nurse only an hour or so later, telling me I had a visitor.

"So, you look like you took it pretty hard in that fight." Fox closed the door behind himself before approaching my bedside.

"I wasn't expecting an exploding arrow…" I growled

"Now there is no need for the attitude, I am still your superior and you still have a mission." Fox stated, squaring his shoulders to accent his authority.

"Excuse me?" I asked a bit confused.

"That girl, Rebecca, I ordered you to keep an eye on her. Something about her still doesn't sit right with me and since you two have become such good friends, you are in the best position to find out what she is hiding. I want you to go with those three to Katzen tomorrow, your official mission is to track down and recover the weapons that Cayden gave to the Nirka during his partnership with the Albedo." Fox's rigid tone was as cold as ever, here he was sending me on a mission right after I woke up from nearly being blown apart.

"Fine, but I don't think I will find out anything about Rebecca Kasimi that will be worth anything." I said looking him in the eye.

"Oh trust me there is something, after spending as many years as I have in the intelligence business you learn to pick up on these things. I have already made arrangements for your travel, just be at the port tomorrow morning, you can do the rest of your recovery on the long boat-ride to Katzen." With that Fox started for the door of my hospital room. "Oh and be careful with that sword of yours, I have seen weapons like those before, they can alter the birthright of the wielder. Even you who was born with no affinity for the Lykos gift are affected, just be careful, anyone that would give you a weapon like that is no friend of yours." Fox's words echoed in my ears hours after he had departed and before I knew it the sun was already beginning to rise.

The next morning I left the hospital without waiting for my family's visit; this would only be harder if I had to try to explain the situation to them. I found myself down at the Garrison, after everything that had happened recently I couldn't believe how normal everything looked around the city. It was hard, harder than I thought, to enjoy the comforts up here and know that there's an entire community just below my feet that was being denied even their basic rights. I felt a little bit of guilt, Cayden may have gone about it the wrong way but he was still trying his hardest to do what was right for people that were not getting fair and just treatment. Now they had only the small hope that Albert might be able to prove their worth to their people and invite them back into the sun. As I looked through the stone archway at the Garrison that loomed tall in the early morning light, the thought occurred to me that Cayden himself was probably being held here since it was the most secure facility in the city. I headed through the arch, this time the guards did not move to even check who I was, I guess after everything I was kind of hard to miss. Out in the back left corner of the district was the large building that served as the city's dedicated prison. The guard at the entrance didn't seem like he wanted to cooperate due to the obstinate look on his face when I approached.

"I need to see Vel, this is Kyn business, let me pass." I demanded, the guard stepped back though I could see the air of disgust in his face as I walked by and through the door.

The passageways in this prison kind of reminded me of the old fort where I first saw Mark on my mission to assassinate his general. There were inset torches in the walls, still lit as the sun was just now coming up, and the shuffling of the patrols as they made rounds. I headed for the high security wing in hopes that Cayden would be there for the severity of his crime. My hunch paid off, I found Cayden in a solitary cell at the very heart of the prison, sitting next to Canaan on a stone bench in silence. When I approached the barred door it was Canaan who looked up first, the wild expression he wore was not what I had expected after all I had heard of the man.

"P..P..Please, it was all her doing. You have to tell them that they have the wrong person... I just wanted respect, to be somebody, and she said she could help me so long as I followed her orders." Canaan slowly walked up to the bars of his cell, keeping steady eye contact as he made his plea, though it rang hollow until the last sentence he spoke.

"You were the Albedo, you spoke for your entire breed! Why would you let those promises draw you away from doing what you know is right so easily?" I growled.

"You don't understand, I was nothing before her..., she gave me everything that I have, I owe it all to her." I could see the shock and remorse of his situation setting in as the wild look faded from his eyes and they dropped to the floor.

"Who...? Who is the woman?" I asked intently.

"Kay..." The disgraced Albedo muttered.

I was a little puzzled until it dawned on me; Rebecca called out that name to the woman who shot the exploding arrow at us in the forest. Something was going on here with her, Fox was right. I looked up to Cayden for confirmation from a sound mind, but he was still sitting on his bench, though he had turned and was now staring at the small window in the cell on the far end of the prison hall. Before I had the chance to question either of them further, I heard the hallway door swing open and when I turned around there was a young Kokin standing in the threshold wearing a white lab coat.

"You must be Albert." I stated as the young man approached.

At hearing my words, Cayden finally rose from his seat and came to the bars where Canaan had stood, though now he had trudged over to the wall and slumped down on the floor. Albert didn't say a word until he came to stand beside me, facing his brother. There was an awkwardly tense silence as both brothers stood staring each other down, Cayden decided to speak first.

"Look Al, I did what I had to do. Just don't do anything stupid because of me, okay?" I had never heard Cayden talk like this, like he actually had anyone to answer too.

"I wouldn't dream of it, one of us has to be smart about things. Do you have any idea what is going to happen now?! You were lucky to get the prison colony and I not only have to watch you go, but denounce you publically in order to keep from failing at what I am trying to do for our people!" Albert's angry words resounded in the halls and his fists shook with anger until a hand came through the bars just far enough to rest on his shoulder.

"It's alright little brother, you'll do great just keep working. Your Kat friend told me about you when he came down to the Undercity, and after everything he said I've never been more proud of you for all you've accomplished. That Rick nearly convinced me to leave the city and become a farmer, haha…" Both brothers laughed weakly at Rick's suggestion. "Maybe I should have taken him up on that, too late now though I guess." Cayden sighed.

"Well you know, you'd have to be a pretty good farmer to make anything grow in Fessel, and who knows, you may be able to come back in a few years if I can change things, convince Parliament to overturn their verdict." Albert gave a fake smile to his brother as they both silently accepted that there was little to no chance they would ever see each other again.

"You will change things, just make them see every breed as equal, I know you can do it Albert." Cayden's shoulders squared as he stood up straight, showing respect for his brother. "Alright well you'd better go, take care of yourself and don't worry about me, I'll be fine.

Both brothers shook each other's hand firmly and Albert turned back down the hallway after giving me a silent nod, acknowledging my presence for the first time since he came and then left me alone before Cayden again. "Do you know the woman, 'Kay' that was working with Cayden?" I asked gravely.

"I only know what my guys reported to me when I had them spying on Canaan, not much. I can tell you, she is dangerous, and whatever she is planning with the Nirka is big and probably not over yet. Watch yourself Dorian and keep an eye out, if you have the chance to stop her then take it before she puts any more of our people at risk." Cayden nodded darkly.

Cayden's ominous warning haunted me as I headed down the main street of Crown Lykou to join up with my 'friends', I didn't know what to think about them anymore. I finally got to the port just a little early and found the three of them, Mark, Rebecca, and Rick, loading up the ship. "Hey guys, thought you would be leaving without me?" I asked when they all turned and saw me coming up the ramp onto the deck of the ship.

"What are you doing here?" Rebecca asked, unable to hide the smile on her face.

"I have my next mission, I am supposed to recover those weapons that Cayden and Canaan stole and gave to the Nirka. So it looks like you guys are stuck with me again, haha…" They all seemed to accept my half truth, though I felt a little guilty. The honest look of joy on Rebecca's face only made my suspicions dig in deeper.

"Wait, did you say goodbye to your family?" Rick asked as we all stood on the deck, enjoying the breeze off of the water.

"Eh sort of, I left them a letter. I thought it was best since they would want an explanation why I was leaving the country before I was fully healed." I explained, though when I looked Rick in the eye I couldn't help but feel like I didn't trust him the same way, if he gave me a weapon knowing it could be dangerous then what could he be planning? I shook off my paranoia when I noticed Mark staring and looked out to the ocean as the sun sat pushed further above the horizon when I heard someone calling out to us from the dock as the ship began to pull away.

"Hey!!! Be safe and come back soon!" A young Kokin girl yelled from the edge of the dock. Margot's smiled as she waved goodbye to the four of us with Wayne standing next to her, I guess Cayden asked him to bring her up here to say goodbye. Seeing them made me think of my parents, they would probably be reading my goodbye letter right now.

Mum and Dad,

I am sorry I couldn't be there in person for this but I was asked to leave on very short notice. I am headed to Katzen with my friends, Rebecca, Rick, and Mark. Thank you for letting them stay at the house after what happened to the place they were staying. They really are good people, Rick is very smart and always helpful if not a little self absorbed, Mark, well he is pretty rough around the edges but he always tries to do the right thing, and Rebecca is an amazing girl though a sometimes she can be annoying and immature, I know that she has a lot to offer the world. I am going with them as a request from Parliament to show Lykos support for their people so that we might be able to foster some sort of relationship with the people in Katzen. Thank you again for everything and even though I know I haven't quite turned out as you hoped I would, I really do want to make you proud.

I love you both very much, Dorian Vesco

www.ingramcontent.com/pod-product-compliance
Lightning Source LLC
Chambersburg PA
CBHW060359260626
47160CB00006B/2364